Best Short Stories of

ANTON CHEKOV

JAICO PUBLISHING HOUSE

Ahmedabad Bangalore Bhopal Bhubaneswar Chennai
Delhi Hyderabad Kolkata Lucknow Mumbai

Published by Jaico Publishing House
A-2 Jash Chambers, 7-A Sir Phirozshah Mehta Road
Fort, Mumbai - 400 001
jaicopub@jaicobooks.com
www.jaicobooks.com

BEST SHORT STORIES OF ANTON CHEKOV
ISBN 978-81-8495-854-6

First Jaico Impression: 2016
Third Jaico Impression: 2018

Page design and layout: R. Ajith Kumar, Delhi

CONTENTS

The Lady with the Toy Dog

I T was reported that a new face had been seen on the quay; a lady with a little dog. Dmitri Dimitrich Gomov, who had been a fortnight at Yalta and had got used to it, had begun to show an interest in new faces. As he sat in the pavilion at Verné's he saw a young lady, blond and fairly tall, and wearing a broad-brimmed hat, pass along the quay. After her ran a white Pomeranian.

Later he saw her in the park and in the square several times a day. She walked by herself, always in the same broad-brimmed hat, and with this white dog. Nobody knew who she was, and she was spoken of as the lady with the toy dog.

"If," thought Gomov, "if she is here without a husband or a friend, it would be as well to make her acquaintance."

He was not yet forty, but he had a daughter of twelve and two boys at school. He had married young, in his second year at the University, and now his wife seemed half as old again as himself. She was a tall woman, with dark eyebrows, erect, grave, stolid, and she thought herself an intellectual woman. She read a great deal, called her husband not Dmitri, but Dimitri, and in his private mind he thought her short-witted, narrow-minded, and ungracious. He was afraid of her and disliked being at home. He had begun to betray her with other women long ago, betrayed her frequently, and, probably for that reason nearly always spoke ill of women, and when they were discussed in his presence he would maintain that they were an inferior race.

It seemed to him that his experience was bitter enough to give him the right to call them any name he liked, but he could not live a couple of days without the "inferior race." With men he was bored and ill at ease, cold and unable to talk, but when he was with women, he felt easy and knew what to talk about, and how to behave, and even when he was silent with them he felt quite comfortable. In his appearance as in his character, indeed in his whole nature, there was something attractive, indefinable, which drew women to him and charmed them; he knew it, and he, too, was drawn by some mysterious power to them.

His frequent, and, indeed, bitter experiences had taught him long ago that every affair of that kind, at first a divine diversion, a delicious smooth adventure, is in the end a source of worry for a decent man, especially for men like those at Moscow who are slow to move, irresolute, domesticated, for it becomes at last an acute and extraordinary complicated problem and a nuisance. But whenever he met and was interested in a new woman, then his experience would slip away from his memory, and he would long to live, and everything would seem so simple and amusing.

And it so happened that one evening he dined in the gardens, and the lady in the broad-brimmed hat came up at a leisurely pace and sat at the next table. Her expression, her gait, her dress, her coiffure told him that she belonged to society, that she was married, that she was paying her first visit to Yalta, that she was alone, and that she was bored.... There is a great deal of untruth in the gossip about the immorality of the place. He scorned such tales, knowing that they were for the most part concocted by people who would be only too ready to sin if they had the chance, but when the lady sat down at the next table, only a yard or two away from him, his thoughts were filled with tales of easy conquests, of trips to the mountains; and he was suddenly possessed by the alluring idea of a quick transitory liaison, a moment's affair with an unknown woman whom he knew not even by name.

He beckoned to the little dog, and when it came up to him, wagged his finger at it. The dog began to growl. Gomov again wagged his finger.

The lady glanced at him and at once cast her eyes down.

"He won't bite," she said and blushed.

"May I give him a bone?"—and when she nodded emphatically, he asked affably: "Have you been in Yalta long?"

"About five days."

"And I am just dragging through my second week."

They were silent for a while.

"Time goes quickly," she said, "and it is amazingly boring here."

"It is the usual thing to say that it is boring here. People live quite happily in dull holes like Belyov or Zhidra, but as soon as they come here they say: 'How boring it is! The very dregs of dullness!' One would think they came from Spain."

She smiled. Then both went on eating in silence as though they did not know each other; but after dinner they went off together—and then began an easy, playful conversation as though they were perfectly happy, and it was all one to them where they went or what they talked of. They walked and talked of how the sea was strangely luminous; the water lilac, so soft and warm, and athwart it the moon cast a golden streak. They said how stifling it was after the hot day. Gomov told her how he came from Moscow and was a philologist by education, but in a bank by profession; and how he had once wanted to sing in opera, but gave it up; and how he had two houses in Moscow.... And from her he learned that she came from Petersburg, was born there, but married at S. where she had been living for the last two years; that she would stay another month at Yalta, and perhaps her husband would come for her, because, he too, needed a rest. She could not tell him what her husband was—Provincial Administration or Zemstvo Council—and she seemed to think it funny. And Gomov found out that her name was Anna Sergueyevna.

In his room at night, he thought of her and how they would meet next day. They must do so. As he was going to sleep, it struck him that she could only lately have left school, and had been at her lessons even as his daughter was then; he remembered how bashful and gauche she was when she laughed and talked with a stranger—it must be, he thought, the first time she had been alone, and in such a place with men walking after her and looking at her and talking to her, all with the same secret purpose which she could not but guess. He thought of her slender white neck and her pretty, grey eyes.

"There is something touching about her," he thought as he began to fall asleep.

II

A week passed. It was a blazing day. Indoors it was stifling, and in the streets the dust whirled along. All day long he was plagued with thirst and he came into the pavilion every few minutes and offered Anna Sergueyevna an iced drink or an ice. It was impossibly hot.

In the evening, when the air was fresher, they walked to the jetty to see the steamer come in. There was quite a crowd all gathered to meet somebody, for they carried bouquets. And among them were clearly marked the peculiarities of Talta: the elderly ladies were youngly dressed and there were many generals.

The sea was rough and the steamer was late, and before it turned into the jetty it had to do a great deal of manoeuvring. Anna Sergueyevna looked through her lorgnette at the steamer and the passengers as though she were looking for friends, and when she turned to Gomov, her eyes shone. She talked much and her questions were abrupt, and she forgot what she had said; and then she lost her lorgnette in the crowd.

The well-dressed people went away, the wind dropped, and Gomov and Anna Sergueyevna stood as though they were waiting for somebody to come from the steamer. Anna Sergueyevna was silent. She smelled her flowers and did not look at Gomov.

"The weather has got pleasanter toward evening," he said. "Where shall we go now? Shall we take a carriage?"

She did not answer.

He fixed his eyes on her and suddenly embraced her and kissed her lips, and he was kindled with the perfume and the moisture of the flowers; at once he started and looked round; had not some one seen?

"Let us go to your—" he murmured.

And they walked quickly away.

Her room was stifling, and smelled of scents which she had bought at the Japanese shop. Gomov looked at her and thought: "What strange chances there are in life!" From the past there came the memory of earlier good-natured women, gay in their love, grateful to him for their happiness, short though it might be; and of others—like his wife—who loved without sincerity, and talked overmuch and affectedly, hysterically, as though they were protesting that it was not love, nor passion, but something more important; and of the few beautiful cold women, into whose eyes there would flash suddenly a fierce expression, a stubborn desire to take, to snatch from life more than it can give; they were no longer in their first youth, they were capricious, unstable, domineering, imprudent, and when Gomov became cold toward them then their beauty roused him to hatred, and the lace on their lingerie reminded him of the scales of fish.

But here there was the shyness and awkwardness of inexperienced youth, a feeling of constraint; an impression of perplexity and wonder, as though some one had suddenly knocked at the door. Anna Sergueyevna, "the lady with the toy dog" took what had happened somehow seriously, with a particular gravity, as though thinking that this was her downfall and very strange and improper. Her features seemed to sink and wither, and on either side of her face her long hair hung mournfully down; she sat crestfallen and musing, exactly like a woman taken in sin in some old picture.

"It is not right," she said. "You are the first to lose respect for me."

There was a melon on the table. Gomov cut a slice and began to eat it slowly. At least half an hour passed in silence.

Anna Sergueyevna was very touching; she irradiated the purity of a simple, devout, inexperienced woman; the solitary candle on the table hardly lighted her face, but it showed her very wretched.

"Why should I cease to respect you?" asked Gomov. "You don't know what you are saying."

"God forgive me!" she said, and her eyes filled with tears. "It is horrible."

"You seem to want to justify yourself."

"How can I justify myself? I am a wicked, low woman and I despise myself. I have no thought of justifying myself. It is not my husband that I have deceived, but myself. And not only now but for a long time past. My husband may be a good honest man, but he is a lackey. I do not know what work he does, but I do know that he is a lackey in his soul. I was twenty when I married him. I was overcome by curiosity. I longed for something. 'Surely,' I said to myself, 'there is another kind of life.' I longed to live! To live, and to live.... Curiosity burned me up.... You do not understand it, but I swear by God, I could no longer control myself. Something strange was going on in me. I could not hold myself in. I told my husband that I was ill and came here.... And here I have been walking about dizzily, like a lunatic.... And now I have become a low, filthy woman whom everybody may despise."

Gomov was already bored; her simple words irritated him with their unexpected and inappropriate repentance; but for the tears in her eyes he might have thought her to be joking or playing a part.

"I do not understand," he said quietly. "What do you want?"

She hid her face in his bosom and pressed close to him.

"Believe, believe me, I implore you," she said. "I love a pure, honest life, and sin is revolting to me. I don't know myself what I am doing. Simple people say: 'The devil entrapped me,' and I can say of myself: 'The Evil One tempted me.'"

"Don't, don't," he murmured.

He looked into her staring, frightened eyes, kissed her, spoke quietly and tenderly, and gradually quieted her and she was happy again, and they both began to laugh.

Later, when they went out, there was not a soul on the quay; the town with its cypresses looked like a city of the dead, but the sea still roared and broke against the shore; a boat swung on the waves; and in it sleepily twinkled the light of a lantern.

They found a cab and drove out to the Oreanda.

"Just now in the hall," said Gomov, "I discovered your name written on the board—von Didenitz. Is your husband a German?"

"No. His grandfather, I believe, was a German, but he himself is an Orthodox Russian."

At Oreanda they sat on a bench, not far from the church, looked down at the sea and were silent. Yalta was hardly visible through the morning mist. The tops of the hills were shrouded in motionless white clouds. The leaves of the trees never stirred, the cicadas trilled, and the monotonous dull sound of the sea, coming up from below, spoke of the rest, the eternal sleep awaiting us. So the sea roared when there was neither Yalta nor Oreanda, and so it roars and will roar, dully, indifferently when we shall be no more. And in this continual indifference to the life and death of each of us, there lies hid, the pledge of our eternal salvation, of the uninterrupted movement of life on earth and its unceasing perfection. Sitting side by side with a young woman, who in the dawn seemed so beautiful, Gomov, appeased and enchanted by the sight of the fairy scene, the sea, the mountains, the clouds, the wide sky, thought how at bottom, if it were thoroughly explored, everything on earth was beautiful, everything, except what we ourselves think and do when we forget the higher purposes of life and our own human dignity.

A man came up—a coast-guard—gave a look at them, then went away. He, too, seemed mysterious and enchanted.

A steamer came over from Theodosia, by the light of the morning star, its own lights already put out.

"There is dew on the grass," said Anna Sergueyevna after a silence.

"Yes. It is time to go home."

They returned to the town.

Then every afternoon they met on the quay, and lunched together, dined, walked, enjoyed the sea. She complained that she slept badly, that her heart beat alarmingly. She would ask the same question over and over again, and was troubled now by jealousy, now by fear that he did not sufficiently respect her. And often in the square or the gardens, when there was no one near, he would draw her close and kiss her passionately. Their complete idleness, these kisses in the full daylight, given timidly and fearfully lest any one should see, the heat, the smell of the sea and the continual brilliant parade of leisured, well-dressed, well-fed people almost regenerated him. He would tell Anna Sergueyevna how delightful she was, how tempting. He was impatiently passionate, never left her side, and she would often brood, and even asked him to confess that he did not respect her, did not love her at all, and only saw in her a loose woman. Almost every evening, rather late, they would drive out of the town, to Oreanda, or to the waterfall; and these drives were always delightful, and the impressions won during them were always beautiful and sublime.

They expected her husband to come. But he sent a letter in which he said that his eyes were bad and implored his wife to come home. Anna Sergueyevna began to worry.

"It is a good thing I am going away," she would say to Gomov. "It is fate."

She went in a carriage and he accompanied her. They

drove for a whole day. When she took her seat in the car of an express-train and when the second bell sounded, she said:

"Let me have another look at you.... Just one more look. Just as you are."

She did not cry, but was sad and low-spirited, and her lips trembled.

"I will think of you—often," she said. "Good-bye. Good-bye. Don't think ill of me. We part for ever. We must, because we ought not to have met at all. Now, good-bye."

The train moved off rapidly. Its lights disappeared, and in a minute or two the sound of it was lost, as though everything were agreed to put an end to this sweet, oblivious madness. Left alone on the platform, looking into the darkness, Gomov heard the trilling of the grasshoppers and the humming of the telegraph-wires, and felt as though he had just woke up. And he thought that it had been one more adventure, one more affair, and it also was finished and had left only a memory. He was moved, sad, and filled with a faint remorse; surely the young woman, whom he would never see again, had not been happy with him; he had been kind to her, friendly, and sincere, but still in his attitude toward her, in his tone and caresses, there had always been a thin shadow of raillery, the rather rough arrogance of the successful male aggravated by the fact that he was twice as old as she. And all the time she had called him kind, remarkable, noble, so that he was never really himself to her, and had involuntarily deceived her....

Here at the station, the smell of autumn was in the air, and the evening was cool.

"It is time for me to go North," thought Gomov, as he left the platform.

"It is time."

III

At home in Moscow, it was already like winter; the stoves were heated, and in the mornings, when the children were getting ready to go toschool, and had their tea, it was dark and their nurse lighted the lamp for a short while. The frost had already begun. When the first snow falls, the first day of driving in sledges, it is good to see the white earth, the white roofs; one breathes easily, eagerly, and then one remembers the days of youth. The old lime-trees and birches, white with hoarfrost, have a kindly expression; they are nearer to the heart than cypresses and palm-trees, and with the dear familiar trees there is no need to think of mountains and the sea.

Gomov was a native of Moscow. He returned to Moscow on a fine frosty day, and when he donned his fur coat and warm gloves, and took a stroll through Petrovka, and when on Saturday evening he heard the church-bells ringing, then his recent travels and the places he had visited lost all their charm. Little by little he sank back into Moscow life, read eagerly three newspapers a day, and said that he did not read Moscow papers as a matter of principle. He was drawn into a round of restaurants, clubs, dinner-parties, parties, and he was flattered to have his house frequented by famous lawyers and actors, and to play cards with a professor at the University club. He could eat a whole plateful of hot salt fish and cabbage.

So a month would pass, and Anna Sergueyevna, he thought, would be lost in the mists of memory and only rarely would she visit his dreams with her touching smile, just as other women had done. But more than a month passed, full winter came, and in his memory everything was clear, as though he had parted from Anna Sergueyevna only yesterday. And his memory was lit by a light that grew ever stronger. No matter how, through the voices of his children saying their lessons, penetrating to the evening stillness of his study, through hearing a song, or the music in a restaurant, or the snow-storm howling in the chimney, suddenly the whole thing would come to life again in his memory: the meeting on the jetty, the early morning with the mists on the mountains, the steamer from Theodosia and their kisses. He would pace up and down his room and remember it all and smile, and then his memories would drift into dreams, and the past was confused in his imagination with the future. He did not dream at night of Anna Sergueyevna, but she followed him everywhere, like a shadow, watching him. As he shut his eyes, he could see her, vividly, and she seemed handsomer, tenderer, younger than in reality; and he seemed to himself better than he had been at Yalta. In the evenings she would look at him from the bookcase, from the fireplace, from the corner; he could hear her breathing and the soft rustle of her dress. In the street he would gaze at women's faces to see if there were not one like her....

He was filled with a great longing to share his memories with some one. But at home it was impossible to speak of his love, and away from home—there was no one. Impossible to talk of her to the other people in the house and the men at the bank. And talk of what? Had he loved then? Was there anything fine, romantic, or elevating or even interesting in his relations with Anna Sergueyevna? And he would speak vaguely of love, of women, and nobody guessed what was the matter, and only his wife would raise her dark eyebrows and say:

"Dimitri, the rôle of coxcomb does not suit you at all."

One night, as he was coming out of the club with his partner, an official, he could not help saying: "If only I could tell what a fascinating woman I met at Yalta."

The official seated himself in his sledge and drove off, but suddenly called: "Dmitri Dimitrich!"

"Yes."

"You were right. The sturgeon was tainted."

These banal words suddenly roused Gomov's indignation. They seemed to him degrading and impure. What barbarous customs and people!

What preposterous nights, what dull, empty days! Furious card-playing, gourmandising, drinking, endless conversations about the same things, futile activities and conversations taking up the best part of the day and all the best of a man's forces, leaving only a stunted, wingless life, just rubbish; and to go away and escape was impossible— one mightas well be in a lunatic asylum or in prison with hard labour.

Gomov did not sleep that night, but lay burning with indignation, and then all next day he had a headache. And the following night he slept badly, sitting up in bed and thinking, or pacing from corner to corner of his room. His children bored him, the bank bored him, and he had no desire to go out or to speak to any one.

In December when the holidays came he prepared to go on a journey and told his wife he was going to Petersburg to present a petition for a young friend of his—and went to S. Why? He did not know. He wanted to see Anna Sergueyevna, to talk to her, and if possible to arrange an assignation.

He arrived at S. in the morning and occupied the best room in the hotel, where the whole floor was covered with a grey canvas, and on the table there stood an inkstand grey with dust, adorned with a horseman on a headless horse holding a net in his raised hand. The porter gave him the necessary information: von Didenitz; Old Goucharno Street, his own house—not far from the hotel; lives well, has his own horses, every one knows him.

Gomov walked slowly to Old Goucharno Street and found the house. In front of it was a long, grey fence spiked with nails.

"No getting over a fence like that," thought Gomov, glancing from the windows to the fence.

He thought: "To-day is a holiday and her husband is probably at home. Besides it would be tactless to call and upset her. If he sent a note then it might fall into her husband's hands and spoil everything. It would be better to wait for an opportunity." And he kept on walking up and down the street, and round the fence, waiting for his opportunity. He saw a beggar go in at the gate and the dogs attack him. He heard a piano and the sounds came faintly to his ears. It must be Anna Sergueyevna playing. The door suddenly opened and out of it came an old woman, and after her ran the familiar white Pomeranian. Gomov wanted to call the dog, but his heart suddenly began to thump and in his agitation he could not remember the dog's name.

He walked on, and more and more he hated the grey fence and thought with a gust of irritation that Anna Sergueyevna had already forgotten him, and was perhaps already amusing herself with some one else, as would be only natural in a young woman forced from morning to night to behold the accursed fence. He returned to his room and sat for a long time on the sofa, not knowing what to do. Then he dined and afterward slept for a long while.

"How idiotic and tiresome it all is," he thought as he awoke and saw the dark windows; for it was evening. "I've had sleep enough, and what shall I do to-night?"

He sat on his bed which was covered with a cheap, grey

blanket, exactly like those used in a hospital, and tormented himself.

"So much for the lady with the toy dog.... So much for the great adventure.... Here you sit."

However, in the morning, at the station, his eye had been caught by a poster with large letters: "First Performance of 'The Geisha.'" He remembered that and went to the theatre.

"It is quite possible she will go to the first performance," he thought.

The theatre was full and, as usual in all provincial theatres, there was a thick mist above the lights, the gallery was noisily restless; in the first row before the opening of the performance stood the local dandies with their hands behind their backs, and there in the governor's box, in front, sat the governor's daughter, and the governor himself sat modestly behind the curtain and only his hands were visible. The curtain quivered; the orchestra tuned up for a long time, and while the audience were coming in and taking their seats, Gomov gazed eagerly round.

At last Anna Sergueyevna came in. She took her seat in the third row, and when Gomov glanced at her his heart ached and he knew that for him there was no one in the whole world nearer, dearer, and more important than she; she was lost in this provincial rabble, the little undistinguished woman, with a common lorgnette in her hands, yet she filled his whole life; she was his grief, his joy, his only happiness, and he longed for her; and through the noise of the bad orchestra with its tenth-rate fiddles, he thought how dear she was to him. He thought and dreamed.

With Anna Sergueyevna there came in a young man with short side-whiskers, very tall, stooping; with every movement he shook and bowed continually. Probably he was the husband whom in a bitter mood at Yalta she had called a lackey. And, indeed, in his long figure, his side-whiskers, the little bald patch on the top of his head, there was something of the lackey; he had a modest sugary smile and in his buttonhole he wore a University badge exactly like a lackey's number.

In the first entr'acte the husband went out to smoke, and she was left alone. Gomov, who was also in the pit, came up to her and said in a trembling voice with a forced smile:

"How do you do?"

She looked up at him and went pale. Then she glanced at him again in terror, not believing her eyes, clasped her fan and lorgnette tightly together, apparently struggling to keep herself from fainting. Both were silent. She sat, he stood; frightened by her emotion, not daring to sit down beside her. The fiddles and flutes began to play and suddenly it seemed to them as though all the people in the boxes were looking at them. She got up and walked quickly to the exit; he followed, and both walked absently along the corridors, down the stairs, up the stairs, with the crowd shifting and shimmering before their eyes; all kinds of uniforms, judges, teachers, crown-estates, and all with badges; ladies shone and shimmered before them, like fur coats on moving rows of clothes-pegs, and there was a draught howling through the place laden with the smell of tobacco and cigar-ends. And Gomov, whose heart was thudding wildly, thought:

"Oh, Lord! Why all these men and that beastly orchestra?"

At that very moment he remembered how when he had seen Anna Sergueyevna off that evening at the station he had said to himself that everything was over between them, and they would never meet again. And now how far off they were from the end!

On a narrow, dark staircase over which was written: "This Way to the Amphitheatre," she stopped: "How you frightened me!" she said, breathing heavily, still pale and apparently stupefied. "Oh! how you frightened me! I am nearly dead. Why did you come? Why?"

"Understand me, Anna," he whispered quickly. "I implore you to understand...."

She looked at him fearfully, in entreaty, with love in her eyes, gazing fixedly to gather up in her memory every one of his features.

"I suffer so!" she went on, not listening to him. "All the time, I thought only of you. I lived with thoughts of you.... And I wanted to forget, to forget, but why, why did you come?"

A little above them, on the landing, two schoolboys stood and smoked and looked down at them, but Gomov did not care. He drew her to him and began to kiss her cheeks, her hands.

"What are you doing? What are you doing?" she said in terror, thrusting him away.... "We were both mad. Go away to-night. You must go away at once.... I implore you, by everything you hold sacred, I implore you.... The people are coming—"

Some one passed them on the stairs.

"You must go away," Anna Sergueyevna went on in a whisper. "Do you hear, Dmitri Dimitrich? I'll come to you in Moscow. I never was happy. Now I am unhappy and I shall never, never be happy, never! Don't make me suffer even more! I swear, I'll come to Moscow. And now let us part. My dear, dearest darling, let us part!"

She pressed his hand and began to go quickly down-stairs, all the while looking back at him, and in her eyes plainly showed that she was most unhappy. Gomov stood for a while, listened, then, when all was quiet he found his coat and left the theatre.

IV

And Anna Sergueyevna began to come to him in Moscow. Once every two or three months she would leave S., telling her husband that she was going to consult a specialist in women's diseases. Her husband half believed and half disbelieved her. At Moscow she would stay at the "Slaviansky Bazaar" and send a message at once to Gomov. He would come to her, and nobody in Moscow knew.

Once as he was going to her as usual one winter morning—he had not received her message the night before—he had his daughter with him, for he was taking her to school which was on the way. Great wet flakes of snow were falling.

"Three degrees above freezing," he said, "and still the snow is falling. But the warmth is only on the surface of the earth. In the upper strata of the atmosphere there is quite a different temperature."

"Yes, papa. Why is there no thunder in winter?"

He explained this too, and as he spoke he thought of his assignation, and that not a living soul knew of it, or ever would know. He had two lives; one obvious, which every one could see and know, if they were sufficiently interested, a life full of conventional truth and conventional fraud, exactly like the lives of his friends and acquaintances; and another, which moved underground. And by a strange conspiracy of circumstances, everything that was to him important, interesting, vital, everything that enabled him to be sincere and denied self-deception and was the very core of his being, must dwell hidden away from others, and everything that made him false, a mere shape in which he hid himself in order to conceal the truth, as for instance his work in the bank, arguments at the club, his favourite gibe about women, going to parties with his wife—all this was open.

And, judging others by himself, he did not believe the things he saw, and assumed that everybody else also had his real vital life passing under a veil of mystery as under the cover of the night. Every man's intimate existence is kept mysterious, and perhaps, in part, because of that civilised people are so nervously anxious that a personal secret should be respected.

When he had left his daughter at school, Gomov went to the "Slaviansky Bazaar." He took off his fur coat down-stairs, went up and knocked quietly at the door. Anna Sergueyevna, wearing his favourite grey dress, tired by the journey, had been expecting him to come all night. She was pale, and looked at him without a smile, and flung herself on his breast as soon as he entered. Their kiss was long and lingering as though they had not seen each other for a couple of years.

"Well, how are you getting on down there?" he asked. "What is your news?"

"Wait. I'll tell you presently.... I cannot."

She could not speak, for she was weeping. She turned her face from him and dried her eyes.

"Well, let her cry a bit.... I'll wait," he thought, and sat down.

Then he rang and ordered tea, and then, as he drank it, she stood and gazed out of the window.... She was weeping in distress, in the bitter knowledge that their life had fallen out so sadly; only seeing each other in secret, hiding themselves away like thieves! Was not their life crushed?

"Don't cry.... Don't cry," he said.

It was clear to him that their love was yet far from its end, which there was no seeing. Anna Sergueyevna was more and more passionately attached to him; she adored him and it was inconceivable that he should tell her that their love must some day end; she would not believe it.

He came up to her and patted her shoulder fondly and at that moment he saw himself in the mirror.

His hair was already going grey. And it seemed strange to him that in the last few years he should have got so old and ugly. Her shoulders were warm and trembled to his touch. He was suddenly filled with pity for her life, still so warm and beautiful, but probably beginning to fade and wither, like his own. Why should she love him so much? He always seemed to women not what he really was, and they loved in him, not himself, but the creature of their imagination, the thing they hankered for in life, and when they had discovered their mistake, still they loved him. And not one of them was happy with him. Time passed; he met women and was friends with them, went further and parted, but never once did he love; there was everything but love.

And now at last when his hair was grey he had fallen in love, real love—for the first time in his life.

Anna Sergueyevna and he loved one another, like dear kindred, like husband and wife, like devoted friends; it seemed to them that Fate had destined them for one another, and it was inconceivable that he should have a wife, she a husband; they were like two birds of passage, a male and a female, which had been caught and forced to live in separate cages. They had forgiven each other all the past of which they were ashamed; they forgave everything in the present, and they felt that their love had changed both of them.

Formerly, when he felt a melancholy compunction, he used to comfort himself with all kinds of arguments, just as they happened to cross his mind, but now he was far removed from any such ideas; he was filled with a profound pity, and he desired to be tender and sincere....

"Don't cry, my darling," he said. "You have cried enough.... Now let us talk and see if we can't find some way out."

Then they talked it all over, and tried to discover some means of avoiding the necessity for concealment and deception, and the torment of living in different towns, and of not seeing each other for a long time. How could they shake off these intolerable fetters?

"How? How?" he asked, holding his head in his hands. "How?"

And it seemed that but a little while and the solution would be found and there would begin a lovely new life; and to both of them it was clear that the end was still very far off, and that their hardest and most difficult period was only just beginning.

Small Fry

"HONORED Sir, Father and Benefactor!" a petty clerk called Nevyrazimov was writing a rough copy of an Easter congratulatory letter. "I trust that you may spend this Holy Day even as many more to come, in good health and prosperity. And to your family also I..."

The lamp, in which the kerosene was getting low, was smoking and smelling. A stray cockroach was running about the table in alarm near Nevyrazimov's writing hand. Two rooms away from the office Paramon the porter was for the third time cleaning his best boots, and with such energy that the sound of the blacking-brush and of his expectorations was audible in all the rooms.

"What else can I write to him, the rascal?" Nevyrazimov wondered, raising his eyes to the smutty ceiling.

On the ceiling he saw a dark circle—the shadow of the lamp-shade. Below it was the dusty cornice, and lower still the wall, which had once been painted a bluish muddy color. And the office seemed to him such a place of desolation that he felt sorry, not only for himself, but even for the cockroach.

"When I am off duty I shall go away, but he'll be on duty

here all his cockroach-life," he thought, stretching. "I am bored! Shall I clean my boots?"

And stretching once more, Nevyrazimov slouched lazily to the porter's room. Paramon had finished cleaning his boots. Crossing himself with one hand and holding the brush in the other, he was standing at the open window-pane, listening.

"They're ringing," he whispered to Nevyrazimov, looking at him with eyes intent and wide open. "Already!"

Nevyrazimov put his ear to the open pane and listened. The Easter chimes floated into the room with a whiff of fresh spring air. The booming of the bells mingled with the rumble of carriages, and above the chaos of sounds rose the brisk tenor tones of the nearest church and a loud shrill laugh.

"What a lot of people!" sighed Nevyrazimov, looking down into the street, where shadows of men flitted one after another by the illumination lamps. "They're all hurrying to the midnight service.... Our fellows have had a drink by now, you may be sure, and are strolling about the town. What a lot of laughter, what a lot of talk! I'm the only unlucky one, to have to sit here on such a day: And I have to do it every year!"

"Well, nobody forces you to take the job. It's not your turn to be on duty today, but Zastupov hired you to take his place. When other folks are enjoying themselves you hire yourself out. It's greediness!"

"Devil a bit of it! Not much to be greedy over—two roubles is all he gives me; a necktie as an extra.... It's poverty, not greediness. And it would be jolly, now, you know, to be going with a party to the service, and then to break the fast.... To drink and to have a bit of supper and tumble off to sleep.... One sits down to the table, there's an Easter cake and the samovar hissing, and some charming little thing beside you.... You drink a glass and chuck her under the chin, and it's first-rate.... You feel you're somebody.... Ech h-h!... I've made a mess of things! Look at that hussy driving by in her carriage, while I have to sit here and brood."

"We each have our lot in life, Ivan Danilitch. Please God, you'll be promoted and drive about in your carriage one day."

"I? No, brother, not likely. I shan't get beyond a 'titular,' not if I try till I burst. I'm not an educated man."

"Our General has no education either, but..."

"Well, but the General stole a hundred thousand before he got his position. And he's got very different manners and deportment from me, brother. With my manners and deportment one can't get far! And such a scoundrelly surname, Nevyrazimov! It's a hopeless position, in fact. One may go on as one is, or one may hang oneself..."

He moved away from the window and walked wearily about the rooms. The din of the bells grew louder and louder.... There was no need to stand by the window to hear it. And the better he could hear the bells and the louder the roar of the carriages, the darker seemed the muddy walls and the smutty cornice and the more the lamp smoked.

"Shall I hook it and leave the office?" thought Nevyrazimov.

But such a flight promised nothing worth having.... After coming out of the office and wandering about the town, Nevyrazimov would have gone home to his lodging, and in his lodging it was even grayer and more depressing than in the office.... Even supposing he were to spend that day pleasantly and with comfort, what had he beyond? Nothing but the same gray walls, the same stop-gap duty and complimentary letters....

Nevyrazimov stood still in the middle of the office and sank into thought. The yearning for a new, better life gnawed at his heart with an intolerable ache. He had a passionate longing to find himself suddenly in the street, to mingle with the living crowd, to take part in the solemn festivity for the sake of which all those bells were clashing and those carriages were rumbling. He longed for what he had known in childhood—the family circle, the festive faces of his own people, the white cloth, light, warmth...! He thought of the carriage in which the lady had just driven by, the overcoat in which the head clerk was so smart, the gold chain that adorned the secretary's chest.... He thought of a warm bed, of the Stanislav order, of new boots, of a uniform without holes in the elbows.... He thought of all those things because he had none of them.

"Shall I steal?" he thought. "Even if stealing is an easy matter, hiding is what's difficult. Men run away to America, they say, with what they've stolen, but the devil knows where that blessed America is. One must have education even to steal, it seems."

The bells died down. He heard only a distant noise of carriages and Paramon's cough, while his depression and anger grew more and more intense and unbearable. The clock in the office struck half-past twelve.

"Shall I write a secret report? Proshkin did, and he rose rapidly."

Nevyrazimov sat down at his table and pondered. The lamp in which the kerosene had quite run dry was smoking violently and threatening to go out. The stray cockroach was still running about the table and had found no resting-place.

"One can always send in a secret report, but how is one to make it up? I should want to make all sorts of innuendoes and insinuations, like Proshkin, and I can't do it. If I made up anything I should be the first to get into trouble for it. I'm an ass, damn my soul!"

And Nevyrazimov, racking his brain for a means of escape from his hopeless position, stared at the rough copy he had written. The letter was written to a man whom he feared and hated with his whole soul, and from whom he had for the last ten years been trying to wring a post worth eighteen roubles a month, instead of the one he had at sixteen roubles.

"Ah, I'll teach you to run here, you devil!" He viciously slapped the palm of his hand on the cockroach, who had the misfortune to catch his eye. "Nasty thing!"

The cockroach fell on its back and wriggled its legs in despair. Nevyrazimov took it by one leg and threw it into the lamp. The lamp flared up and spluttered.

And Nevyrazimov felt better.

The Requiem

IN the village church of Verhny Zaprudy mass was just over. The people had begun moving and were trooping out of church. The only one who did not move was Andrey Andreyitch, a shopkeeper and old inhabitant of Verhny Zaprudy. He stood waiting, with his elbows on the railing of the right choir. His fat and shaven face, covered with indentations left by pimples, expressed on this occasion two contradictory feelings: resignation in the face of inevitable destiny, and stupid, unbounded disdain for the smocks and striped kerchiefs passing by him. As it was Sunday, he was dressed like a dandy. He wore a long cloth overcoat with yellow bone buttons, blue trousers not thrust into his boots, and sturdy goloshes—the huge clumsy goloshes only seen on the feet of practical and prudent persons of firm religious convictions.

His torpid eyes, sunk in fat, were fixed upon the ikon stand. He saw the long familiar figures of the saints, the verger Matvey puffing out his cheeks and blowing out the candles, the darkened candle stands, the threadbare carpet, the sacristan Lopuhov running impulsively from the altar and carrying the holy bread to the churchwarden.... All these things he had seen for years, and seen over and over again like the five fingers of his hand.... There was only one thing, however, that was somewhat strange and unusual. Father Grigory, still in his vestments, was standing at the north door, twitching his thick eyebrows angrily.

"Who is it he is winking at? God bless him!" thought the shopkeeper. "And he is beckoning with his finger! And he stamped his foot! What next! What's the matter, Holy Queen and Mother! Whom does he mean it for?"

Andrey Andreyitch looked round and saw the church completely deserted. There were some ten people standing at the door, but they had their backs to the altar.

"Do come when you are called! Why do you stand like a graven image?" he heard Father Grigory's angry voice. "I am calling you."

The shopkeeper looked at Father Grigory's red and wrathful face, and only then realized that the twitching eyebrows and beckoning finger might refer to him. He started, left the railing, and hesitatingly walked towards the altar, tramping with his heavy goloshes.

"Andrey Andreyitch, was it you asked for prayers for the rest of Mariya's soul?" asked the priest, his eyes angrily transfixing the shopkeeper's fat, perspiring face.

"Yes, Father."

"Then it was you wrote this? You?" And Father Grigory angrily thrust before his eyes the little note.

And on this little note, handed in by Andrey Andreyitch before mass, was written in big, as it were staggering, letters:

"For the rest of the soul of the servant of God, the harlot Mariya."

"Yes, certainly I wrote it,..." answered the shopkeeper.

"How dared you write it?" whispered the priest, and in his husky whisper there was a note of wrath and alarm.

The shopkeeper looked at him in blank amazement; he was perplexed, and he, too, was alarmed. Father Grigory had never in his life spoken in such a tone to a leading resident of Verhny Zaprudy. Both were silent for a minute, staring into each other's face. The shopkeeper's amazement was so great that his fat face spread in all directions like spilt dough.

"How dared you?" repeated the priest.

"Wha...what?" asked Andrey Andreyitch in bewilderment.

"You don't understand?" whispered Father Grigory, stepping back in astonishment and clasping his hands. "What have you got on your shoulders, a head or some other object? You send a note up to the altar, and write a word in it which it would be unseemly even to utter in the street! Why are you rolling your eyes? Surely you know the meaning of the word?"

"Are you referring to the word harlot?" muttered the shopkeeper, flushing crimson and blinking. "But you know, the Lord in His mercy... forgave this very thing,... forgave a harlot.... He has prepared a place for her, and indeed from the life of the holy saint, Mariya of Egypt, one may see in what sense the word is used—excuse me..."

The shopkeeper wanted to bring forward some other argument in his justification, but took fright and wiped his lips with his sleeve.

"So that's what you make of it!" cried Father Grigory, clasping his hands. "But you see God has forgiven her—do you understand? He has forgiven, but you judge her, you slander her, call her by an unseemly name, and whom! Your own deceased daughter! Not only in Holy Scripture, but even in worldly literature you won't read of such a sin! I tell you again, Andrey, you mustn't be over-subtle! No, no, you mustn't be over-subtle, brother! If God has given you an inquiring mind, and if you cannot direct it, better not go into things.... Don't go into things, and hold your peace!"

"But you know, she,... excuse my mentioning it, was an actress!" articulated Andrey Andreyitch, overwhelmed.

"An actress! But whatever she was, you ought to forget it all now she is dead, instead of writing it on the note."

"Just so,...." the shopkeeper assented.

"You ought to do penance," boomed the deacon from the depths of the altar, looking contemptuously at Andrey Andreyitch's embarrassed face, "that would teach you to leave off being so clever! Your daughter was a well-known actress. There were even notices of her death in the newspapers.... Philosopher!"

"To be sure,... certainly," muttered the shopkeeper, "the word is not a seemly one; but I did not say it to judge her, Father Grigory, I only meant to speak spiritually,... that it might be clearer to you for whom you were praying. They write in the memorial notes the various callings, such as the infant John, the drowned woman Pelagea, the warrior Yegor, the murdered Pavel, and so on.... I meant to do the same."

"It was foolish, Andrey! God will forgive you, but beware another time. Above all, don't be subtle, but think like other people. Make ten bows and go your way."

"I obey," said the shopkeeper, relieved that the lecture was over, and allowing his face to resume its expression of importance and dignity. "Ten bows? Very good, I understand. But now, Father, allow me to ask you a favor.... Seeing that I am, anyway, her father,... you know yourself, whatever she was, she was still my daughter, so I was,... excuse me, meaning to ask you to sing the requiem today. And allow me to ask you, Father Deacon!"

"Well, that's good," said Father Grigory, taking off his

vestments. "That I commend. I can approve of that! Well, go your way. We will come out immediately."

Andrey Andreyitch walked with dignity from the altar, and with a solemn, requiem-like expression on his red face took his stand in the middle of the church. The verger Matvey set before him a little table with the memorial food upon it, and a little later the requiem service began.

There was perfect stillness in the church. Nothing could be heard but the metallic click of the censer and slow singing.... Near Andrey Andreyitch stood the verger Matvey, the midwife Makaryevna, and her one-armed son Mitka. There was no one else. The sacristan sang badly in an unpleasant, hollow bass, but the tune and the words were so mournful that the shopkeeper little by little lost the expression of dignity and was plunged in sadness. He thought of his Mashutka,... he remembered she had been born when he was still a lackey in the service of the owner of Verhny Zaprudy. In his busy life as a lackey he had not noticed how his girl had grown up. That long period during which she was being shaped into a graceful creature, with a little flaxen head and dreamy eyes as big as kopeck-pieces passed unnoticed by him. She had been brought up like all the children of favorite lackeys, in ease and comfort in the company of the young ladies. The gentry, to fill up their idle time, had taught her to read, to write, to dance; he had had no hand in her bringing up. Only from time to time casually meeting her at the gate or on the landing of the stairs, he would remember that she was his daughter, and would, so far as he had leisure for it, begin teaching her the prayers and the scripture. Oh, even then he had the reputation of an authority on the church rules and the holy scriptures! Forbidding and stolid as her father's face was, yet the girl listened readily. She repeated the prayers after him yawning, but on the other hand, when he, hesitating and trying to express himself elaborately, began telling her stories, she was all attention. Esau's pottage, the punishment of Sodom, and the troubles of the boy Joseph made her turn pale and open her blue eyes wide.

Afterwards when he gave up being a lackey, and with the money he had saved opened a shop in the village, Mashutka had gone away to Moscow with his master's family....

Three years before her death she had come to see her father. He had scarcely recognized her. She was a graceful young woman with the manners of a young lady, and dressed like one. She talked cleverly, as though from a book, smoked, and slept till midday. When Andrey Andreyitch asked her what she was doing, she had announced, looking him boldly straight in the face: "I am an actress." Such frankness struck the former flunkey as the acme of cynicism. Mashutka had begun boasting of her successes and her stage life; but seeing that her father only turned crimson and threw up his hands, she ceased. And they spent a fortnight together without speaking or looking at one another till the day she went away. Before she went away she asked her father to come for a walk on the bank of the river. Painful as it was for him to walk in the light of day, in the sight of all honest people, with a daughter who was an actress, he yielded to her request.

"What a lovely place you live in!" she said enthusiastically. "What ravines and marshes! Good heavens, how lovely my native place is!"

And she had burst into tears.

"The place is simply taking up room,..." Andrey Andreyvitch had thought, looking blankly at the ravines, not understanding his daughter's enthusiasm. "There is no more profit from them than milk from a billy-goat."

And she had cried and cried, drawing her breath greedily with her whole chest, as though she felt she had not a long time left to breathe.

Andrey Andreyitch shook his head like a horse that has been bitten, and to stifle painful memories began rapidly crossing himself....

"Be mindful, O Lord," he muttered, "of Thy departed servant, the harlot Mariya, and forgive her sins, voluntary or involuntary...."

The unseemly word dropped from his lips again, but he did not notice it: what is firmly imbedded in the consciousness cannot be driven out by Father Grigory's exhortations or even knocked out by a nail. Makaryevna sighed and whispered something, drawing in a deep breath, while one-armed Mitka was brooding over something....

"Where there is no sickness, nor grief, nor sighing," droned the sacristan, covering his right cheek with his hand.

Bluish smoke coiled up from the censer and bathed in the broad, slanting patch of sunshine which cut across the gloomy, lifeless emptiness of the church. And it seemed as though the soul of the dead woman were soaring into the sunlight together with the smoke. The coils of smoke like a child's curls eddied round and round, floating upwards to the window and, as it were, holding aloof from the woes and tribulations of which that poor soul was full.

The Bet

I T was a dark autumn night. The old banker was walking up and down his study and remembering how, fifteen years before, he had given a party one autumn evening. There had been many clever men there, and there had been interesting conversations. Among other things they had talked of capital punishment. The majority of the guests, among whom were many journalists and intellectual men, disapproved of the death penalty. They considered that form of punishment out of date, immoral, and unsuitable for Christian States. In the opinion of some of them the death penalty ought to be replaced everywhere by imprisonment for life.

"I don't agree with you," said their host the banker. "I have not tried either the death penalty or imprisonment for life, but if one may judge *à priori*, the death penalty is more moral and more humane than imprisonment for life. Capital punishment kills a man at once, but lifelong imprisonment kills him slowly. Which executioner is the more humane, he who kills you in a few minutes or he who drags the life out of you in the course of many years?"

"Both are equally immoral," observed one of the guests, "for they both have the same object—to take away life. The State is not God. It has not the right to take away what it cannot restore when it wants to."

Among the guests was a young lawyer, a young man of five-and-twenty. When he was asked his opinion, he said:

"The death sentence and the life sentence are equally immoral, but if I had to choose between the death penalty and imprisonment for life, I would certainly choose the second. To live anyhow is better than not at all."

A lively discussion arose. The banker, who was younger and more nervous in those days, was suddenly carried away by excitement; he struck the table with his fist and shouted at the young man:

"It's not true! I'll bet you two millions you wouldn't stay in solitary confinement for five years."

"If you mean that in earnest," said the young man, "I'll take the bet, but I would stay not five but fifteen years."

"Fifteen? Done!" cried the banker. "Gentlemen, I stake two millions!"

"Agreed! You stake your millions and I stake my freedom!" said the young man.

And this wild, senseless bet was carried out! The banker, spoilt and frivolous, with millions beyond his reckoning, was delighted at the bet. At supper he made fun of the young man, and said:

"Think better of it, young man, while there is still time. To me two millions are a trifle, but you are losing three or four of the best years of your life. I say three or four, because you won't stay longer. Don't forget either, you unhappy man, that voluntary confinement is a great deal harder to bear than compulsory. The thought that you have the right to step out in liberty at any moment will poison your whole existence in prison. I am sorry for you."

And now the banker, walking to and fro, remembered all

this, and asked himself: "What was the object of that bet? What is the good of that man's losing fifteen years of his life and my throwing away two millions? Can it prove that the death penalty is better or worse than imprisonment for life? No, no. It was all nonsensical and meaningless. On my part it was the caprice of a pampered man, and on his part simple greed for money...."

Then he remembered what followed that evening. It was decided that the young man should spend the years of his captivity under the strictest supervision in one of the lodges in the banker's garden. It was agreed that for fifteen years he should not be free to cross the threshold of the lodge, to see human beings, to hear the human voice, or to receive letters and newspapers. He was allowed to have a musical instrument and books, and was allowed to write letters, to drink wine, and to smoke. By the terms of the agreement, the only relations he could have with the outer world were by a little window made purposely for that object. He might have anything he wanted—books, music, wine, and so on— in any quantity he desired by writing an order, but could only receive them through the window. The agreement provided for every detail and every trifle that would make his imprisonment strictly solitary, and bound the young man to stay there _exactly_ fifteen years, beginning from twelve o'clock of November 14, 1870, and ending at twelve o'clock of November 14, 1885. The slightest attempt on his part to break the conditions, if only two minutes before the end, released the banker from the obligation to pay him two millions.

For the first year of his confinement, as far as one could judge from his brief notes, the prisoner suffered severely from loneliness and depression. The sounds of the piano could be heard continually day and night from his lodge. He refused wine and tobacco. Wine, he wrote, excites the desires, and desires are the worst foes of the prisoner; and besides, nothing could be more dreary than drinking good wine and seeing no one. And tobacco spoilt the air of his room. In the first year the books he sent for were principally of a light character; novels with a complicated love plot, sensational and fantastic stories, and so on.

In the second year the piano was silent in the lodge, and the prisoner asked only for the classics. In the fifth year music was audible again, and the prisoner asked for wine. Those who watched him through the window said that all that year he spent doing nothing but eating and drinking and lying on his bed, frequently yawning and angrily talking to himself. He did not read books. Sometimes at night he would sit down to write; he would spend hours writing, and in the morning tear up all that he had written. More than once he could be heard crying.

In the second half of the sixth year the prisoner began zealously studying languages, philosophy, and history. He threw himself eagerly into these studies—so much so that the banker had enough to do to get him the books he ordered. In the course of four years some six hundred volumes were procured at his request. It was during this period that the banker received the following letter from his prisoner:

"My dear Jailer, I write you these lines in six languages. Show them to people who know the languages. Let them read them. If they find not one mistake I implore you to fire a shot in the garden. That shot will show me that my efforts have not been thrown away. The geniuses of all ages and of all lands speak different languages, but the same flame burns in them all. Oh, if you only knew what unearthly happiness my soul feels now from being able to understand them!" The prisoner's desire was fulfilled. The banker ordered two shots to be fired in the garden.

Then after the tenth year, the prisoner sat immovably at

the table and read nothing but the Gospel. It seemed strange
to the banker that a man who in four years had mastered six
hundred learned volumes should waste nearly a year over
one thin book easy of comprehension. Theology and histories
of religion followed the Gospels.

In the last two years of his confinement the prisoner
read an immense quantity of books quite indiscriminately.
At one time he was busy with the natural sciences, then he
would ask for Byron or Shakespeare. There were notes in
which he demanded at the same time books on chemistry,
and a manual of medicine, and a novel, and some treatise
on philosophy or theology. His reading suggested a man
swimming in the sea among the wreckage of his ship, and
trying to save his life by greedily clutching first at one spar
and then at another.

II

The old banker remembered all this, and thought:

"To-morrow at twelve o'clock he will regain his freedom.
By our agreement I ought to pay him two millions. If I do pay
him, it is all over with me: I shall be utterly ruined."

Fifteen years before, his millions had been beyond his
reckoning; now he was afraid to ask himself which were
greater, his debts or his assets. Desperate gambling on
the Stock Exchange, wild speculation and the excitability
which he could not get over even in advancing years, had
by degrees led to the decline of his fortune and the proud,
fearless, self-confident millionaire had become a banker
of middling rank, trembling at every rise and fall in his
investments. "Cursed bet!" muttered the old man, clutching
his head in despair "Why didn't the man die? He is only forty
now. He will take my last penny from me, he will marry, will

enjoy life, will gamble on the Exchange; while I shall look at him with envy like a beggar, and hear from him every day the same sentence: 'I am indebted to you for the happiness of my life, let me help you!' No, it is too much! The one means of being saved from bankruptcy and disgrace is the death of that man!"

It struck three o'clock, the banker listened; everyone was asleep in the house and nothing could be heard outside but the rustling of the chilled trees. Trying to make no noise, he took from a fireproof safe the key of the door which had not been opened for fifteen years, put on his overcoat, and went out of the house.

It was dark and cold in the garden. Rain was falling. A damp cutting wind was racing about the garden, howling and giving the trees no rest. The banker strained his eyes, but could see neither the earth nor the white statues, nor the lodge, nor the trees. Going to the spot where the lodge stood, he twice called the watchman. No answer followed. Evidently the watchman had sought shelter from the weather, and was now asleep somewhere either in the kitchen or in the greenhouse.

"If I had the pluck to carry out my intention," thought the old man, "Suspicion would fall first upon the watchman."

He felt in the darkness for the steps and the door, and went into the entry of the lodge. Then he groped his way into a little passage and lighted a match. There was not a soul there. There was a bedstead with no bedding on it, and in the corner there was a dark cast-iron stove. The seals on the door leading to the prisoner's rooms were intact.

When the match went out the old man, trembling with emotion, peeped through the little window. A candle was burning dimly in the prisoner's room. He was sitting at the table. Nothing could be seen but his back, the hair on his head, and his hands. Open books were lying on the table, on the two easy-chairs, and on the carpet near the table.

Five minutes passed and the prisoner did not once stir. Fifteen years' imprisonment had taught him to sit still. The banker tapped at the window with his finger, and the prisoner made no movement whatever in response. Then the banker cautiously broke the seals off the door and put the key in the keyhole. The rusty lock gave a grating sound and the door creaked. The banker expected to hear at once footsteps and a cry of astonishment, but three minutes passed and it was as quiet as ever in the room. He made up his mind to go in.

At the table a man unlike ordinary people was sitting motionless. He was a skeleton with the skin drawn tight over his bones, with long curls like a woman's and a shaggy beard. His face was yellow with an earthy tint in it, his cheeks were hollow, his back long and narrow, and the hand on which his shaggy head was propped was so thin and delicate that it was dreadful to look at it. His hair was already streaked with silver, and seeing his emaciated, aged-looking face, no one would have believed that he was only forty. He was asleep.... In front of his bowed head there lay on the table a sheet of paper on which there was something written in fine handwriting.

"Poor creature!" thought the banker, "he is asleep and most likely dreaming of the millions. And I have only to take this half-dead man, throw him on the bed, stifle him a little with the pillow, and the most conscientious expert would find no sign of a violent death. But let us first read what he has written here...."

The banker took the page from the table and read as follows:

"To-morrow at twelve o'clock I regain my freedom and the right to associate with other men, but before I leave this room and see the sunshine, I think it necessary to say a few words to you. With a clear conscience I tell you, as before God, who beholds me, that I despise freedom and life and health, and all that in your books is called the good things of the world.

"For fifteen years I have been intently studying earthly life. It is true I have not seen the earth nor men, but in your books I have drunk fragrant wine, I have sung songs, I have hunted stags and wild boars in the forests, have loved women.... Beauties as ethereal as clouds, created by the magic of your poets and geniuses, have visited me at night, and have whispered in my ears wonderful tales that have set my brain in a whirl. In your books I have climbed to the peaks of Elburz and Mont Blanc, and from there I have seen the sun rise and have watched it at evening flood the sky, the ocean, and the mountain-tops with gold and crimson. I have watched from there the lightning flashing over my head and cleaving the storm-clouds. I have seen green forests, fields, rivers, lakes, towns. I have heard the singing of the sirens, and the strains of the shepherds' pipes; I have touched the wings of comely devils who flew down to converse with me of God.... In your books I have flung myself into the bottomless pit, performed miracles, slain, burned towns, preached new religions, conquered whole kingdoms....

"Your books have given me wisdom. All that the unresting thought of man has created in the ages is compressed into a small compass in my brain. I know that I am wiser than all of you.

"And I despise your books, I despise wisdom and the blessings of this world. It is all worthless, fleeting, illusory, and deceptive, like a mirage. You may be proud, wise, and fine, but death will wipe you off the face of the earth as though you were no more than mice burrowing under the floor, and your posterity, your history, your immortal geniuses will burn or freeze together with the earthly globe.

"You have lost your reason and taken the wrong path. You have taken lies for truth, and hideousness for beauty. You would marvel if, owing to strange events of some sorts, frogs and lizards suddenly grew on apple and orange trees instead of fruit, or if roses began to smell like a sweating horse; so I marvel at you who exchange heaven for earth. I don't want to understand you.

"To prove to you in action how I despise all that you live by, I renounce the two millions of which I once dreamed as of paradise and which now I despise. To deprive myself of the right to the money I shall go out from here five hours before the time fixed, and so break the compact...."

When the banker had read this he laid the page on the table, kissed the strange man on the head, and went out of the lodge, weeping. At no other time, even when he had lost heavily on the Stock Exchange, had he felt so great a contempt for himself. When he got home he lay on his bed, but his tears and emotion kept him for hours from sleeping.

Next morning the watchmen ran in with pale faces, and told him they had seen the man who lived in the lodge climb out of the window into the garden, go to the gate, and disappear. The banker went at once with the servants to the lodge and made sure of the flight of his prisoner. To avoid arousing unnecessary talk, he took from the table the writing in which the millions were renounced, and when he got home locked it up in the fireproof safe.

Misery

"TO WHOM SHALL I TELL MY GRIEF?"

THE twilight of evening. Big flakes of wet snow are whirling lazily about the street lamps, which have just been lighted, and lying in a thin soft layer on roofs, horses' backs, shoulders, caps. Iona Potapov, the sledge-driver, is all white like a ghost. He sits on the box without stirring, bent as double as the living body can be bent. If a regular snowdrift fell on him it seems as though even then he would not think it necessary to shake it off.... His little mare is white and motionless too. Her stillness, the angularity of her lines, and the stick-like straightness of her legs make her look like a halfpenny gingerbread horse. She is probably lost in thought. Anyone who has been torn away from the plough, from the familiar gray landscapes, and cast into this slough, full of monstrous lights, of unceasing uproar and hurrying people, is bound to think.

It is a long time since Iona and his nag have budged. They came out of the yard before dinnertime and not a single fare yet. But now the shades of evening are falling on the town. The pale light of the street lamps changes to a vivid color, and the bustle of the street grows noisier.

"Sledge to Vyborgskaya!" Iona hears. "Sledge!"

Iona starts, and through his snow-plastered eyelashes sees an officer in a military overcoat with a hood over his head.

"To Vyborgskaya," repeats the officer. "Are you asleep? To Vyborgskaya!"

In token of assent Iona gives a tug at the reins which sends cakes of snow flying from the horse's back and shoulders. The officer gets into the sledge. The sledge-driver clicks to the horse, cranes his neck like a swan, rises in his seat, and more from habit than necessity brandishes his whip. The mare cranes her neck, too, crooks her stick-like legs, and hesitatingly sets of....

"Where are you shoving, you devil?" Iona immediately hears shouts from the dark mass shifting to and fro before him. "Where the devil are you going? Keep to the r-right!"

"You don't know how to drive! Keep to the right," says the officer angrily.

A coachman driving a carriage swears at him; a pedestrian crossing the road and brushing the horse's nose with his shoulder looks at him angrily and shakes the snow off his sleeve. Iona fidgets on the box as though he were sitting on thorns, jerks his elbows, and turns his eyes about like one possessed as though he did not know where he was or why he was there.

"What rascals they all are!" says the officer jocosely. "They are simply doing their best to run up against you or fall under the horse's feet. They must be doing it on purpose."

Iona looks as his fare and moves his lips.... Apparently he means to say something, but nothing comes but a sniff.

"What?" inquires the officer.

Iona gives a wry smile, and straining his throat, brings out huskily: "My son... er... my son died this week, sir."

"H'm! What did he die of?"

Iona turns his whole body round to his fare, and says:

"Who can tell! It must have been from fever.... He lay three days in the hospital and then he died.... God's will."

"Turn round, you devil!" comes out of the darkness. "Have you gone cracked, you old dog? Look where you are going!"

"Drive on! drive on!..." says the officer. "We shan't get there till to-morrow going on like this. Hurry up!"

The sledge-driver cranes his neck again, rises in his seat, and with heavy grace swings his whip. Several times he looks round at the officer, but the latter keeps his eyes shut and is apparently disinclined to listen. Putting his fare down at Vyborgskaya, Iona stops by a restaurant, and again sits huddled up on the box.... Again the wet snow paints him and his horse white. One hour passes, and then another....

Three young men, two tall and thin, one short and hunchbacked, come up, railing at each other and loudly stamping on the pavement with their goloshes.

"Cabby, to the Police Bridge!" the hunchback cries in a cracked voice. "The three of us,... twenty kopecks!"

Iona tugs at the reins and clicks to his horse. Twenty kopecks is not a fair price, but he has no thoughts for that. Whether it is a rouble or whether it is five kopecks does not matter to him now so long as he has a fare.... The three young men, shoving each other and using bad language, go up to the sledge, and all three try to sit down at once. The question remains to be settled: Which are to sit down and which one is to stand? After a long altercation, ill-temper, and abuse, they come to the conclusion that the hunchback must stand because he is the shortest.

"Well, drive on," says the hunchback in his cracked voice,

settling himself and breathing down Iona's neck. "Cut along! What a cap you've got, my friend! You wouldn't find a worse one in all Petersburg...."

"He-he!... he-he!..." laughs Iona. "It's nothing to boast of!"

"Well, then, nothing to boast of, drive on! Are you going to drive like this all the way? Eh? Shall I give you one in the neck?"

"My head aches," says one of the tall ones. "At the Dukmasovs' yesterday Vaska and I drank four bottles of brandy between us."

"I can't make out why you talk such stuff," says the other tall one angrily. "You lie like a brute."

"Strike me dead, it's the truth!..."

"It's about as true as that a louse coughs."

"He-he!" grins Iona. "Me-er-ry gentlemen!"

"Tfoo! the devil take you!" cries the hunchback indignantly. "Will you get on, you old plague, or won't you? Is that the way to drive? Give her one with the whip. Hang it all, give it her well."

Iona feels behind his back the jolting person and quivering voice of the hunchback. He hears abuse addressed to him, he sees people, and the feeling of loneliness begins little by little to be less heavy on his heart. The hunchback swears at him, till he chokes over some elaborately whimsical string of epithets and is overpowered by his cough. His tall companions begin talking of a certain Nadyezhda Petrovna. Iona looks round at them. Waiting till there is a brief pause, he looks round once more and says:

"This week... er... my... er... son died!"

"We shall all die,...." says the hunchback with a sigh, wiping his lips after coughing. "Come, drive on! drive on!

My friends, I simply cannot stand crawling like this! When will he get us there?"

"Well, you give him a little encouragement... one in the neck!"

"Do you hear, you old plague? I'll make you smart. If one stands on ceremony with fellows like you one may as well walk. Do you hear, you old dragon? Or don't you care a hang what we say?"

And Iona hears rather than feels a slap on the back of his neck.

"He-he!..." he laughs. "Merry gentlemen.... God give you health!"

"Cabman, are you married?" asks one of the tall ones.

"I? He he! Me-er-ry gentlemen. The only wife for me now is the damp earth.... He-ho-ho!.... The grave that is!... Here my son's dead and I am alive.... It's a strange thing, death has come in at the wrong door.... Instead of coming for me it went for my son...."

And Iona turns round to tell them how his son died, but at that point the hunchback gives a faint sigh and announces that, thank God! they have arrived at last. After taking his twenty kopecks, Iona gazes for a long while after the revelers, who disappear into a dark entry. Again he is alone and again there is silence for him.... The misery which has been for a brief space eased comes back again and tears his heart more cruelly than ever. With a look of anxiety and suffering Iona's eyes stray restlessly among the crowds moving to and fro on both sides of the street: can he not find among those thousands someone who will listen to him? But the crowds flit by heedless of him and his misery.... His misery is immense, beyond all bounds. If Iona's heart were to burst and his misery to flow out, it would flood the whole world, it seems, but yet it is not seen. It has found a hiding-place in such an insignificant shell that one would not have found it with a candle by daylight....

Iona sees a house-porter with a parcel and makes up his mind to address him.

"What time will it be, friend?" he asks.

"Going on for ten.... Why have you stopped here? Drive on!"

Iona drives a few paces away, bends himself double, and gives himself up to his misery. He feels it is no good to appeal to people. But before five minutes have passed he draws himself up, shakes his head as though he feels a sharp pain, and tugs at the reins.... He can bear it no longer.

"Back to the yard!" he thinks. "To the yard!"

And his little mare, as though she knew his thoughts, falls to trotting. An hour and a half later Iona is sitting by a big dirty stove. On the stove, on the floor, and on the benches are people snoring. The air is full of smells and stuffiness. Iona looks at the sleeping figures, scratches himself, and regrets that he has come home so early....

"I have not earned enough to pay for the oats, even," he thinks. "That's why I am so miserable. A man who knows how to do his work,... who has had enough to eat, and whose horse has had enough to eat, is always at ease...."

In one of the corners a young cabman gets up, clears his throat sleepily, and makes for the water-bucket.

"Want a drink?" Iona asks him.

"Seems so."

"May it do you good.... But my son is dead, mate.... Do you hear? This week in the hospital.... It's a queer business...."

Iona looks to see the effect produced by his words, but he

sees nothing. The young man has covered his head over and is already asleep. The old man sighs and scratches himself.... Just as the young man had been thirsty for water, he thirsts for speech. His son will soon have been dead a week, and he has not really talked to anybody yet.... He wants to talk of it properly, with deliberation.... He wants to tell how his son was taken ill, how he suffered, what he said before he died, how he died.... He wants to describe the funeral, and how he went to the hospital to get his son's clothes. He still has his daughter Anisya in the country.... And he wants to talk about her too.... Yes, he has plenty to talk about now. His listener ought to sigh and exclaim and lament.... It would be even better to talk to women. Though they are silly creatures, they blubber at the first word.

"Let's go out and have a look at the mare," Iona thinks. "There is always time for sleep.... You'll have sleep enough, no fear...."

He puts on his coat and goes into the stables where his mare is standing. He thinks about oats, about hay, about the weather.... He cannot think about his son when he is alone.... To talk about him with someone is possible, but to think of him and picture him is insufferable anguish....

"Are you munching?" Iona asks his mare, seeing her shining eyes. "There, munch away, munch away.... Since we have not earned enough for oats, we will eat hay.... Yes,... I have grown too old to drive.... My son ought to be driving, not I.... He was a real cabman.... He ought to have lived...."

Iona is silent for a while, and then he goes on:

"That's how it is, old girl.... Kuzma Ionitch is gone.... He said good-by to me.... He went and died for no reason.... Now, suppose you had a little colt, and you were own mother to that little colt. ... And all at once that same little colt went and died.... You'd be sorry, wouldn't you?..."

The little mare munches, listens, and breathes on her master's hands. Iona is carried away and tells her all about it.

At Christmas Time

"WHAT shall I write?" said Yegor, and he dipped his pen in the ink.

Vasilisa had not seen her daughter for four years. Her daughter Yefimya had gone after her wedding to Petersburg, had sent them two letters, and since then seemed to vanish out of their lives; there had been no sight nor sound of her. And whether the old woman were milking her cow at dawn, or heating her stove, or dozing at night, she was always thinking of one and the same thing—what was happening to Yefimya, whether she were alive out yonder. She ought to have sent a letter, but the old father could not write, and there was no one to write.

But now Christmas had come, and Vasilisa could not bear it any longer, and went to the tavern to Yegor, the brother of the innkeeper's wife, who had sat in the tavern doing nothing ever since he came back from the army; people said that he could write letters very well if he were properly paid. Vasilisa talked to the cook at the tavern, then to the mistress of the house, then to Yegor himself. They agreed upon fifteen kopecks.

And now—it happened on the second day of the holidays,

in the tavern kitchen—Yegor was sitting at the table, holding the pen in his hand. Vasilisa was standing before him, pondering with an expression of anxiety and woe on her face. Pyotr, her husband, a very thin old man with a brownish bald patch, had come with her; he stood looking straight before him like a blind man. On the stove a piece of pork was being braised in a saucepan; it was spurting and hissing, and seemed to be actually saying: "Flu-flu-flu." It was stifling.

"What am I to write?" Yegor asked again.

"What?" asked Vasilisa, looking at him angrily and suspiciously. "Don't worry me! You are not writing for nothing; no fear, you'll be paid for it. Come, write: 'To our dear son-in-law, Andrey Hrisanfitch, and to our only beloved daughter, Yefimya Petrovna, with our love we send a low bow and our parental blessing abiding for ever.'"

"Written; fire away."

"'And we wish them a happy Christmas; we are alive and well, and I wish you the same, please the Lord... the Heavenly King.'"

Vasilisa pondered and exchanged glances with the old man.

"'And I wish you the same, please the Lord the Heavenly King,'" she repeated, beginning to cry.

She could say nothing more. And yet before, when she lay awake thinking at night, it had seemed to her that she could not get all she had to say into a dozen letters. Since the time when her daughter had gone away with her husband much water had flowed into the sea, the old people had lived feeling bereaved, and sighed heavily at night as though they had buried their daughter. And how many events had occurred in the village since then, how many marriages and deaths! How long the winters had been! How long the nights!

"It's hot," said Yegor, unbuttoning his waistcoat. "It must be seventy degrees. What more?" he asked.

The old people were silent.

"What does your son-in-law do in Petersburg?" asked Yegor.

"He was a soldier, my good friend," the old man answered in a weak voice. "He left the service at the same time as you did. He was a soldier, and now, to be sure, he is at Petersburg at a hydropathic establishment. The doctor treats the sick with water. So he, to be sure, is house-porter at the doctor's."

"Here it is written down," said the old woman, taking a letter out of her pocket. "We got it from Yefimya, goodness knows when. Maybe they are no longer in this world."

Yegor thought a little and began writing rapidly:

"At the present time"—he wrote—"since your destiny through your own doing allotted you to the Military Career, we counsel you to look into the Code of Disciplinary Offences and Fundamental Laws of the War Office, and you will see in that law the Civilization of the Officials of the War Office."

He wrote and kept reading aloud what was written, while Vasilisa considered what she ought to write: how great had been their want the year before, how their corn had not lasted even till Christmas, how they had to sell their cow. She ought to ask for money, ought to write that the old father was often ailing and would soon no doubt give up his soul to God... but how to express this in words? What must be said first and what afterwards?

"Take note," Yegor went on writing, "in volume five of the Army Regulations soldier is a common noun and a proper one, a soldier of the first rank is called a general, and of the last a private...."

The old man stirred his lips and said softly:

"It would be all right to have a look at the grandchildren."

"What grandchildren?" asked the old woman, and she looked angrily at him; "perhaps there are none."

"Well, but perhaps there are. Who knows?"

"And thereby you can judge," Yegor hurried on, "what is the enemy without and what is the enemy within. The foremost of our enemies within is Bacchus." The pen squeaked, executing upon the paper flourishes like fish-hooks. Yegor hastened and read over every line several times. He sat on a stool sprawling his broad feet under the table, well-fed, bursting with health, with a coarse animal face and a red bull neck. He was vulgarity itself: coarse, conceited, invincible, proud of having been born and bred in a pot-house; and Vasilisa quite understood the vulgarity, but could not express it in words, and could only look angrily and suspiciously at Yegor. Her head was beginning to ache, and her thoughts were in confusion from the sound of his voice and his unintelligible words, from the heat and the stuffiness, and she said nothing and thought nothing, but simply waited for him to finish scribbling. But the old man looked with full confidence. He believed in his old woman who had brought him there, and in Yegor; and when he had mentioned the hydropathic establishment it could be seen that he believed in the establishment and the healing efficacy of water.

Having finished the letter, Yegor got up and read the whole of it through from the beginning. The old man did not understand, but he nodded his head trustfully.

"That's all right; it is smooth..." he said. "God give you health. That's all right...."

They laid on the table three five-kopeck pieces and went out of the tavern; the old man looked immovably straight before him as though he were blind, and perfect trustfulness was written on his face; but as Vasilisa came out of the tavern she waved angrily at the dog, and said angrily:

"Ugh, the plague."

The old woman did not sleep all night; she was disturbed by thoughts, and at daybreak she got up, said her prayers, and went to the station to send off the letter.

It was between eight and nine miles to the station.

II

Dr. B. O. Mozelweiser's hydropathic establishment worked on New Year's Day exactly as on ordinary days; the only difference was that the porter, Andrey Hrisanfitch, had on a uniform with new braiding, his boots had an extra polish, and he greeted every visitor with "A Happy New Year to you!"

It was the morning; Andrey Hrisanfitch was standing at the door, reading the newspaper. Just at ten o'clock there arrived a general, one of the habitual visitors, and directly after him the postman; Andrey Hrisanfitch helped the general off with his great-coat, and said:

"A Happy New Year to your Excellency!"

"Thank you, my good fellow; the same to you."

And at the top of the stairs the general asked, nodding towards the door (he asked the same question every day and always forgot the answer):

"And what is there in that room?"

"The massage room, your Excellency."

When the general's steps had died away Andrey Hrisanfitch looked at the post that had come, and found one addressed to himself. He tore it open, read several lines, then, looking at the newspaper, he walked without haste to his own room, which was downstairs close by at the end of the passage. His wife Yefimya was sitting on the bed, feeding her baby; another child, the eldest, was standing by, laying its curly head on her knee; a third was asleep on the bed.

Going into the room, Andrey gave his wife the letter and said:

"From the country, I suppose."

Then he walked out again without taking his eyes from the paper. He could hear Yefimya with a shaking voice reading the first lines. She read them and could read no more; these lines were enough for her. She burst into tears, and hugging her eldest child, kissing him, she began saying—and it was hard to say whether she were laughing or crying:

"It's from granny, from grandfather," she said. "From the country.... The Heavenly Mother, Saints and Martyrs! The snow lies heaped up under the roofs now... the trees are as white as white. The boys slide on little sledges... and dear old bald grandfather is on the stove... and there is a little yellow dog.... My own darlings!"

Andrey Hrisanfitch, hearing this, recalled that his wife had on three or four occasions given him letters and asked him to send them to the country, but some important business had always prevented him; he had not sent them, and the letters somehow got lost.

"And little hares run about in the fields," Yefimya went on chanting, kissing her boy and shedding tears. "Grandfather is kind and gentle; granny is good, too—kind-hearted. They are warm-hearted in the country, they are God-fearing... and there is a little church in the village; the peasants sing in the choir. Queen of Heaven, Holy Mother and Defender, take us away from here!"

Andrey Hrisanfitch returned to his room to smoke a little

till there was another ring at the door, and Yefimya ceased speaking, subsided, and wiped her eyes, though her lips were still quivering. She was very much frightened of him— oh, how frightened of him! She trembled and was reduced to terror by the sound of his steps, by the look in his eyes, and dared not utter a word in his presence.

Andrey Hrisanfitch lighted a cigarette, but at that very moment there was a ring from upstairs. He put out his cigarette, and, assuming a very grave face, hastened to his front door.

The general was coming downstairs, fresh and rosy from his bath.

"And what is there in that room?" he asked, pointing to a door.

Andrey Hrisanfitch put his hands down swiftly to the seams of his trousers, and pronounced loudly:

"Charcot douche, your Excellency!"

The Huntsman

A sultry, stifling midday. Not a cloudlet in the sky.... The sun-baked grass had a disconsolate, hopeless look: even if there were rain it could never be green again.... The forest stood silent, motionless, as though it were looking at something with its tree-tops or expecting something.

At the edge of the clearing a tall, narrow-shouldered man of forty in a red shirt, in patched trousers that had been a gentleman's, and in high boots, was slouching along with a lazy, shambling step. He was sauntering along the road. On the right was the green of the clearing, on the left a golden sea of ripe rye stretched to the very horizon. He was red and perspiring, a white cap with a straight jockey peak, evidently a gift from some open-handed young gentleman, perched jauntily on his handsome flaxen head. Across his shoulder hung a game-bag with a blackcock lying in it. The man held a double-barrelled gun cocked in his hand, and screwed up his eyes in the direction of his lean old dog who was running on ahead sniffing the bushes. There was stillness all round, not a sound... everything living was hiding away from the heat.

"Yegor Vlassitch!" the huntsman suddenly heard a soft voice.

He started and, looking round, scowled. Beside him, as though she had sprung out of the earth, stood a pale-faced woman of thirty with a sickle in her hand. She was trying to look into his face, and was smiling diffidently.

"Oh, it is you, Pelagea!" said the huntsman, stopping and deliberately uncocking the gun. "H'm!... How have you come here?"

"The women from our village are working here, so I have come with them.... As a labourer, Yegor Vlassitch."

"Oh..." growled Yegor Vlassitch, and slowly walked on.

Pelagea followed him. They walked in silence for twenty paces.

"I have not seen you for a long time, Yegor Vlassitch..." said Pelagea looking tenderly at the huntsman's moving shoulders. "I have not seen you since you came into our hut at Easter for a drink of water... you came in at Easter for a minute and then God knows how... drunk... you scolded and beat me and went away... I have been waiting and waiting... I've tired my eyes out looking for you. Ah, Yegor Vlassitch, Yegor Vlassitch! you might look in just once!"

"What is there for me to do there?"

"Of course there is nothing for you to do... though to be sure... there is the place to look after.... To see how things are going.... You are the master.... I say, you have shot a blackcock, Yegor Vlassitch! You ought to sit down and rest!"

As she said all this Pelagea laughed like a silly girl and looked up at Yegor's face. Her face was simply radiant with happiness.

"Sit down? If you like..." said Yegor in a tone of indifference, and he chose a spot between two fir-trees. "Why are you standing? You sit down too."

Pelagea sat a little way off in the sun and, ashamed of

her joy, put her hand over her smiling mouth. Two minutes passed in silence.

"You might come for once," said Pelagea.

"What for?" sighed Yegor, taking off his cap and wiping his red forehead with his hand. "There is no object in my coming. To go for an hour or two is only waste of time, it's simply upsetting you, and to live continually in the village my soul could not endure.... You know yourself I am a pampered man.... I want a bed to sleep in, good tea to drink, and refined conversation.... I want all the niceties, while you live in poverty and dirt in the village.... I couldn't stand it for a day. Suppose there were an edict that I must live with you, I should either set fire to the hut or lay hands on myself. From a boy I've had this love for ease; there is no help for it."

"Where are you living now?"

"With the gentleman here, Dmitry Ivanitch, as a huntsman. I furnish his table with game, but he keeps me... more for his pleasure than anything."

"That's not proper work you're doing, Yegor Vlassitch.... For other people it's a pastime, but with you it's like a trade... like real work."

"You don't understand, you silly," said Yegor, gazing gloomily at the sky. "You have never understood, and as long as you live you will never understand what sort of man I am.... You think of me as a foolish man, gone to the bad, but to anyone who understands I am the best shot there is in the whole district. The gentry feel that, and they have even printed things about me in a magazine. There isn't a man to be compared with me as a sportsman.... And it is not because I am pampered and proud that I look down upon your village work. From my childhood, you know, I have never had any calling apart from guns and dogs. If they took away my gun, I used to go out with the fishing-hook, if they took the hook I caught things with my hands. And I went in for horse-dealing too, I used to go to the fairs when I had the money, and you know that if a peasant goes in for being a sportsman, or a horse-dealer, it's good-bye to the plough. Once the spirit of freedom has taken a man you will never root it out of him. In the same way, if a gentleman goes in for being an actor or for any other art, he will never make an official or a landowner. You are a woman, and you do not understand, but one must understand that."

"I understand, Yegor Vlassitch."

"You don't understand if you are going to cry...."

"I... I'm not crying," said Pelagea, turning away. "It's a sin, Yegor Vlassitch! You might stay a day with luckless me, anyway. It's twelve years since I was married to you, and... and... there has never once been love between us!... I... I am not crying."

"Love..." muttered Yegor, scratching his hand. "There can't be any love. It's only in name we are husband and wife; we aren't really. In your eyes I am a wild man, and in mine you are a simple peasant woman with no understanding. Are we well matched? I am a free, pampered, profligate man, while you are a working woman, going in bark shoes and never straightening your back. The way I think of myself is that I am the foremost man in every kind of sport, and you look at me with pity.... Is that being well matched?"

"But we are married, you know, Yegor Vlassitch," sobbed Pelagea.

"Not married of our free will.... Have you forgotten? You have to thank Count Sergey Paylovitch and yourself. Out of envy, because I shot better than he did, the Count kept giving me wine for a whole month, and when a man's drunk you could make him change his religion, let alone getting married. To pay me out he married me to you when I was drunk.... A huntsman to a herd-girl! You saw I was drunk, why did you marry me? You were not a serf, you know; you could have resisted. Of course it was a bit of luck for a herd-girl to marry a huntsman, but you ought to have thought about it. Well, now be miserable, cry. It's a joke for the Count, but a crying matter for you.... Beat yourself against the wall."

A silence followed. Three wild ducks flew over the clearing. Yegor followed them with his eyes till, transformed into three scarcely visible dots, they sank down far beyond the forest.

"How do you live?" he asked, moving his eyes from the ducks to Pelagea.

"Now I am going out to work, and in the winter I take a child from the Foundling Hospital and bring it up on the bottle. They give me a rouble and a half a month."

"Oh...."

Again a silence. From the strip that had been reaped floated a soft song which broke off at the very beginning. It was too hot to sing.

"They say you have put up a new hut for Akulina," said Pelagea.

Yegor did not speak.

"So she is dear to you...."

"It's your luck, it's fate!" said the huntsman, stretching. "You must put up with it, poor thing. But good-bye, I've been chattering long enough.... I must be at Boltovo by the evening."

Yegor rose, stretched himself, and slung his gun over his shoulder; Pelagea got up.

"And when are you coming to the village?" she asked softly.

"I have no reason to, I shall never come sober, and you have little to gain from me drunk; I am spiteful when I am drunk. Good-bye!"

"Good-bye, Yegor Vlassitch."

Yegor put his cap on t he back of his head and, clicking to his dog, went on his way. Pelagea stood still looking after him.... She saw his moving shoulder-blades, his jaunty cap, his lazy, careless step, and her eyes were full of sadness and tender affection.... Her gaze flitted over her husband's tall, lean figure and caressed and fondled it.... He, as though he felt that gaze, stopped and looked round.... He did not speak, but from his face, from his shrugged shoulders, Pelagea could see that he wanted to say something to her. She went up to him timidly and looked at him with imploring eyes.

"Take it," he said, turning round.

He gave her a crumpled rouble note and walked quickly away.

"Good-bye, Yegor Vlassitch," she said, mechanically taking the rouble.

He walked by a long road, straight as a taut strap. She, pale and motionless as a statue, stood, her eyes seizing every step he took. But the red of his shirt melted into the dark colour of his trousers, his step could not be seen, and the dog could not be distinguished from the boots. Nothing could be seen but the cap, and... suddenly Yegor turned off sharply into the clearing and the cap vanished in the greenness.

"Good-bye, Yegor Vlassitch," whispered Pelagea, and she stood on tiptoe to see the white cap once more.

A Malefactor

AN exceedingly lean little peasant, in a striped hempen shirt and patched drawers, stands facing the investigating magistrate. His face overgrown with hair and pitted with smallpox, and his eyes scarcely visible under thick, overhanging eyebrows have an expression of sullen moroseness. On his head there is a perfect mop of tangled, unkempt hair, which gives him an even more spider-like air of moroseness. He is barefooted.

"Denis Grigoryev!" the magistrate begins. "Come nearer, and answer my questions. On the seventh of this July the railway watchman, Ivan Semyonovitch Akinfov, going along the line in the morning, found you at the hundred-and-forty-first mile engaged in unscrewing a nut by which the rails are made fast to the sleepers. Here it is, the nut!... With the aforesaid nut he detained you. Was that so?"

"Wha-at?"

"Was this all as Akinfov states?"

"To be sure, it was."

"Very good; well, what were you unscrewing the nut for?"

"Wha-at?"

"Drop that 'wha-at' and answer the question; what were

you unscrewing the nut for?"

"If I hadn't wanted it I shouldn't have unscrewed it," croaks Denis, looking at the ceiling.

"What did you want that nut for?"

"The nut? We make weights out of those nuts for our lines."

"Who is 'we'?"

"We, people.... The Klimovo peasants, that is."

"Listen, my man; don't play the idiot to me, but speak sensibly. It's no use telling lies here about weights!"

"I've never been a liar from a child, and now I'm telling lies..." mutters Denis, blinking. "But can you do without a weight, your honour? If you put live bait or maggots on a hook, would it go to the bottom without a weight?... I am telling lies," grins Denis.... "What the devil is the use of the worm if it swims on the surface! The perch and the pike and the eel-pout always go to the bottom, and a bait on the surface is only taken by a shillisper, not very often then, and there are no shillispers in our river.... That fish likes plenty of room."

"Why are you telling me about shillispers?"

"Wha-at? Why, you asked me yourself! The gentry catch fish that way too in our parts. The silliest little boy would not try to catch a fish without a weight. Of course anyone who did not understand might go to fish without a weight. There is no rule for a fool."

"So you say you unscrewed this nut to make a weight for your fishing line out of it?"

"What else for? It wasn't to play knuckle-bones with!"

"But you might have taken lead, a bullet... a nail of some sort...."

"You don't pick up lead in the road, you have to buy it, and a nail's no good. You can't find anything better than a nut.... It's heavy, and there's a hole in it."

"He keeps pretending to be a fool! as though he'd been born yesterday or dropped from heaven! Don't you understand, you blockhead, what unscrewing these nuts leads to? If the watchman had not noticed it the train might have run off the rails, people would have been killed—you would have killed people."

"God forbid, your honour! What should I kill them for? Are we heathens or wicked people? Thank God, good gentlemen, we have lived all our lives without ever dreaming of such a thing.... Save, and have mercy on us, Queen of Heaven!... What are you saying?"

"And what do you suppose railway accidents do come from? Unscrew two or three nuts and you have an accident."

Denis grins, and screws up his eye at the magistrate incredulously.

"Why! how many years have we all in the village been unscrewing nuts, and the Lord has been merciful; and you talk of accidents, killing people. If I had carried away a rail or put a log across the line, say, then maybe it might have upset the train, but... pouf! a nut!"

"But you must understand that the nut holds the rail fast to the sleepers!"

"We understand that.... We don't unscrew them all... we leave some.... We don't do it thoughtlessly... we understand...."

Denis yawns and makes the sign of the cross over his mouth.

"Last year the train went off the rails here," says the magistrate. "Now I see why!"

"What do you say, your honour?"

"I am telling you that now I see why the train went off the rails last year.... I understand!"

"That's what you are educated people for, to understand, you kind gentlemen. The Lord knows to whom to give understanding.... Here you have reasoned how and what, but the watchman, a peasant like ourselves, with no understanding at all, catches one by the collar and hauls one along.... You should reason first and then haul me off. It's a saying that a peasant has a peasant's wit.... Write down, too, your honour, that he hit me twice—in the jaw and in the chest."

"When your hut was searched they found another nut.... At what spot did you unscrew that, and when?"

"You mean the nut which lay under the red box?"

"I don't know where it was lying, only it was found. When did you unscrew it?"

"I didn't unscrew it; Ignashka, the son of one-eyed Semyon, gave it me. I mean the one which was under the box, but the one which was in the sledge in the yard Mitrofan and I unscrewed together."

"What Mitrofan?"

"Mitrofan Petrov.... Haven't you heard of him? He makes nets in our village and sells them to the gentry. He needs a lot of those nuts. Reckon a matter of ten for each net."

"Listen. Article 1081 of the Penal Code lays down that every wilful damage of the railway line committed when it can expose the traffic on that line to danger, and the guilty party knows that an accident must be caused by it... (Do you understand? Knows! And you could not help knowing what this unscrewing would lead to...) is liable to penal servitude."

"Of course, you know best.... We are ignorant people.... What do we understand?"

"You understand all about it! You are lying, shamming!"

"What should I lie for? Ask in the village if you don't believe me. Only a bleak is caught without a weight, and there is no fish worse than a gudgeon, yet even that won't bite without a weight."

"You'd better tell me about the shillisper next," said the magistrate, smiling.

"There are no shillispers in our parts.... We cast our line without a weight on the top of the water with a butterfly; a mullet may be caught that way, though that is not often."

"Come, hold your tongue."

A silence follows. Denis shifts from one foot to the other, looks at the table with the green cloth on it, and blinks his eyes violently as though what was before him was not the cloth but the sun. The magistrate writes rapidly.

"Can I go?" asks Denis after a long silence.

"No. I must take you under guard and send you to prison."

Denis leaves off blinking and, raising his thick eyebrows, looks inquiringly at the magistrate.

"How do you mean, to prison? Your honour! I have no time to spare, I must go to the fair; I must get three roubles from Yegor for some tallow!..."

"Hold your tongue; don't interrupt."

"To prison.... If there was something to go for, I'd go; but just to go for nothing! What for? I haven't stolen anything, I believe, and I've not been fighting.... If you are in doubt about the arrears, your honour, don't believe the elder.... You ask the agent... he's a regular heathen, the elder, you know."

"Hold your tongue."

"I am holding my tongue, as it is," mutters Denis; "but

that the elder has lied over the account, I'll take my oath for it.... There are three of us brothers: Kuzma Grigoryev, then Yegor Grigoryev, and me, Denis Grigoryev."

"You are hindering me.... Hey, Semyon," cries the magistrate, "take him away!"

"There are three of us brothers," mutters Denis, as two stalwart soldiers take him and lead him out of the room. "A brother is not responsible for a brother. Kuzma does not pay, so you, Denis, must answer for it.... Judges indeed! Our master the general is dead—the Kingdom of Heaven be his— or he would have shown you judges.... You ought to judge sensibly, not at random.... Flog if you like, but flog someone who deserves it, flog with conscience."

Ward No. 6

I

IN the hospital yard there stands a small lodge surrounded by a perfect forest of burdocks, nettles, and wild hemp. Its roof is rusty, the chimney is tumbling down, the steps at the front-door are rotting away and overgrown with grass, and there are only traces left of the stucco. The front of the lodge faces the hospital; at the back it looks out into the open country, from which it is separated by the grey hospital fence with nails on it. These nails, with their points upwards, and the fence, and the lodge itself, have that peculiar, desolate, God-forsaken look which is only found in our hospital and prison buildings.

If you are not afraid of being stung by the nettles, come by the narrow footpath that leads to the lodge, and let us see what is going on inside. Opening the first door, we walk into the entry. Here along the walls and by the stove every sort of hospital rubbish lies littered about. Mattresses, old tattered dressing-gowns, trousers, blue striped shirts, boots and shoes no good for anything—all these remnants are piled up in heaps, mixed up and crumpled, mouldering and giving out a sickly smell.

The porter, Nikita, an old soldier wearing rusty good-conduct stripes, is always lying on the litter with a pipe between his teeth. He has a grim, surly, battered-looking face, overhanging eyebrows which give him the expression of a sheep-dog of the steppes, and a red nose; he is short and looks thin and scraggy, but he is of imposing deportment and his fists are vigorous. He belongs to the class of simple-hearted, practical, and dull-witted people, prompt in carrying out orders, who like discipline better than anything in the world, and so are convinced that it is their duty to beat people. He showers blows on the face, on the chest, on the back, on whatever comes first, and is convinced that there would be no order in the place if he did not.

Next you come into a big, spacious room which fills up the whole lodge except for the entry. Here the walls are painted a dirty blue, the ceiling is as sooty as in a hut without a chimney—it is evident that in the winter the stove smokes and the room is full of fumes. The windows are disfigured by iron gratings on the inside. The wooden floor is grey and full of splinters. There is a stench of sour cabbage, of smouldering wicks, of bugs, and of ammonia, and for the first minute this stench gives you the impression of having walked into a menagerie.

There are bedsteads screwed to the floor. Men in blue hospital dressing-gowns, and wearing nightcaps in the old style, are sitting and lying on them. These are the lunatics.

There are five of them in all here. Only one is of the upper class, the rest are all artisans. The one nearest the door—a tall, lean workman with shining red whiskers and tear-stained eyes—sits with his head propped on his hand, staring at the same point. Day and night he grieves, shaking his head, sighing and smiling bitterly. He takes a part in conversation and usually makes no answer to questions; he eats and drinks mechanically when food is offered him. From his agonizing, throbbing cough, his thinness, and the flush on his cheeks, one may judge that he is in the first stage of consumption. Next to him is a little, alert, very lively old man, with a pointed beard and curly black hair like a negro's. By day he walks up and down the ward from window to window, or sits on his bed, cross-legged like a Turk, and, ceaselessly as a bullfinch whistles, softly sings and titters. He shows his childish gaiety and lively character at night also when he gets up to say his prayers—that is, to beat himself on the chest with his fists, and to scratch with his fingers at the door. This is the Jew Moiseika, an imbecile, who went crazy twenty years ago when his hat factory was burnt down.

And of all the inhabitants of Ward No. 6, he is the only one who is allowed to go out of the lodge, and even out of the yard into the street. He has enjoyed this privilege for years, probably because he is an old inhabitant of the hospital—a quiet, harmless imbecile, the buffoon of the town, where people are used to seeing him surrounded by boys and dogs. In his wretched gown, in his absurd night-cap, and in slippers, sometimes with bare legs and even without trousers, he walks about the streets, stopping at the gates and little shops, and begging for a copper. In one place they will give him some kvass, in another some bread, in another a copper, so that he generally goes back to the ward feeling rich and well fed. Everything that he brings back Nikita takes from him for his own benefit. The soldier does this roughly, angrily turning the Jew's pockets inside out, and calling God to witness that he will not let him go into the street again, and that breach of the regulations is worse to him than anything in the world.

Moiseika likes to make himself useful. He gives his companions water, and covers them up when they are asleep; he promises each of them to bring him back a kopeck, and to make him a new cap; he feeds with a spoon his neighbour on the left, who is paralyzed. He acts in this way, not from compassion nor from any considerations of a humane kind, but through imitation, unconsciously dominated by Gromov, his neighbour on the right hand.

Ivan Dmitritch Gromov, a man of thirty-three, who is a gentleman by birth, and has been a court usher and provincial secretary, suffers from the mania of persecution. He either lies curled up in bed, or walks from corner to corner as though for exercise; he very rarely sits down. He is always excited, agitated, and overwrought by a sort of vague, undefined expectation. The faintest rustle in the entry or shout in the yard is enough to make him raise his head and begin listening: whether they are coming for him, whether they are looking for him. And at such times his face expresses the utmost uneasiness and repulsion.

I like his broad face with its high cheek-bones, always pale and unhappy, and reflecting, as though in a mirror, a soul tormented by conflict and long-continued terror. His grimaces are strange and abnormal, but the delicate lines traced on his face by profound, genuine suffering show intelligence and sense, and there is a warm and healthy light in his eyes. I like the man himself, courteous, anxious to be of use, and extraordinarily gentle to everyone except Nikita. When anyone drops a button or a spoon, he jumps up from his bed quickly and picks it up; every day he says good-morning to his companions, and when he goes to bed he wishes them good-night.

Besides his continually overwrought condition and his grimaces, his madness shows itself in the following way also. Sometimes in the evenings he wraps himself in his dressing-gown, and, trembling all over, with his teeth chattering, begins walking rapidly from corner to corner and between the bedsteads. It seems as though he is in a violent fever. From the way he suddenly stops and glances at his companions, it can be seen that he is longing to say something very important, but, apparently reflecting that they would not listen, or would not understand him, he shakes his head impatiently and goes on pacing up and down. But soon the desire to speak gets the upper hand of every consideration, and he will let himself go and speak fervently and passionately. His talk is disordered and feverish like delirium, disconnected, and not always intelligible, but, on the other hand, something extremely fine may be felt in it, both in the words and the voice. When he talks you recognize in him the lunatic and the man. It is difficult to reproduce on paper his insane talk. He speaks of the baseness of mankind, of violence trampling on justice, of the glorious life which will one day be upon earth, of the window-gratings, which remind him every minute of the stupidity and cruelty of oppressors. It makes a disorderly, incoherent potpourri of themes old but not yet out of date.

II

Some twelve or fifteen years ago an official called Gromov, a highly respectable and prosperous person, was living in his own house in the principal street of the town. He had two sons, Sergey and Ivan. When Sergey was a student in his fourth year he was taken ill with galloping consumption and died, and his death was, as it were, the first of a whole series of calamities which suddenly showered on the Gromov family. Within a week of Sergey's funeral the old father was put on trial for fraud and misappropriation, and he died of typhoid in the prison hospital soon afterwards. The house, with all their belongings, was sold by auction, and Ivan Dmitritch and his mother were left entirely without means.

Hitherto in his father's lifetime, Ivan Dmitritch, who was studying in the University of Petersburg, had received an allowance of sixty or seventy roubles a month, and had had no conception of poverty; now he had to make an abrupt change in his life. He had to spend his time from morning to night giving lessons for next to nothing, to work at copying, and with all that to go hungry, as all his earnings were sent to keep his mother. Ivan Dmitritch could not stand such a life; he lost heart and strength, and, giving up the university, went home.

Here, through interest, he obtained the post of teacher in the district school, but could not get on with his colleagues, was not liked by the boys, and soon gave up the post. His mother died. He was for six months without work, living on nothing but bread and water; then he became a court usher. He kept this post until he was dismissed owing to his illness.

He had never even in his young student days given the impression of being perfectly healthy. He had always been pale, thin, and given to catching cold; he ate little and slept badly. A single glass of wine went to his head and made him hysterical. He always had a craving for society, but, owing to his irritable temperament and suspiciousness, he never became very intimate with anyone, and had no friends. He always spoke with contempt of his fellow-townsmen, saying that their coarse ignorance and sleepy animal existence seemed to him loathsome and horrible. He spoke in a loud tenor, with heat, and invariably either with scorn and indignation, or with wonder and enthusiasm, and always with perfect sincerity. Whatever one talked to him about he always brought it round to the same subject: that life was dull and stifling in the town; that the townspeople had no lofty interests, but lived a dingy, meaningless life, diversified by violence, coarse profligacy, and hypocrisy; that scoundrels were well fed and clothed, while honest men lived from hand to mouth; that they needed schools, a progressive local paper, a theatre, public lectures, the co-ordination of the intellectual elements; that society must see its failings and be horrified. In his criticisms of people he laid on the colours thick, using only black and white, and no fine shades; mankind was divided for him into honest men and scoundrels: there was nothing in between. He always spoke with passion and enthusiasm of women and of love, but he had never been in love.

In spite of the severity of his judgments and his nervousness, he was liked, and behind his back was spoken of affectionately as Vanya. His innate refinement and readiness to be of service, his good breeding, his moral purity, and his shabby coat, his frail appearance and family misfortunes, aroused a kind, warm, sorrowful feeling. Moreover, he was well educated and well read; according to the townspeople's notions, he knew everything, and was in their eyes something like a walking encyclopedia.

He had read a great deal. He would sit at the club, nervously pulling at his beard and looking through the magazines and books; and from his face one could see that he was not reading, but devouring the pages without giving himself time to digest what he read. It must be supposed that reading was one of his morbid habits, as he fell upon anything that came into his hands with equal avidity, even last year's newspapers and calendars. At home he always read lying down.

III

One autumn morning Ivan Dmitritch, turning up the collar of his greatcoat and splashing through the mud, made his way by side-streets and back lanes to see some artisan, and to collect some payment that was owing. He was in a gloomy mood, as he always was in the morning. In one of the side-streets he was met by two convicts in fetters and four soldiers with rifles in charge of them. Ivan Dmitritch had very often met convicts before, and they had always excited feelings of compassion and discomfort in him; but now this meeting made a peculiar, strange impression on him. It suddenly seemed to him for some reason that he, too, might be put into fetters and led through the mud to prison like that. After visiting the artisan, on the way home he met near the post office a police superintendent of his acquaintance, who greeted him and walked a few paces along the street with him, and for some reason this seemed to him suspicious. At home he could not get the convicts or the soldiers with their rifles out of his head all day, and an unaccountable inward agitation prevented him from reading or concentrating his mind. In the evening he did not light his lamp, and at night he could not sleep, but kept thinking that he might be arrested, put into fetters, and thrown into prison. He did not know of any harm he had done, and could be certain that he would never be guilty of murder, arson, or theft in the future either; but was it not easy to commit a crime by accident, unconsciously, and was not false witness always possible, and, indeed, miscarriage of justice? It was not without good reason that the agelong experience of the simple people teaches that beggary and prison are ills none can be safe from. A judicial mistake is very possible as legal proceedings are conducted nowadays, and there is nothing to be wondered at in it. People who have an official, professional relation to other men's sufferings—for instance, judges, police officers, doctors—in course of time, through habit, grow so callous that they cannot, even if they wish it, take any but a formal attitude to their clients; in this respect they are not different from the peasant who slaughters sheep and calves in the back-yard, and does not notice the blood. With this formal, soulless attitude to human personality the judge needs but one thing—time—in order to deprive an innocent man of all rights of property, and to condemn him to penal servitude. Only the time spent on performing certain formalities for which the judge is paid his salary, and then—it is all over. Then you may look in vain for justice and protection in this dirty, wretched little town a hundred and fifty miles from a railway station! And, indeed, is it not absurd even to think of justice when every kind of violence is accepted by society as a rational and consistent necessity, and every act of mercy—for instance, a verdict of acquittal—calls forth a perfect outburst of dissatisfied and revengeful feeling?

In the morning Ivan Dmitritch got up from his bed in a state of horror, with cold perspiration on his forehead, completely convinced that he might be arrested any minute. Since his gloomy thoughts of yesterday had haunted him so long, he thought, it must be that there was some truth in them. They could not, indeed, have come into his mind without any grounds whatever.

A policeman walking slowly passed by the windows: that was not for nothing. Here were two men standing still and silent near the house. Why were they silent? And agonizing days and nights followed for Ivan Dmitritch. Everyone who passed by the windows or came into the yard seemed to him a spy or a detective. At midday the chief of the police usually drove down the street with a pair of horses; he was going from his estate near the town to the police department; but Ivan Dmitritch fancied every time that he was driving especially quickly, and that he had a peculiar expression: it was evident that he was in haste to announce that there was a very important criminal in the town. Ivan Dmitritch started at every ring at the bell and knock at the gate, and was agitated whenever he came upon anyone new at his landlady's; when he met police officers and gendarmes he smiled and began whistling so as to seem unconcerned. He could not sleep for whole nights in succession expecting to be arrested, but he snored loudly and sighed as though in deep sleep, that his landlady might think he was asleep; for if he could not sleep it meant that he was tormented by the stings of conscience—what a piece of evidence! Facts and common sense persuaded him that all these terrors were nonsense and morbidity, that if one looked at the matter more broadly there was nothing really terrible in arrest and imprisonment—so long as the conscience is at ease; but the more sensibly and logically he reasoned, the more acute and agonizing his mental distress became. It might be compared with the story of a hermit who tried to cut a dwelling-place for himself in a virgin forest; the more zealously he worked with his axe, the thicker the forest grew. In the end Ivan Dmitritch, seeing it was useless, gave up reasoning altogether, and abandoned himself entirely to despair and terror.

He began to avoid people and to seek solitude. His official work had been distasteful to him before: now it became unbearable to him. He was afraid they would somehow get him into trouble, would put a bribe in his pocket unnoticed and then denounce him, or that he would accidentally make a mistake in official papers that would appear to be fraudulent, or would lose other people's money. It is strange that his imagination had never at other times been so agile and inventive as now, when every day he thought of thousands of different reasons for being seriously anxious over his freedom and honour; but, on the other hand, his interest in the outer world, in books in particular, grew sensibly fainter, and his memory began to fail him.

In the spring when the snow melted there were found in the ravine near the cemetery two half-decomposed corpses— the bodies of an old woman and a boy bearing the traces of death by violence. Nothing was talked of but these bodies and their unknown murderers. That people might not think he had been guilty of the crime, Ivan Dmitritch walked about the streets, smiling, and when he met acquaintances he turned pale, flushed, and began declaring that there was no greater crime than the murder of the weak and defenceless. But this duplicity soon exhausted him, and after some reflection he decided that in his position the best thing to do was to hide in his landlady's cellar. He sat in the cellar all day and then all night, then another day, was fearfully cold, and waiting till dusk, stole secretly like a thief back to his room. He stood in the middle of the room till daybreak, listening without stirring. Very early in the morning, before sunrise, some workmen came into the house. Ivan Dmitritch knew perfectly well that they had come to mend the stove in the kitchen, but terror told him that they were police officers disguised as workmen. He slipped stealthily out of the flat, and, overcome by terror, ran along the street without his cap and coat. Dogs raced after him barking, a peasant shouted somewhere behind him, the wind whistled in his ears, and it seemed to Ivan Dmitritch that the force and violence of the whole world was massed together behind his back and was chasing after him.

He was stopped and brought home, and his landlady sent for a doctor. Doctor Andrey Yefimitch, of whom we shall have more to say hereafter, prescribed cold compresses on his head and laurel drops, shook his head, and went away, telling the landlady he should not come again, as one should not interfere with people who are going out of their minds. As he had not the means to live at home and be nursed, Ivan Dmitritch was soon sent to the hospital, and was there put into the ward for venereal patients. He could not sleep at night, was full of whims and fancies, and disturbed the patients, and was soon afterwards, by Andrey Yefimitch's orders, transferred to Ward No. 6.

Within a year Ivan Dmitritch was completely forgotten in the town, and his books, heaped up by his landlady in a sledge in the shed, were pulled to pieces by boys.

IV

Ivan Dmitritch's neighbour on the left hand is, as I have said already, the Jew Moiseika; his neighbour on the right hand is a peasant so rolling in fat that he is almost spherical, with a blankly stupid face, utterly devoid of thought. This is a motionless, gluttonous, unclean animal who has long ago lost all powers of thought or feeling. An acrid, stifling stench always comes from him.

Nikita, who has to clean up after him, beats him terribly with all his might, not sparing his fists; and what is dreadful is not his being beaten—that one can get used to—but the fact that this stupefied creature does not respond to the blows with a sound or a movement, nor by a look in the eyes, but only sways a little like a heavy barrel.

The fifth and last inhabitant of Ward No. 6 is a man of the artisan class who had once been a sorter in the post office, a thinnish, fair little man with a good-natured but rather sly face. To judge from the clear, cheerful look in his calm and intelligent eyes, he has some pleasant idea in his mind, and has some very important and agreeable secret. He has under his pillow and under his mattress something that he never shows anyone, not from fear of its being taken from him and stolen, but from modesty. Sometimes he goes to the window, and turning his back to his companions, puts something on his breast, and bending his head, looks at it; if you go up to him at such a moment, he is overcome with confusion and snatches something off his breast. But it is not difficult to guess his secret.

"Congratulate me," he often says to Ivan Dmitritch; "I have been presented with the Stanislav order of the second degree with the star. The second degree with the star is only given to foreigners, but for some reason they want to make an exception for me," he says with a smile, shrugging his shoulders in perplexity. "That I must confess I did not expect."

"I don't understand anything about that," Ivan Dmitritch replies morosely.

"But do you know what I shall attain to sooner or later?" the former sorter persists, screwing up his eyes slyly. "I shall certainly get the Swedish 'Polar Star.' That's an order it is worth working for, a white cross with a black ribbon. It's very beautiful."

Probably in no other place is life so monotonous as in this ward. In the morning the patients, except the paralytic and the fat peasant, wash in the entry at a big tab and wipe themselves with the skirts of their dressing-gowns; after that they drink tea out of tin mugs which Nikita brings them out of the main building. Everyone is allowed one mugful. At midday they have soup made out of sour cabbage and boiled grain, in the evening their supper consists of grain left from dinner. In the intervals they lie down, sleep, look out of window, and walk from one corner to the other. And so every day. Even the former sorter always talks of the same orders.

Fresh faces are rarely seen in Ward No. 6. The doctor has not taken in any new mental cases for a long time, and the people who are fond of visiting lunatic asylums are few in this world. Once every two months Semyon Lazaritch, the barber, appears in the ward. How he cuts the patients' hair, and how Nikita helps him to do it, and what a trepidation the lunatics are always thrown into by the arrival of the drunken, smiling barber, we will not describe.

No one even looks into the ward except the barber. The patients are condemned to see day after day no one but Nikita.

A rather strange rumour has, however, been circulating in the hospital of late.

It is rumoured that the doctor has begun to visit Ward No. 6.

V

A STRANGE RUMOUR!

Dr. Andrey Yefimitch Ragin is a strange man in his way. They say that when he was young he was very religious, and prepared himself for a clerical career, and that when he had finished his studies at the high school in 1863 he intended to enter a theological academy, but that his father, a surgeon and doctor of medicine, jeered at him and declared point-blank that he would disown him if he became a priest. How far this is true I don't know, but Andrey Yefimitch himself has more than once confessed that he has never had a natural bent for medicine or science in general.

However that may have been, when he finished his studies in the medical faculty he did not enter the priesthood. He showed no special devoutness, and was no more like a priest at the beginning of his medical career than he is now.

His exterior is heavy—coarse like a peasant's, his face, his beard, his flat hair, and his coarse, clumsy figure, suggest an overfed, intemperate, and harsh innkeeper on the highroad. His face is surly-looking and covered with blue veins, his eyes are little and his nose is red. With his height and broad shoulders he has huge hands and feet; one would think that a blow from his fist would knock the life out of anyone, but his step is soft, and his walk is cautious and insinuating; when he meets anyone in a narrow passage he is always the first to stop and make way, and to say, not in a bass, as one would expect, but in a high, soft tenor: "I beg your pardon!"

He has a little swelling on his neck which prevents him from wearing stiff starched collars, and so he always goes about in soft linen or cotton shirts. Altogether he does not dress like a doctor. He wears the same suit for ten years, and the new clothes, which he usually buys at a Jewish shop, look as shabby and crumpled on him as his old ones; he sees patients and dines and pays visits all in the same coat; but this is not due to niggardliness, but to complete carelessness about his appearance.

When Andrey Yefimitch came to the town to take up his duties the "institution founded to the glory of God" was in a terrible condition. One could hardly breathe for the stench in the wards, in the passages, and in the courtyards of the hospital. The hospital servants, the nurses, and their children slept in the wards together with the patients. They complained that there was no living for beetles, bugs, and mice. The surgical wards were never free from erysipelas. There were only two scalpels and not one thermometer in the whole hospital; potatoes were kept in the baths. The superintendent, the housekeeper, and the medical assistant robbed the patients, and of the old doctor, Andrey Yefimitch's predecessor, people declared that he secretly sold the hospital alcohol, and that he kept a regular harem consisting of nurses and female patients. These disorderly proceedings were perfectly well known in the town, and were even exaggerated, but people took them calmly; some justified them on the ground that there were only peasants and working men in the hospital, who could not be dissatisfied, since they were much worse off at home than in the hospital—they couldn't be fed on woodcocks! Others said in excuse that the town alone, without help from the Zemstvo, was not equal to maintaining a good hospital; thank God for having one at all, even a poor one. And the newly formed Zemstvo did not open infirmaries either in the town or the neighbourhood, relying on the fact that the town already had its hospital.

After looking over the hospital Andrey Yefimitch came to the conclusion that it was an immoral institution and extremely prejudicial to the health of the townspeople. In his opinion the most sensible thing that could be done was to let out the patients and close the hospital. But he reflected that his will alone was not enough to do this, and that it would be useless; if physical and moral impurity were driven out of one place, they would only move to another; one must wait for it to wither away of itself, Besides, if people open a hospital and put up with having it, it must be because they need it; superstition and all the nastiness and abominations of daily life were necessary, since in process of time they worked out to something sensible, just as manure turns into black earth. There was nothing on earth so good that it had not something nasty about its first origin.

When Andrey Yefimitch undertook his duties he was apparently not greatly concerned about the irregularities at the hospital. He only asked the attendants and nurses not to sleep in the wards, and had two cupboards of instruments put up; the superintendent, the housekeeper, the medical assistant, and the erysipelas remained unchanged.

Andrey Yefimitch loved intelligence and honesty intensely, but he had no strength of will nor belief in his right to organize an intelligent and honest life about him. He was absolutely unable to give orders, to forbid things, and to insist. It seemed as though he had taken a vow never to raise his voice and never to make use of the imperative. It was difficult for him to say. "Fetch" or "Bring"; when he wanted his meals he would cough hesitatingly and say to the cook, "How about tea?. . ." or "How about dinner? . . ." To dismiss the superintendent or to tell him to leave off stealing, or to abolish the unnecessary parasitic post altogether, was absolutely beyond his powers. When Andrey Yefimitch was deceived or flattered, or accounts he knew to be cooked were brought him to sign, he would turn as red as a crab and feel guilty, but yet he would sign the accounts. When the patients complained to him of being hungry or of the roughness of the nurses, he would be confused and mutter guiltily: "Very well, very well, I will go into it later . . . . Most likely there is some misunderstanding. . ."

At first Andrey Yefimitch worked very zealously. He saw patients every day from morning till dinner-time, performed operations, and even attended confinements. The ladies said of him that he was attentive and clever at diagnosing diseases, especially those of women and children. But in process of time the work unmistakably wearied him by its monotony and obvious uselessness. To-day one sees thirty patients, and to-morrow they have increased to thirty-five, the next day forty, and so on from day to day, from year to year, while the mortality in the town did not decrease and the patients did not leave off coming. To be any real help to forty patients between morning and dinner was not physically possible, so it could but lead to deception. If twelve thousand patients were seen in a year it meant, if one looked at it simply, that twelve thousand men were deceived. To put those who were seriously ill into wards, and to treat them according to the principles of science, was impossible, too, because though there were principles there was no science; if he were to put aside philosophy and pedantically follow the rules as other doctors did, the things above all necessary were cleanliness and ventilation instead of dirt, wholesome nourishment instead of broth made of stinking, sour cabbage, and good assistants instead of thieves; and, indeed, why hinder people dying if death is the normal and legitimate end of everyone? What is gained if some shop-keeper or clerk lives an extra five or ten years? If the aim of medicine is by drugs to alleviate suffering, the question forces itself on one: why alleviate it? In the first place, they say that suffering leads man to perfection; and in the second, if mankind really learns to alleviate its sufferings with pills and drops, it will completely abandon religion and philosophy, in which it has hitherto found not merely protection from all sorts of trouble, but even happiness. Pushkin suffered terrible agonies before his death, poor Heine lay paralyzed for several years; why, then, should not some Andrey Yefimitch or Matryona Savishna be ill, since their lives had nothing of importance in them, and would have been entirely empty and like the life of an amoeba except for suffering?

Oppressed by such reflections, Andrey Yefimitch relaxed his efforts and gave up visiting the hospital every day.

VI

His life was passed like this. As a rule he got up at eight o'clock in the morning, dressed, and drank his tea. Then he sat down in his study to read, or went to the hospital. At the hospital the out-patients were sitting in the dark, narrow little corridor waiting to be seen by the doctor. The nurses and the attendants, tramping with their boots over the brick floors, ran by them; gaunt-looking patients in dressing-gowns passed; dead bodies and vessels full of filth were carried by; the children were crying, and there was a cold draught. Andrey Yefimitch knew that such surroundings were torture to feverish, consumptive, and impressionable patients; but what could be done? In the consulting-room he was met by his assistant, Sergey Sergeyitch—a fat little man with a plump, well-washed shaven face, with soft, smooth manners, wearing a new loosely cut suit, and looking more like a senator than a medical assistant. He had an immense practice in the town, wore a white tie, and considered himself more proficient than the doctor, who had no practice. In the corner of the consulting-room there stood a large ikon in a shrine with a heavy lamp in front of it, and near it a candle-stand with a white cover on it. On the walls hung portraits of bishops, a view of the Svyatogorsky Monastery, and wreaths of dried cornflowers. Sergey Sergeyitch was religious, and liked solemnity and decorum. The ikon had been put up at his expense; at his instructions some one of the patients read the hymns of praise in the consulting-room on Sundays, and after the reading Sergey Sergeyitch himself went through the wards with a censer and burned incense.

There were a great many patients, but the time was short, and so the work was confined to the asking of a few brief questions and the administration of some drugs, such as castor-oil or volatile ointment. Andrey Yefimitch would sit with his cheek resting in his hand, lost in thought and asking questions mechanically. Sergey Sergeyitch sat down too, rubbing his hands, and from time to time putting in his word.

"We suffer pain and poverty," he would say, "because we do not pray to the merciful God as we should. Yes!"

Andrey Yefimitch never performed any operation when he was seeing patients; he had long ago given up doing so, and the sight of blood upset him. When he had to open a child's mouth in order to look at its throat, and the child cried and tried to defend itself with its little hands, the noise in his ears made his head go round and brought tears to his eyes. He would make haste to prescribe a drug, and motion to the woman to take the child away.

He was soon wearied by the timidity of the patients and their incoherence, by the proximity of the pious Sergey Sergeyitch, by the portraits on the walls, and by his own questions which he had asked over and over again for twenty years. And he would go away after seeing five or six patients.

The rest would be seen by his assistant in his absence.

With the agreeable thought that, thank God, he had no private practice now, and that no one would interrupt him, Andrey Yefimitch sat down to the table immediately on reaching home and took up a book. He read a great deal and always with enjoyment. Half his salary went on buying books, and of the six rooms that made up his abode three were heaped up with books and old magazines. He liked best of all works on history and philosophy; the only medical publication to which he subscribed was _The Doctor_, of which he always read the last pages first. He would always go on reading for several hours without a break and without being weary. He did not read as rapidly and impulsively as Ivan Dmitritch had done in the past, but slowly and with concentration, often pausing over a passage which he liked or did not find intelligible. Near the books there always stood a decanter of vodka, and a salted cucumber or a pickled apple lay beside it, not on a plate, but on the baize table-cloth. Every half-hour he would pour himself out a glass of vodka and drink it without taking his eyes off the book. Then without looking at it he would feel for the cucumber and bite off a bit.

At three o'clock he would go cautiously to the kitchen door; cough, and say, "Daryushka, what about dinner? . ."

After his dinner—a rather poor and untidily served one— Andrey Yefimitch would walk up and down his rooms with his arms folded, thinking. The clock would strike four, then five, and still he would be walking up and down thinking. Occasionally the kitchen door would creak, and the red and sleepy face of Daryushka would appear.

"Andrey Yefimitch, isn't it time for you to have your beer?" she would ask anxiously.

"No, it's not time yet . . ." he would answer. "I'll wait a little . . . . I'll wait a little. . ."

Towards the evening the postmaster, Mihail Averyanitch, the only man in town whose society did not bore Andrey Yefimitch, would come in. Mihail Averyanitch had once been a very rich landowner, and had served in the calvary, but had come to ruin, and was forced by poverty to take a job in the post office late in life. He had a hale and hearty appearance, luxuriant grey whiskers, the manners of a well-bred man, and a loud, pleasant voice. He was good-natured and emotional, but hot-tempered. When anyone in the post office made a protest, expressed disagreement, or even began to argue, Mihail Averyanitch would turn crimson, shake all over, and shout in a voice of thunder, "Hold your tongue!" so that the post office had long enjoyed the reputation of an institution which it was terrible to visit. Mihail Averyanitch liked and respected Andrey Yefimitch for his culture and the loftiness of his soul; he treated the other inhabitants of the town superciliously, as though they were his subordinates.

"Here I am," he would say, going in to Andrey Yefimitch. "Good evening, my dear fellow! I'll be bound, you are getting sick of me, aren't you?"

"On the contrary, I am delighted," said the doctor. "I am always glad to see you."

The friends would sit on the sofa in the study and for some time would smoke in silence.

"Daryushka, what about the beer?" Andrey Yefimitch would say.

They would drink their first bottle still in silence, the doctor brooding and Mihail Averyanitch with a gay and animated face, like a man who has something very interesting to tell. The doctor was always the one to begin the conversation.

"What a pity," he would say quietly and slowly, not looking his friend in the face (he never looked anyone in the face)—"what a great pity it is that there are no people in our town who are capable of carrying on intelligent and interesting conversation, or care to do so. It is an immense privation for us. Even the educated class do not rise above vulgarity; the level of their development, I assure you, is not a bit higher than that of the lower orders."

"Perfectly true. I agree."

"You know, of course," the doctor went on quietly and deliberately, "that everything in this world is insignificant and uninteresting except the higher spiritual manifestations of the human mind. Intellect draws a sharp line between the animals and man, suggests the divinity of the latter, and to some extent even takes the place of the immortality which does not exist. Consequently the intellect is the only possible source of enjoyment. We see and hear of no trace of intellect about us, so we are deprived of enjoyment. We have books, it is true, but that is not at all the same as living talk and converse. If you will allow me to make a not quite apt comparison: books are the printed score, while talk is the singing."

"Perfectly true."

A silence would follow. Daryushka would come out of the kitchen and with an expression of blank dejection would stand in the doorway to listen, with her face propped on her fist.

"Eh!" Mihail Averyanitch would sigh. "To expect intelligence of this generation!"

And he would describe how wholesome, entertaining, and interesting life had been in the past. How intelligent the educated class in Russia used to be, and what lofty ideas it had of honour and friendship; how they used to lend money without an IOU, and it was thought a disgrace not to give a helping hand to a comrade in need; and what campaigns, what adventures, what skirmishes, what comrades, what women! And the Caucasus, what a marvellous country! The wife of a battalion commander, a queer woman, used to put on an officer's uniform and drive off into the mountains in the evening, alone, without a guide. It was said that she had a love affair with some princeling in the native village.

"Queen of Heaven, Holy Mother..." Daryushka would sigh.

"And how we drank! And how we ate! And what desperate liberals we were!"

Andrey Yefimitch would listen without hearing; he was musing as he sipped his beer.

"I often dream of intellectual people and conversation with them," he said suddenly, interrupting Mihail Averyanitch. "My father gave me an excellent education, but under the influence of the ideas of the sixties made me become a doctor. I believe if I had not obeyed him then, by now I should have been in the very centre of the intellectual movement. Most likely I should have become a member of some university. Of course, intellect, too, is transient and not eternal, but you know why I cherish a partiality for it. Life is a vexatious trap; when a thinking man reaches maturity and attains to full consciousness he cannot help feeling that he is in a trap from which there is no escape. Indeed, he is summoned without his choice by fortuitous circumstances from non-existence into life . . . what for? He tries to find out the meaning and object of his existence; he is told nothing, or he is told absurdities; he knocks and it is not opened to him; death comes to him—also without his choice. And so, just as in prison men held together by common misfortune feel more at ease when they are together, so one does not notice the trap in life when people with a bent for analysis and generalization meet together and pass their time in the interchange of proud and free ideas. In that sense the intellect is the source of an enjoyment nothing can replace."

"Perfectly true."

Not looking his friend in the face, Andrey Yefimitch would go on, quietly and with pauses, talking about intellectual people and conversation with them, and Mihail Averyanitch would listen attentively and agree: "Perfectly true."

"And you do not believe in the immortality of the soul?" he would ask suddenly.

"No, honoured Mihail Averyanitch; I do not believe it, and have no grounds for believing it."

"I must own I doubt it too. And yet I have a feeling as though I should never die. Oh, I think to myself: 'Old fogey, it is time you were dead!' But there is a little voice in my soul says: 'Don't believe it; you won't die.'"

Soon after nine o'clock Mihail Averyanitch would go away. As he put on his fur coat in the entry he would say with a sigh:

"What a wilderness fate has carried us to, though, really! What's most vexatious of all is to have to die here. Ech! . ."

VII

After seeing his friend out Andrey Yefimitch would sit down at the table and begin reading again. The stillness of the evening, and afterwards of the night, was not broken by a single sound, and it seemed as though time were standing still and brooding with the doctor over the book, and as though there were nothing in existence but the books and the lamp with the green shade. The doctor's coarse peasant-like face was gradually lighted up by a smile of delight and enthusiasm over the progress of the human intellect. Oh, why is not man immortal? he thought. What is the good of the brain centres and convolutions, what is the good of

sight, speech, self-consciousness, genius, if it is all destined
to depart into the soil, and in the end to grow cold together
with the earth's crust, and then for millions of years to fly
with the earth round the sun with no meaning and no object?
To do that there was no need at all to draw man with his lofty,
almost godlike intellect out of non-existence, and then, as
though in mockery, to turn him into clay. The transmutation of
substances! But what cowardice to comfort oneself with that
cheap substitute for immortality! The unconscious processes
that take place in nature are lower even than the stupidity of
man, since in stupidity there is, anyway, consciousness and
will, while in those processes there is absolutely nothing.
Only the coward who has more fear of death than dignity
can comfort himself with the fact that his body will in time
live again in the grass, in the stones, in the toad. To find one's
immortality in the transmutation of substances is as strange
as to prophesy a brilliant future for the case after a precious
violin has been broken and become useless.

When the clock struck, Andrey Yefimitch would sink back
into his chair and close his eyes to think a little. And under
the influence of the fine ideas of which he had been reading
he would, unawares, recall his past and his present. The past
was hateful—better not to think of it. And it was the same
in the present as in the past. He knew that at the very time
when his thoughts were floating together with the cooling
earth round the sun, in the main building beside his abode
people were suffering in sickness and physical impurity:
someone perhaps could not sleep and was making war
upon the insects, someone was being infected by erysipelas,
or moaning over too tight a bandage; perhaps the patients
were playing cards with the nurses and drinking vodka.
According to the yearly return, twelve thousand people
had been deceived; the whole hospital rested as it had done
twenty years ago on thieving, filth, scandals, gossip, on

gross quackery, and, as before, it was an immoral institution extremely injurious to the health of the inhabitants. He knew that Nikita knocked the patients about behind the barred windows of Ward No. 6, and that Moiseika went about the town every day begging alms.

On the other hand, he knew very well that a magical change had taken place in medicine during the last twenty-five years. When he was studying at the university he had fancied that medicine would soon be overtaken by the fate of alchemy and metaphysics; but now when he was reading at night the science of medicine touched him and excited his wonder, and even enthusiasm. What unexpected brilliance, what a revolution! Thanks to the antiseptic system operations were performed such as the great Pirogov had considered impossible even *in spe*. Ordinary Zemstvo doctors were venturing to perform the resection of the kneecap; of abdominal operations only one per cent. was fatal; while stone was considered such a trifle that they did not even write about it. A radical cure for syphilis had been discovered. And the theory of heredity, hypnotism, the discoveries of Pasteur and of Koch, hygiene based on statistics, and the work of Zemstvo doctors!

Psychiatry with its modern classification of mental diseases, methods of diagnosis, and treatment, was a perfect Elborus in comparison with what had been in the past. They no longer poured cold water on the heads of lunatics nor put strait-waistcoats upon them; they treated them with humanity, and even, so it was stated in the papers, got up balls and entertainments for them. Andrey Yefimitch knew that with modern tastes and views such an abomination as Ward No. 6 was possible only a hundred and fifty miles from a railway in a little town where the mayor and all the town council were half-illiterate tradesmen who looked upon the doctor as an oracle who must be believed without any criticism even if he had poured molten lead into their mouths; in any other place the public and the newspapers would long ago have torn this little Bastille to pieces.

"But, after all, what of it?" Andrey Yefimitch would ask himself, opening his eyes. "There is the antiseptic system, there is Koch, there is Pasteur, but the essential reality is not altered a bit; ill-health and mortality are still the same. They get up balls and entertainments for the mad, but still they don't let them go free; so it's all nonsense and vanity, and there is no difference in reality between the best Vienna clinic and my hospital." But depression and a feeling akin to envy prevented him from feeling indifferent; it must have been owing to exhaustion. His heavy head sank on to the book, he put his hands under his face to make it softer, and thought: "I serve in a pernicious institution and receive a salary from people whom I am deceiving. I am not honest, but then, I of myself am nothing, I am only part of an inevitable social evil: all local officials are pernicious and receive their salary for doing nothing. . . . And so for my dishonesty it is not I who am to blame, but the times.... If I had been born two hundred years later I should have been different. . ."

When it struck three he would put out his lamp and go into his bedroom; he was not sleepy.

VIII

Two years before, the Zemstvo in a liberal mood had decided to allow three hundred roubles a year to pay for additional medical service in the town till the Zemstvo hospital should be opened, and the district doctor, Yevgeny Fyodoritch Hobotov, was invited to the town to assist Andrey Yefimitch. He was a very young man—not yet thirty—tall and dark, with broad cheek-bones and little eyes; his forefathers had probably come from one of the many alien races of Russia. He arrived in the town without a farthing, with a small portmanteau, and a plain young woman whom he called his cook. This woman had a baby at the breast. Yevgeny Fyodoritch used to go about in a cap with a peak, and in high boots, and in the winter wore a sheepskin. He made great friends with Sergey Sergeyitch, the medical assistant, and with the treasurer, but held aloof from the other officials, and for some reason called them aristocrats. He had only one book in his lodgings, "The Latest Prescriptions of the Vienna Clinic for 1881." When he went to a patient he always took this book with him. He played billiards in the evening at the club: he did not like cards. He was very fond of using in conversation such expressions as "endless bobbery," "canting soft soap," "shut up with your finicking. . ."

He visited the hospital twice a week, made the round of the wards, and saw out-patients. The complete absence of antiseptic treatment and the cupping roused his indignation, but he did not introduce any new system, being afraid of offending Andrey Yefimitch. He regarded his colleague as a sly old rascal, suspected him of being a man of large means, and secretly envied him. He would have been very glad to have his post.

IX

On a spring evening towards the end of March, when there was no snow left on the ground and the starlings were singing in the hospital garden, the doctor went out to see his friend the postmaster as far as the gate. At that very moment the Jew Moiseika, returning with his booty, came into the yard. He had no cap on, and his bare feet were thrust into goloshes; in his hand he had a little bag of coppers.

"Give me a kopeck!" he said to the doctor, smiling, and shivering with cold. Andrey Yefimitch, who could never refuse anyone anything, gave him a ten-kopeck piece.

"How bad that is!" he thought, looking at the Jew's bare feet with their thin red ankles. "Why, it's wet."

And stirred by a feeling akin both to pity and disgust, he went into the lodge behind the Jew, looking now at his bald head, now at his ankles. As the doctor went in, Nikita jumped up from his heap of litter and stood at attention.

"Good-day, Nikita," Andrey Yefimitch said mildly. "That Jew should be provided with boots or something, he will catch cold."

"Certainly, your honour. I'll inform the superintendent."

"Please do; ask him in my name. Tell him that I asked."

The door into the ward was open. Ivan Dmitritch, lying propped on his elbow on the bed, listened in alarm to the unfamiliar voice, and suddenly recognized the doctor. He trembled all over with anger, jumped up, and with a red and wrathful face, with his eyes starting out of his head, ran out into the middle of the road.

"The doctor has come!" he shouted, and broke into a laugh. "At last! Gentlemen, I congratulate you. The doctor is honouring us with a visit! Cursed reptile!" he shrieked, and stamped in a frenzy such as had never been seen in the ward before. "Kill the reptile! No, killing's too good. Drown him in the midden-pit!"

Andrey Yefimitch, hearing this, looked into the ward from the entry and asked gently: "What for?"

"What for?" shouted Ivan Dmitritch, going up to him with a menacing air and convulsively wrapping himself in his dressing-gown. "What for? Thief!" he said with a look of repulsion, moving his lips as though he would spit at him. "Quack! Hangman!"

"Calm yourself," said Andrey Yefimitch, smiling guiltily. "I assure you I have never stolen anything; and as to the rest, most likely you greatly exaggerate. I see you are angry with me. Calm yourself, I beg, if you can, and tell me coolly what are you angry for?"

"What are you keeping me here for?"

"Because you are ill."

"Yes, I am ill. But you know dozens, hundreds of madmen are walking about in freedom because your ignorance is incapable of distinguishing them from the sane. Why am I and these poor wretches to be shut up here like scapegoats for all the rest? You, your assistant, the superintendent, and all your hospital rabble, are immeasurably inferior to every one of us morally; why then are we shut up and you not? Where's the logic of it?"

"Morality and logic don't come in, it all depends on chance. If anyone is shut up he has to stay, and if anyone is not shut up he can walk about, that's all. There is neither morality nor logic in my being a doctor and your being a mental patient, there is nothing but idle chance."

"That twaddle I don't understand. . ." Ivan Dmitritch brought out in a hollow voice, and he sat down on his bed.

Moiseika, whom Nikita did not venture to search in the presence of the doctor, laid out on his bed pieces of bread, bits of paper, and little bones, and, still shivering with cold, began rapidly in a singsong voice saying something in Yiddish. He most likely imagined that he had opened a shop.

"Let me out," said Ivan Dmitritch, and his voice quivered.

"I cannot."

"But why, why?"

"Because it is not in my power. Think, what use will it be to you if I do let you out? Go. The townspeople or the police will detain you or bring you back."

"Yes, yes, that's true," said Ivan Dmitritch, and he rubbed his forehead. "It's awful! But what am I to do, what?"

Andrey Yefimitch liked Ivan Dmitritch's voice and his intelligent young face with its grimaces. He longed to be kind to the young man and soothe him; he sat down on the bed beside him, thought, and said:

"You ask me what to do. The very best thing in your position would be to run away. But, unhappily, that is useless. You would be taken up. When society protects itself from the criminal, mentally deranged, or otherwise inconvenient people, it is invincible. There is only one thing left for you: to resign yourself to the thought that your presence here is inevitable."

"It is no use to anyone."

"So long as prisons and madhouses exist someone must be shut up in them. If not you, I. If not I, some third person. Wait till in the distant future prisons and madhouses no longer exist, and there will be neither bars on the windows nor hospital gowns. Of course, that time will come sooner or later."

Ivan Dmitritch smiled ironically.

"You are jesting," he said, screwing up his eyes. "Such gentlemen as you and your assistant Nikita have nothing to do with the future, but you may be sure, sir, better days will come! I may express myself cheaply, you may laugh, but the dawn of a new life is at hand; truth and justice will triumph, and—our turn will come! I shall not live to see it, I shall perish, but some people's great-grandsons will see it. I greet them with all my heart and rejoice, rejoice with them! Onward! God be your help, friends!"

With shining eyes Ivan Dmitritch got up, and stretching his hands towards the window, went on with emotion in his voice:

"From behind these bars I bless you! Hurrah for truth and justice! I rejoice!"

"I see no particular reason to rejoice," said Andrey Yefimitch, who thought Ivan Dmitritch's movement theatrical, though he was delighted by it. "Prisons and madhouses there will not be, and truth, as you have just expressed it, will triumph; but the reality of things, you know, will not change, the laws of nature will still remain the same. People will suffer pain, grow old, and die just as they do now. However magnificent a dawn lighted up your life, you would yet in the end be nailed up in a coffin and thrown into a hole."

"And immortality?"

"Oh, come, now!"

"You don't believe in it, but I do. Somebody in Dostoevsky or Voltaire said that if there had not been a God men would have invented him. And I firmly believe that if there is no immortality the great intellect of man will sooner or later invent it."

"Well said," observed Andrey Yefimitch, smiling with pleasure; its a good thing you have faith. With such a belief one may live happily even shut up within walls. You have studied somewhere, I presume?"

"Yes, I have been at the university, but did not complete my studies."

"You are a reflecting and a thoughtful man. In any surroundings you can find tranquillity in yourself. Free and deep thinking which strives for the comprehension of life, and complete contempt for the foolish bustle of the world—those are two blessings beyond any that man has ever known. And you can possess them even though you lived behind threefold bars. Diogenes lived in a tub, yet he was happier than all the kings of the earth."

"Your Diogenes was a blockhead," said Ivan Dmitritch morosely. "Why do you talk to me about Diogenes and some foolish comprehension of life?" he cried, growing suddenly angry and leaping up. "I love life; I love it passionately. I have the mania of persecution, a continual agonizing terror; but I have moments when I am overwhelmed by the thirst for life, and then I am afraid of going mad. I want dreadfully to live, dreadfully!"

He walked up and down the ward in agitation, and said, dropping his voice:

"When I dream I am haunted by phantoms. People come to me, I hear voices and music, and I fancy I am walking through woods or by the seashore, and I long so passionately for movement, for interests . . . . Come, tell me, what news is there?" asked Ivan Dmitritch; "what's happening?"

"Do you wish to know about the town or in general?"

"Well, tell me first about the town, and then in general."

"Well, in the town it is appallingly dull. . . . There's no one to say a word to, no one to listen to. There are no new people. A young doctor called Hobotov has come here recently."

"He had come in my time. Well, he is a low cad, isn't he?"

"Yes, he is a man of no culture. It's strange, you know. . . . Judging by every sign, there is no intellectual stagnation in our capital cities; there is a movement—so there must be real people there too; but for some reason they always send us such men as I would rather not see. It's an unlucky town!"

"Yes, it is an unlucky town," sighed Ivan Dmitritch, and he laughed. "And how are things in general? What are they writing in the papers and reviews?"

It was by now dark in the ward. The doctor got up, and, standing, began to describe what was being written abroad and in Russia, and the tendency of thought that could be noticed now. Ivan Dmitritch listened attentively and put questions, but suddenly, as though recalling something terrible, clutched at his head and lay down on the bed with his back to the doctor.

"What's the matter?" asked Andrey Yefimitch.

"You will not hear another word from me," said Ivan Dmitritch rudely. "Leave me alone."

"Why so?"

"I tell you, leave me alone. Why the devil do you persist?"

Andrey Yefimitch shrugged his shoulders, heaved a sigh, and went out. As he crossed the entry he said: "You might clear up here, Nikita . . . there's an awfully stuffy smell."

"Certainly, your honour."

"What an agreeable young man!" thought Andrey Yefimitch, going back to his flat. "In all the years I have been living here I do believe he is the first I have met with whom one can talk. He is capable of reasoning and is interested in just the right things."

While he was reading, and afterwards, while he was going to bed, he kept thinking about Ivan Dmitritch, and when he woke next morning he remembered that he had the day before made the acquaintance of an intelligent and interesting man, and determined to visit him again as soon as possible.

X

Ivan Dmitritch was lying in the same position as on the previous day, with his head clutched in both hands and his legs drawn up. His face was not visible.

"Good-day, my friend," said Andrey Yefimitch. "You are not asleep, are you?"

"In the first place, I am not your friend," Ivan Dmitritch articulated into the pillow; "and in the second, your efforts are useless; you will not get one word out of me."

"Strange," muttered Andrey Yefimitch in confusion. "Yesterday we talked peacefully, but suddenly for some reason you took offence and broke off all at once.... Probably I expressed myself awkwardly, or perhaps gave utterance to some idea which did not fit in with your convictions...."

"Yes, a likely idea!" said Ivan Dmitritch, sitting up and looking at the doctor with irony and uneasiness. His eyes were red. "You can go and spy and probe somewhere else, it's no use your doing it here. I knew yesterday what you had come for."

"A strange fancy," laughed the doctor. "So you suppose me to be a spy?"

"Yes, I do.... A spy or a doctor who has been charged to test me—it's all the same——"

"Oh excuse me, what a queer fellow you are really!"

The doctor sat down on the stool near the bed and shook his head reproachfully.

"But let us suppose you are right," he said, "let us suppose that I am treacherously trying to trap you into saying something so as to betray you to the police. You would be arrested and then tried. But would you be any worse off being tried and in prison than you are here? If you are banished to a settlement, or even sent to penal servitude, would it be worse than being shut up in this ward? I imagine it would be no worse. . . . What, then, are you afraid of?"

These words evidently had an effect on Ivan Dmitritch. He sat down quietly.

It was between four and five in the afternoon—the time when Andrey Yefimitch usually walked up and down his rooms, and Daryushka asked whether it was not time for his beer. It was a still, bright day.

"I came out for a walk after dinner, and here I have come, as you see," said the doctor. "It is quite spring."

"What month is it? March?" asked Ivan Dmitritch.

"Yes, the end of March."

"Is it very muddy?"

"No, not very. There are already paths in the garden."

"It would be nice now to drive in an open carriage somewhere into the country," said Ivan Dmitritch, rubbing his red eyes as though he were just awake, "then to come home to a warm, snug study, and . . . and to have a decent doctor to cure one's headache. . . . It's so long since I have lived like a human being. It's disgusting here! Insufferably disgusting!"

After his excitement of the previous day he was exhausted and listless, and spoke unwillingly. His fingers twitched, and from his face it could be seen that he had a splitting headache.

"There is no real difference between a warm, snug study and this ward," said Andrey Yefimitch. "A man's peace and contentment do not lie outside a man, but in himself."

"What do you mean?"

"The ordinary man looks for good and evil in external things—that is, in carriages, in studies—but a thinking man looks for it in himself."

"You should go and preach that philosophy in Greece, where it's warm and fragrant with the scent of pomegranates, but here it is not suited to the climate. With whom was it I was talking of Diogenes? Was it with you?"

"Yes, with me yesterday."

"Diogenes did not need a study or a warm habitation; it's hot there without. You can lie in your tub and eat oranges and olives. But bring him to Russia to live: he'd be begging to be let indoors in May, let alone December. He'd be doubled up with the cold."

"No. One can be insensible to cold as to every other pain. Marcus Aurelius says: 'A pain is a vivid idea of pain; make an effort of will to change that idea, dismiss it, cease to complain, and the pain will disappear.' That is true. The wise man, or simply the reflecting, thoughtful man, is distinguished precisely by his contempt for suffering; he is always contented and surprised at nothing."

"Then I am an idiot, since I suffer and am discontented and surprised at the baseness of mankind."

"You are wrong in that; if you will reflect more on the subject you will understand how insignificant is all that external world that agitates us. One must strive for the comprehension of life, and in that is true happiness."

"Comprehension . . ." repeated Ivan Dmitritch frowning. "External, internal. . . . Excuse me, but I don t understand it. I only know," he said, getting up and looking angrily at the doctor—"I only know that God has created me of warm blood and nerves, yes, indeed! If organic tissue is capable of life it must react to every stimulus. And I do! To pain I respond with tears and outcries, to baseness with indignation, to filth with loathing. To my mind, that is just what is called life. The lower the organism, the less sensitive it is, and the more feebly it reacts to stimulus; and the higher it is, the more responsively and vigorously it reacts to reality. How is it you don't know that? A doctor, and not know such trifles! To despise suffering, to be always contented, and to be surprised at nothing, one must reach this condition"—and Ivan Dmitritch pointed to the peasant who was a mass of fat—"or to harden oneself by suffering to such a point that one loses all sensibility to it—that is, in other words, to cease to live. You must excuse me, I am not a sage or a philosopher," Ivan Dmitritch continued with irritation, "and I don't understand anything about it. I am not capable of reasoning."

"On the contrary, your reasoning is excellent."

"The Stoics, whom you are parodying, were remarkable people, but their doctrine crystallized two thousand years ago and has not advanced, and will not advance, an inch forward, since it is not practical or living. It had a success only with the minority which spends its life in savouring all sorts of theories and ruminating over them; the majority did not understand it. A doctrine which advocates indifference to wealth and to the comforts of life, and a contempt for suffering and death, is quite unintelligible to the vast majority of men, since that majority has never known wealth or the comforts of life; and to despise suffering would mean to it despising life itself, since the whole existence of man is made up of the sensations of hunger, cold, injury, and a Hamlet-like dread of death. The whole of life lies in these sensations; one may be oppressed by it, one may hate it, but one cannot despise it. Yes, so, I repeat, the doctrine of the Stoics can never have a future; from the beginning of time up to to-day you see continually increasing the struggle, the sensibility to pain, the capacity of responding to stimulus."

Ivan Dmitritch suddenly lost the thread of his thoughts, stopped, and rubbed his forehead with vexation.

"I meant to say something important, but I have lost it," he said. "What was I saying? Oh, yes! This is what I mean: one of the Stoics sold himself into slavery to redeem his neighbour, so, you see, even a Stoic did react to stimulus, since, for such a generous act as the destruction of oneself for the sake of one's neighbour, he must have had a soul capable of pity and indignation. Here in prison I have forgotten everything I have learned, or else I could have recalled something else. Take Christ, for instance: Christ responded to reality by weeping, smiling, being sorrowful and moved to wrath, even overcome by misery. He did not go to meet His sufferings with a smile, He did not despise death, but prayed in the Garden of Gethsemane that this cup might pass Him by."

Ivan Dmitritch laughed and sat down.

"Granted that a man's peace and contentment lie not outside but in himself," he said, "granted that one must despise suffering and not be surprised at anything, yet on what ground do you preach the theory? Are you a sage? A philosopher?"

"No, I am not a philosopher, but everyone ought to preach it because it is reasonable."

"No, I want to know how it is that you consider yourself competent to judge of 'comprehension,' contempt for suffering, and so on. Have you ever suffered? Have you any idea of suffering? Allow me to ask you, were you ever thrashed in your childhood?"

"No, my parents had an aversion for corporal punishment."

"My father used to flog me cruelly; my father was a harsh, sickly Government clerk with a long nose and a yellow neck. But let us talk of you. No one has laid a finger on you all your life, no one has scared you nor beaten you; you are as strong as a bull. You grew up under your father's wing and studied at his expense, and then you dropped at once into a sinecure. For more than twenty years you have lived rent free with

heating, lighting, and service all provided, and had the right
to work how you pleased and as much as you pleased, even
to do nothing. You were naturally a flabby, lazy man, and so
you have tried to arrange your life so that nothing should
disturb you or make you move. You have handed over your
work to the assistant and the rest of the rabble while you
sit in peace and warmth, save money, read, amuse yourself
with reflections, with all sorts of lofty nonsense, and" (Ivan
Dmitritch looked at the doctor's red nose) "with boozing;
in fact, you have seen nothing of life, you know absolutely
nothing of it, and are only theoretically acquainted with
reality; you despise suffering and are surprised at nothing
for a very simple reason: vanity of vanities, the external and
the internal, contempt for life, for suffering and for death,
comprehension, true happiness—that's the philosophy that
suits the Russian sluggard best. You see a peasant beating
his wife, for instance. Why interfere? Let him beat her, they
will both die sooner or later, anyway; and, besides, he who
beats injures by his blows, not the person he is beating, but
himself. To get drunk is stupid and unseemly, but if you drink
you die, and if you don't drink you die. A peasant woman
comes with toothache . . . well, what of it? Pain is the idea
of pain, and besides 'there is no living in this world without
illness; we shall all die, and so, go away, woman, don't hinder
me from thinking and drinking vodka.' A young man asks
advice, what he is to do, how he is to live; anyone else would
think before answering, but you have got the answer ready:
strive for 'comprehension' or for true happiness. And what is
that fantastic 'true happiness'? There's no answer, of course.
We are kept here behind barred windows, tortured, left to
rot; but that is very good and reasonable, because there is no
difference at all between this ward and a warm, snug study.
A convenient philosophy. You can do nothing, and your
conscience is clear, and you feel you are wise . . . . No, sir, it
is not philosophy, it's not thinking, it's not breadth of vision,

but laziness, fakirism, drowsy stupefaction. Yes," cried Ivan Dmitritch, getting angry again, "you despise suffering, but I'll be bound if you pinch your finger in the door you will howl at the top of your voice."

"And perhaps I shouldn't howl," said Andrey Yefimitch, with a gentle smile.

"Oh, I dare say! Well, if you had a stroke of paralysis, or supposing some fool or bully took advantage of his position and rank to insult you in public, and if you knew he could do it with impunity, then you would understand what it means to put people off with comprehension and true happiness."

"That's original," said Andrey Yefimitch, laughing with pleasure and rubbing his hands. "I am agreeably struck by your inclination for drawing generalizations, and the sketch of my character you have just drawn is simply brilliant. I must confess that talking to you gives me great pleasure. Well, I've listened to you, and now you must graciously listen to me."

XI

The conversation went on for about an hour longer, and apparently made a deep impression on Andrey Yefimitch. He began going to the ward every day. He went there in the mornings and after dinner, and often the dusk of evening found him in conversation with Ivan Dmitritch. At first Ivan Dmitritch held aloof from him, suspected him of evil designs, and openly expressed his hostility. But afterwards he got used to him, and his abrupt manner changed to one of condescending irony.

Soon it was all over the hospital that the doctor, Andrey Yefimitch, had taken to visiting Ward No. 6. No one— neither Sergey Sergevitch, nor Nikita, nor the nurses—could conceive why he went there, why he stayed there for hours together, what he was talking about, and why he did not write prescriptions. His actions seemed strange. Often Mihail Averyanitch did not find him at home, which had never happened in the past, and Daryushka was greatly perturbed, for the doctor drank his beer now at no definite time, and sometimes was even late for dinner.

One day—it was at the end of June—Dr. Hobotov went to see Andrey Yefimitch about something. Not finding him at home, he proceeded to look for him in the yard; there he was told that the old doctor had gone to see the mental patients. Going into the lodge and stopping in the entry, Hobotov heard the following conversation:

"We shall never agree, and you will not succeed in converting me to your faith," Ivan Dmitritch was saying irritably; "you are utterly ignorant of reality, and you have never known suffering, but have only like a leech fed beside the sufferings of others, while I have been in continual suffering from the day of my birth till to-day. For that reason, I tell you frankly, I consider myself superior to you and more competent in every respect. It's not for you to teach me."

"I have absolutely no ambition to convert you to my faith," said Andrey Yefimitch gently, and with regret that the other refused to understand him. "And that is not what matters, my friend; what matters is not that you have suffered and I have not. Joy and suffering are passing; let us leave them, never mind them. What matters is that you and I think; we see in each other people who are capable of thinking and reasoning, and that is a common bond between us however different our views. If you knew, my friend, how sick I am of the universal senselessness, ineptitude, stupidity, and with what delight I always talk with you! You are an intelligent man, and I enjoyed your company."

Hobotov opened the door an inch and glanced into the ward; Ivan Dmitritch in his night-cap and the doctor Andrey Yefimitch were sitting side by side on the bed. The madman was grimacing, twitching, and convulsively wrapping himself in his gown, while the doctor sat motionless with bowed head, and his face was red and look helpless and sorrowful. Hobotov shrugged his shoulders, grinned, and glanced at Nikita. Nikita shrugged his shoulders too.

Next day Hobotov went to the lodge, accompanied by the assistant. Both stood in the entry and listened.

"I fancy our old man has gone clean off his chump!" said Hobotov as he came out of the lodge.

"Lord have mercy upon us sinners!" sighed the decorous Sergey Sergeyitch, scrupulously avoiding the puddles that he might not muddy his polished boots. "I must own, honoured Yevgeny Fyodoritch, I have been expecting it for a long time."

XII

After this Andrey Yefimitch began to notice a mysterious air in all around him. The attendants, the nurses, and the patients looked at him inquisitively when they met him, and then whispered together. The superintendent's little daughter Masha, whom he liked to meet in the hospital garden, for some reason ran away from him now when he went up with a smile to stroke her on the head. The postmaster no longer said, "Perfectly true," as he listened to him, but in unaccountable confusion muttered, "Yes, yes, yes . . ." and looked at him with a grieved and thoughtful expression; for some reason he took to advising his friend to give up vodka and beer, but as a man of delicate feeling he did not say this directly, but hinted it, telling him first about the commanding officer of his battalion, an excellent man, and then about the priest of the regiment, a capital fellow, both of whom drank and fell ill, but on giving up drinking completely regained their health. On two or three occasions Andrey Yefimitch was visited by his colleague Hobotov, who also advised him to give up spirituous liquors, and for no apparent reason recommended him to take bromide.

In August Andrey Yefimitch got a letter from the mayor of the town asking him to come on very important business. On arriving at the town hall at the time fixed, Andrey Yefimitch found there the military commander, the superintendent of the district school, a member of the town council, Hobotov, and a plump, fair gentleman who was introduced to him as a doctor. This doctor, with a Polish surname difficult to pronounce, lived at a pedigree stud-farm twenty miles away, and was now on a visit to the town.

"There's something that concerns you," said the member of the town council, addressing Andrey Yefimitch after they had all greeted one another and sat down to the table. "Here Yevgeny Fyodoritch says that there is not room for the dispensary in the main building, and that it ought to be transferred to one of the lodges. That's of no consequence—of course it can be transferred, but the point is that the lodge wants doing up."

"Yes, it would have to be done up," said Andrey Yefimitch after a moment's thought. "If the corner lodge, for instance, were fitted up as a dispensary, I imagine it would cost at least five hundred roubles. An unproductive expenditure!"

Everyone was silent for a space.

"I had the honour of submitting to you ten years ago," Andrey Yefimitch went on in a low voice, "that the hospital in its present form is a luxury for the town beyond its means. It was built in the forties, but things were different then. The town spends too much on unnecessary buildings and superfluous staff. I believe with a different system two model hospitals might be maintained for the same money."

"Well, let us have a different system, then!" the member of the town council said briskly.

"I have already had the honour of submitting to you that the medical department should be transferred to the supervision of the Zemstvo."

"Yes, transfer the money to the Zemstvo and they will steal it," laughed the fair-haired doctor.

"That's what it always comes to," the member of the council assented, and he also laughed.

Andrey Yefimitch looked with apathetic, lustreless eyes at the fair-haired doctor and said: "One should be just."

Again there was silence. Tea was brought in. The military commander, for some reason much embarrassed, touched Andrey Yefimitch's hand across the table and said: "You have quite forgotten us, doctor. But of course you are a hermit: you don't play cards and don't like women. You would be dull with fellows like us."

They all began saying how boring it was for a decent person to live in such a town. No theatre, no music, and at the last dance at the club there had been about twenty ladies and only two gentlemen. The young men did not dance, but spent all the time crowding round the refreshment bar or playing cards.

Not looking at anyone and speaking slowly in a low voice, Andrey Yefimitch began saying what a pity, what a terrible pity it was that the townspeople should waste their vital energy, their hearts, and their minds on cards and gossip, and should have neither the power nor the inclination to spend their time in interesting conversation and reading, and should refuse to take advantage of the enjoyments of the mind. The mind alone was interesting and worthy of attention, all the rest was low and petty. Hobotov listened to his colleague attentively and suddenly asked:

"Andrey Yefimitch, what day of the month is it?"

Having received an answer, the fair-haired doctor and he, in the tone of examiners conscious of their lack of skill, began asking Andrey Yefimitch what was the day of the week, how many days there were in the year, and whether it was true that there was a remarkable prophet living in Ward No. 6.

In response to the last question Andrey Yefimitch turned rather red and said: "Yes, he is mentally deranged, but he is an interesting young man."

They asked him no other questions.

When he was putting on his overcoat in the entry, the military commander laid a hand on his shoulder and said with a sigh:

"It's time for us old fellows to rest!"

As he came out of the hall, Andrey Yefimitch understood that it had been a committee appointed to enquire into his mental condition. He recalled the questions that had been asked him, flushed crimson, and for some reason, for the first time in his life, felt bitterly grieved for medical science.

"My God..." he thought, remembering how these doctors had just examined him; "why, they have only lately been hearing lectures on mental pathology; they had passed an examination—what's the explanation of this crass ignorance? They have not a conception of mental pathology!"

And for the first time in his life he felt insulted and moved to anger.

In the evening of the same day Mihail Averyanitch came to see him. The postmaster went up to him without waiting to greet him, took him by both hands, and said in an agitated voice:

"My dear fellow, my dear friend, show me that you believe in my genuine affection and look on me as your friend!" And preventing Andrey Yefimitch from speaking, he went on, growing excited: "I love you for your culture and nobility of soul. Listen to me, my dear fellow. The rules of their profession compel the doctors to conceal the truth from you, but I blurt out the plain truth like a soldier. You are not well! Excuse me, my dear fellow, but it is the truth; everyone about you has been noticing it for a long time. Dr. Yevgeny Fyodoritch has just told me that it is essential for you to rest and distract your mind for the sake of your health. Perfectly true! Excellent! In a day or two I am taking a holiday and am going away for a sniff of a different atmosphere. Show that you are a friend to me, let us go together! Let us go for a jaunt as in the good old days."

"I feel perfectly well," said Andrey Yefimitch after a moment's thought. "I can't go away. Allow me to show you my friendship in some other way."

To go off with no object, without his books, without his Daryushka, without his beer, to break abruptly through the routine of life, established for twenty years—the idea for the first minute struck him as wild and fantastic, but he remembered the conversation at the Zemstvo committee and the depressing feelings with which he had returned home, and the thought of a brief absence from the town in which stupid people looked on him as a madman was pleasant to him.

"And where precisely do you intend to go?" he asked.

"To Moscow, to Petersburg, to Warsaw. . . . I spent the five happiest years of my life in Warsaw. What a marvellous town! Let us go, my dear fellow!"

XIII

A week later it was suggested to Andrey Yefimitch that he should have a rest—that is, send in his resignation—a suggestion he received with indifference, and a week later still, Mihail Averyanitch and he were sitting in a posting carriage driving to the nearest railway station. The days were cool and bright, with a blue sky and a transparent distance. They were two days driving the hundred and fifty miles to the railway station, and stayed two nights on the way. When at the posting station the glasses given them for their tea had not been properly washed, or the drivers were slow in harnessing the horses, Mihail Averyanitch would turn crimson, and quivering all over would shout:

"Hold your tongue! Don't argue!"

And in the carriage he talked without ceasing for a moment, describing his campaigns in the Caucasus and in Poland. What adventures he had had, what meetings! He talked loudly and opened his eyes so wide with wonder that he might well be thought to be lying. Moreover, as he talked he breathed in Andrey Yefimitch's face and laughed into his ear. This bothered the doctor and prevented him from thinking or concentrating his mind.

In the train they travelled, from motives of economy, third-class in a non-smoking compartment. Half the passengers were decent people. Mihail Averyanitch soon made friends with everyone, and moving from one seat to another, kept saying loudly that they ought not to travel by these appalling lines. It was a regular swindle! A very different thing riding on a good horse: one could do over seventy miles a day and feel fresh and well after it. And our bad harvests were due to the draining of the Pinsk marshes; altogether, the way things were done was dreadful. He got excited, talked loudly, and would not let others speak. This endless chatter to the accompaniment of loud laughter and expressive gestures wearied Andrey Yefimitch.

"Which of us is the madman?" he thought with vexation. "I, who try not to disturb my fellow-passengers in any way, or this egoist who thinks that he is cleverer and more interesting than anyone here, and so will leave no one in peace?"

In Moscow Mihail Averyanitch put on a military coat without epaulettes and trousers with red braid on them. He wore a military cap and overcoat in the street, and soldiers saluted him. It seemed to Andrey Yefimitch, now, that his companion was a man who had flung away all that was good and kept only what was bad of all the characteristics of a country gentleman that he had once possessed. He liked to be waited on even when it was quite unnecessary. The matches would be lying before him on the table, and he would see them and shout to the waiter to give him the matches; he did not hesitate to appear before a maidservant in nothing but his underclothes; he used the familiar mode of address to all footmen indiscriminately, even old men, and when he was angry called them fools and blockheads. This, Andrey Yefimitch thought, was like a gentleman, but disgusting.

First of all Mihail Averyanitch led his friend to the Iversky Madonna. He prayed fervently, shedding tears and bowing down to the earth, and when he had finished, heaved a deep sigh and said:

"Even though one does not believe it makes one somehow easier when one prays a little. Kiss the ikon, my dear fellow."

Andrey Yefimitch was embarrassed and he kissed the image, while Mihail Averyanitch pursed up his lips and prayed in a whisper, and again tears came into his eyes. Then they went to the Kremlin and looked there at the Tsar-cannon and the Tsar-bell, and even touched them with their fingers, admired the view over the river, visited St. Saviour's and the Rumyantsev museum.

They dined at Tyestov's. Mihail Averyanitch looked a long time at the menu, stroking his whiskers, and said in the tone of a gourmand accustomed to dine in restaurants:

"We shall see what you give us to eat to-day, angel!"

XIV

The doctor walked about, looked at things, ate and drank, but he had all the while one feeling: annoyance with Mihail Averyanitch. He longed to have a rest from his friend, to get away from him, to hide himself, while the friend thought it was his duty not to let the doctor move a step away from him, and to provide him with as many distractions as possible. When there was nothing to look at he entertained him with conversation. For two days Andrey Yefimitch endured it, but on the third he announced to his friend that he was ill and wanted to stay at home for the whole day; his friend replied that in that case he would stay too—that really he needed rest, for he was run off his legs already. Andrey Yefimitch lay on the sofa, with his face to the back, and clenching his teeth, listened to his friend, who assured him with heat that sooner or later France would certainly thrash Germany, that there were a great many scoundrels in Moscow, and that it was impossible to judge of a horse's quality by its outward appearance. The doctor began to have a buzzing in his ears and palpitations of the heart, but out of delicacy could not bring himself to beg his friend to go away or hold his tongue. Fortunately Mihail Averyanitch grew weary of sitting in the hotel room, and after dinner he went out for a walk.

As soon as he was alone Andrey Yefimitch abandoned himself to a feeling of relief. How pleasant to lie motionless on the sofa and to know that one is alone in the room! Real happiness is impossible without solitude. The fallen angel betrayed God probably because he longed for solitude, of which the angels know nothing. Andrey Yefimitch wanted to think about what he had seen and heard during the last few days, but he could not get Mihail Averyanitch out of his head.

"Why, he has taken a holiday and come with me out of friendship, out of generosity," thought the doctor with vexation; "nothing could be worse than this friendly supervision. I suppose he is good-natured and generous and a lively fellow, but he is a bore. An insufferable bore. In the same way there are people who never say anything but what is clever and good, yet one feels that they are dull-witted people."

For the following days Andrey Yefimitch declared himself ill and would not leave the hotel room; he lay with his face to the back of the sofa, and suffered agonies of weariness when his friend entertained him with conversation, or rested when his friend was absent. He was vexed with himself for having come, and with his friend, who grew every day more talkative and more free-and-easy; he could not succeed in attuning his thoughts to a serious and lofty level.

"This is what I get from the real life Ivan Dmitritch talked about," he thought, angry at his own pettiness. "It's of no consequence, though. . . . I shall go home, and everything will go on as before . . . ."

It was the same thing in Petersburg too; for whole days together he did not leave the hotel room, but lay on the sofa and only got up to drink beer.

Mihail Averyanitch was all haste to get to Warsaw.

"My dear man, what should I go there for?" said Andrey Yefimitch in an imploring voice. "You go alone and let me get home! I entreat you!"

"On no account," protested Mihail Averyanitch. "It's a marvellous town."

Andrey Yefimitch had not the strength of will to insist on his own way, and much against his inclination went to Warsaw. There he did not leave the hotel room, but lay on the sofa, furious with himself, with his friend, and with the waiters, who obstinately refused to understand Russian; while Mihail Averyanitch, healthy, hearty, and full of spirits as usual, went about the town from morning to night, looking for his old acquaintances. Several times he did not return home at night. After one night spent in some unknown haunt he returned home early in the morning, in a violently excited condition, with a red face and tousled hair. For a long time he walked up and down the rooms muttering something to himself, then stopped and said:

"Honour before everything."

After walking up and down a little longer he clutched his head in both hands and pronounced in a tragic voice: "Yes, honour before everything! Accursed be the moment when the idea first entered my head to visit this Babylon! My dear friend," he added, addressing the doctor, "you may despise me, I have played and lost; lend me five hundred roubles!"

Andrey Yefimitch counted out five hundred roubles and gave them to his friend without a word. The latter, still crimson with shame and anger, incoherently articulated some useless vow, put on his cap, and went out. Returning two hours later he flopped into an easy-chair, heaved a loud sigh, and said:

"My honour is saved. Let us go, my friend; I do not care to remain another hour in this accursed town. Scoundrels! Austrian spies!"

By the time the friends were back in their own town it was November, and deep snow was lying in the streets. Dr.

Hobotov had Andrey Yefimitch's post; he was still living in his old lodgings, waiting for Andrey Yefimitch to arrive and clear out of the hospital apartments. The plain woman whom he called his cook was already established in one of the lodges.

Fresh scandals about the hospital were going the round of the town. It was said that the plain woman had quarrelled with the superintendent, and that the latter had crawled on his knees before her begging forgiveness. On the very first day he arrived Andrey Yefimitch had to look out for lodgings.

"My friend," the postmaster said to him timidly, "excuse an indiscreet question: what means have you at your disposal?"

Andrey Yefimitch, without a word, counted out his money and said: "Eighty-six roubles."

"I don't mean that," Mihail Averyanitch brought out in confusion, misunderstanding him; "I mean, what have you to live on?"

"I tell you, eighty-six roubles . . . I have nothing else."

Mihail Averyanitch looked upon the doctor as an honourable man, yet he suspected that he had accumulated a fortune of at least twenty thousand. Now learning that Andrey Yefimitch was a beggar, that he had nothing to live on he was for some reason suddenly moved to tears and embraced his friend.

XV

Andrey Yefimitch now lodged in a little house with three windows. There were only three rooms besides the kitchen in the little house. The doctor lived in two of them which looked into the street, while Daryushka and the landlady with her three children lived in the third room and the kitchen.

Sometimes the landlady's lover, a drunken peasant who was rowdy and reduced the children and Daryushka to terror, would come for the night. When he arrived and established himself in the kitchen and demanded vodka, they all felt very uncomfortable, and the doctor would be moved by pity to take the crying children into his room and let them lie on his floor, and this gave him great satisfaction.

He got up as before at eight o'clock, and after his morning tea sat down to read his old books and magazines: he had no money for new ones. Either because the books were old, or perhaps because of the change in his surroundings, reading exhausted him, and did not grip his attention as before. That he might not spend his time in idleness he made a detailed catalogue of his books and gummed little labels on their backs, and this mechanical, tedious work seemed to him more interesting than reading. The monotonous, tedious work lulled his thoughts to sleep in some unaccountable way, and the time passed quickly while he thought of nothing. Even sitting in the kitchen, peeling potatoes with Daryushka or picking over the buckwheat grain, seemed to him interesting. On Saturdays and Sundays he went to church. Standing near the wall and half closing his eyes, he listened to the singing and thought of his father, of his mother, of the university, of the religions of the world; he felt calm and melancholy, and as he went out of the church afterwards he regretted that the service was so soon over. He went twice to the hospital to talk to Ivan Dmitritch. But on both occasions Ivan Dmitritch was unusually excited and ill-humoured; he bade the doctor leave him in peace, as he had long been sick of empty chatter, and declared, to make up for all his sufferings, he asked from the damned scoundrels only one favour—solitary confinement. Surely they would not refuse him even that? On both occasions when Andrey Yefimitch was taking leave of him and wishing him good-night, he answered rudely and said:

"Go to hell!"

And Andrey Yefimitch did not know now whether to go to him for the third time or not. He longed to go.

In old days Andrey Yefimitch used to walk about his rooms and think in the interval after dinner, but now from dinner-time till evening tea he lay on the sofa with his face to the back and gave himself up to trivial thoughts which he could not struggle against. He was mortified that after more than twenty years of service he had been given neither a pension nor any assistance. It is true that he had not done his work honestly, but, then, all who are in the Service get a pension without distinction whether they are honest or not. Contemporary justice lies precisely in the bestowal of grades, orders, and pensions, not for moral qualities or capacities, but for service whatever it may have been like. Why was he alone to be an exception? He had no money at all. He was ashamed to pass by the shop and look at the woman who owned it. He owed thirty-two roubles for beer already. There was money owing to the landlady also. Daryushka sold old clothes and books on the sly, and told lies to the landlady, saying that the doctor was just going to receive a large sum of money.

He was angry with himself for having wasted on travelling the thousand roubles he had saved up. How useful that thousand roubles would have been now! He was vexed that people would not leave him in peace. Hobotov thought it his duty to look in on his sick colleague from time to time. Everything about him was revolting to Andrey Yefimitch—his well-fed face and vulgar, condescending tone, and his use of the word "colleague," and his high top-boots; the most revolting thing was that he thought it was his duty to treat Andrey Yefimitch, and thought that he really was treating him. On every visit he brought a bottle of bromide and rhubarb pills.

Mihail Averyanitch, too, thought it his duty to visit his friend and entertain him. Every time he went in to Andrey Yefimitch with an affectation of ease, laughed constrainedly, and began assuring him that he was looking very well to-day, and that, thank God, he was on the highroad to recovery, and from this it might be concluded that he looked on his friend's condition as hopeless. He had not yet repaid his Warsaw debt, and was overwhelmed by shame; he was constrained, and so tried to laugh louder and talk more amusingly. His anecdotes and descriptions seemed endless now, and were an agony both to Andrey Yefimitch and himself.

In his presence Andrey Yefimitch usually lay on the sofa with his face to the wall, and listened with his teeth clenched; his soul was oppressed with rankling disgust, and after every visit from his friend he felt as though this disgust had risen higher, and was mounting into his throat.

To stifle petty thoughts he made haste to reflect that he himself, and Hobotov, and Mihail Averyanitch, would all sooner or later perish without leaving any trace on the world. If one imagined some spirit flying by the earthly globe in space in a million years he would see nothing but clay and bare rocks. Everything—culture and the moral law—would pass away and not even a burdock would grow out of them. Of what consequence was shame in the presence of a shopkeeper, of what consequence was the insignificant Hobotov or the wearisome friendship of Mihail Averyanitch? It was all trivial and nonsensical.

But such reflections did not help him now. Scarcely had he imagined the earthly globe in a million years, when Hobotov in his high top-boots or Mihail Averyanitch with his forced laugh would appear from behind a bare rock, and he even heard the shamefaced whisper: "The Warsaw debt. . . . I will repay it in a day or two, my dear fellow, without fail. . . ."

XVI

One day Mihail Averyanitch came after dinner when Andrey Yefimitch was lying on the sofa. It so happened that Hobotov arrived at the same time with his bromide. Andrey Yefimitch got up heavily and sat down, leaning both arms on the sofa.

"You have a much better colour to-day than you had yesterday, my dear man," began Mihail Averyanitch. "Yes, you look jolly. Upon my soul, you do!"

"It's high time you were well, dear colleague," said Hobotov, yawning. "I'll be bound, you are sick of this bobbery."

"And we shall recover," said Mihail Averyanitch cheerfully. "We shall live another hundred years! To be sure!"

"Not a hundred years, but another twenty," Hobotov said reassuringly. "It's all right, all right, colleague; don't lose heart. . . . Don't go piling it on!"

"We'll show what we can do," laughed Mihail Averyanitch, and he slapped his friend on the knee. "We'll show them yet! Next summer, please God, we shall be off to the Caucasus, and we will ride all over it on horseback—trot, trot, trot! And when we are back from the Caucasus I shouldn't wonder if we will all dance at the wedding." Mihail Averyanitch gave a sly wink. "We'll marry you, my dear boy, we'll marry you. . . ."

Andrey Yefimitch felt suddenly that the rising disgust had mounted to his throat, his heart began beating violently.

"That's vulgar," he said, getting up quickly and walking

away to the window. "Don't you understand that you are talking vulgar nonsense?"

He meant to go on softly and politely, but against his will he suddenly clenched his fists and raised them above his head.

"Leave me alone," he shouted in a voice unlike his own, blushing crimson and shaking all over. "Go away, both of you!"

Mihail Averyanitch and Hobotov got up and stared at him first with amazement and then with alarm.

"Go away, both!" Andrey Yefimitch went on shouting. "Stupid people! Foolish people! I don't want either your friendship or your medicines, stupid man! Vulgar! Nasty!"

Hobotov and Mihail Averyanitch, looking at each other in bewilderment, staggered to the door and went out. Andrey Yefimitch snatched up the bottle of bromide and flung it after them; the bottle broke with a crash on the door-frame.

"Go to the devil!" he shouted in a tearful voice, running out into the passage. "To the devil!"

When his guests were gone Andrey Yefimitch lay down on the sofa, trembling as though in a fever, and went on for a long while repeating: "Stupid people! Foolish people!"

When he was calmer, what occurred to him first of all was the thought that poor Mihail Averyanitch must be feeling fearfully ashamed and depressed now, and that it was all dreadful. Nothing like this had ever happened to him before. Where was his intelligence and his tact? Where was his comprehension of things and his philosophical indifference?

The doctor could not sleep all night for shame and vexation with himself, and at ten o'clock next morning he went to the post office and apologized to the postmaster.

"We won't think again of what has happened," Mihail

Averyanitch, greatly touched, said with a sigh, warmly pressing his hand. "Let bygones be bygones. Lyubavkin," he suddenly shouted so loud that all the postmen and other persons present started, "hand a chair; and you wait," he shouted to a peasant woman who was stretching out a registered letter to him through the grating. "Don't you see that I am busy? We will not remember the past," he went on, affectionately addressing Andrey Yefimitch; "sit down, I beg you, my dear fellow."

For a minute he stroked his knees in silence, and then said:

"I have never had a thought of taking offence. Illness is no joke, I understand. Your attack frightened the doctor and me yesterday, and we had a long talk about you afterwards. My dear friend, why won't you treat your illness seriously? You can't go on like this . . . . Excuse me speaking openly as a friend," whispered Mihail Averyanitch. "You live in the most unfavourable surroundings, in a crowd, in uncleanliness, no one to look after you, no money for proper treatment. . . . My dear friend, the doctor and I implore you with all our hearts, listen to our advice: go into the hospital! There you will have wholesome food and attendance and treatment. Though, between ourselves, Yevgeny Fyodoritch is mauvais ton, yet he does understand his work, you can fully rely upon him. He has promised me he will look after you."

Andrey Yefimitch was touched by the postmaster's genuine sympathy and the tears which suddenly glittered on his cheeks.

"My honoured friend, don't believe it!" he whispered, laying his hand on his heart; "don't believe them. It's all a sham. My illness is only that in twenty years I have only found one intelligent man in the whole town, and he is mad. I am not ill at all, it's simply that I have got into an enchanted circle which there is no getting out of. I don't care; I am ready for anything."

"Go into the hospital, my dear fellow."

"I don't care if it were into the pit."

"Give me your word, my dear man, that you will obey Yevgeny Fyodoritch in everything."

"Certainly I will give you my word. But I repeat, my honoured friend, I have got into an enchanted circle. Now everything, even the genuine sympathy of my friends, leads to the same thing—to my ruin. I am going to my ruin, and I have the manliness to recognize it."

"My dear fellow, you will recover."

"What's the use of saying that?" said Andrey Yefimitch, with irritation. "There are few men who at the end of their lives do not experience what I am experiencing now. When you are told that you have something such as diseased kidneys or enlarged heart, and you begin being treated for it, or are told you are mad or a criminal—that is, in fact, when people suddenly turn their attention to you—you may be sure you have got into an enchanted circle from which you will not escape. You will try to escape and make things worse. You had better give in, for no human efforts can save you. So it seems to me."

Meanwhile the public was crowding at the grating. That he might not be in their way, Andrey Yefimitch got up and began to take leave. Mihail Averyanitch made him promise on his honour once more, and escorted him to the outer door.

Towards evening on the same day Hobotov, in his sheepskin and his high top-boots, suddenly made his appearance, and said to Andrey Yefimitch in a tone as though nothing had happened the day before:

"I have come on business, colleague. I have come to ask

you whether you would not join me in a consultation. Eh?"

Thinking that Hobotov wanted to distract his mind with an outing, or perhaps really to enable him to earn something, Andrey Yefimitch put on his coat and hat, and went out with him into the street. He was glad of the opportunity to smooth over his fault of the previous day and to be reconciled, and in his heart thanked Hobotov, who did not even allude to yesterday's scene and was evidently sparing him. One would never have expected such delicacy from this uncultured man.

"Where is your invalid?" asked Andrey Yefimitch.

"In the hospital. . . . I have long wanted to show him to you. A very interesting case."

They went into the hospital yard, and going round the main building, turned towards the lodge where the mental cases were kept, and all this, for some reason, in silence. When they went into the lodge Nikita as usual jumped up and stood at attention.

"One of the patients here has a lung complication." Hobotov said in an undertone, going into the yard with Andrey Yefimitch. "You wait here, I'll be back directly. I am going for a stethoscope."

And he went away.

XVII

It was getting dusk. Ivan Dmitritch was lying on his bed with his face thrust unto his pillow; the paralytic was sitting motionless, crying quietly and moving his lips. The fat peasant and the former sorter were asleep. It was quiet.

Andrey Yefimitch sat down on Ivan Dmitritch's bed and waited. But half an hour passed, and instead of Hobotov, Nikita came into the ward with a dressing-gown, some underlinen, and a pair of slippers in a heap on his arm.

"Please change your things, your honour," he said softly. "Here is your bed; come this way," he added, pointing to an empty bedstead which had obviously recently been brought into the ward. "It's all right; please God, you will recover."

Andrey Yefimitch understood it all. Without saying a word he crossed to the bed to which Nikita pointed and sat down; seeing that Nikita was standing waiting, he undressed entirely and he felt ashamed. Then he put on the hospital clothes; the drawers were very short, the shirt was long, and the dressing-gown smelt of smoked fish.

"Please God, you will recover," repeated Nikita, and he gathered up Andrey Yefimitch's clothes into his arms, went out, and shut the door after him.

"No matter . . ." thought Andrey Yefimitch, wrapping himself in his dressing-gown in a shamefaced way and feeling that he looked like a convict in his new costume. "It's no matter. . . . It does not matter whether it's a dress-coat or a uniform or this dressing-gown."

But how about his watch? And the notebook that was in the side-pocket? And his cigarettes? Where had Nikita taken his clothes? Now perhaps to the day of his death he would not put on trousers, a waistcoat, and high boots. It was all somehow strange and even incomprehensible at first. Andrey Yefimitch was even now convinced that there was no difference between his landlady's house and Ward No. 6, that everything in this world was nonsense and vanity of vanities. And yet his hands were trembling, his feet were cold, and he was filled with dread at the thought that soon Ivan Dmitritch would get up and see that he was in a dressing-gown. He got up and walked across the room and sat down again.

Here he had been sitting already half an hour, an hour, and he was miserably sick of it: was it really possible to live here a day, a week, and even years like these people? Why, he had been sitting here, had walked about and sat down again; he could get up and look out of window and walk from corner to corner again, and then what? Sit so all the time, like a post, and think? No, that was scarcely possible.

Andrey Yefimitch lay down, but at once got up, wiped the cold sweat from his brow with his sleeve and felt that his whole face smelt of smoked fish. He walked about again.

"It's some misunderstanding . . ." he said, turning out the palms of his hands in perplexity. "It must be cleared up. There is a misunderstanding."

Meanwhile Ivan Dmitritch woke up; he sat up and propped his cheeks on his fists. He spat. Then he glanced lazily at the doctor, and apparently for the first minute did not understand; but soon his sleepy face grew malicious and mocking.

"Aha! so they have put you in here, too, old fellow?" he said in a voice husky from sleepiness, screwing up one eye. "Very glad to see you. You sucked the blood of others, and now they will suck yours. Excellent!"

"It's a misunderstanding . . ." Andrey Yefimitch brought out, frightened by Ivan Dmitritch's words; he shrugged his shoulders and repeated: "It's some misunderstanding."

Ivan Dmitritch spat again and lay down.

"Cursed life," he grumbled, "and what's bitter and insulting, this life will not end in compensation for our sufferings, it will not end with apotheosis as it would in an opera, but with death; peasants will come and drag one's dead body by the arms and the legs to the cellar. Ugh! Well, it does not matter. . . . We shall have our good time in the other world. . . . I shall come here as a ghost from the other world and frighten these reptiles. I'll turn their hair grey."

Moiseika returned, and, seeing the doctor, held out his hand.

"Give me one little kopeck," he said.

XVIII

Andrey Yefimitch walked away to the window and looked out into the open country. It was getting dark, and on the horizon to the right a cold crimson moon was mounting upwards. Not far from the hospital fence, not much more than two hundred yards away, stood a tall white house shut in by a stone wall. This was the prison.

"So this is real life," thought Andrey Yefimitch, and he felt frightened.

The moon and the prison, and the nails on the fence, and the far-away flames at the bone-charring factory were all terrible. Behind him there was the sound of a sigh. Andrey Yefimitch looked round and saw a man with glittering stars and orders on his breast, who was smiling and slyly winking. And this, too, seemed terrible.

Andrey Yefimitch assured himself that there was nothing special about the moon or the prison, that even sane persons wear orders, and that everything in time will decay and turn to earth, but he was suddenly overcome with desire; he clutched at the grating with both hands and shook it with all his might. The strong grating did not yield.

Then that it might not be so dreadful he went to Ivan Dmitritch's bed and sat down.

"I have lost heart, my dear fellow," he muttered, trembling and wiping away the cold sweat, "I have lost heart."

"You should be philosophical," said Ivan Dmitritch ironically.

"My God, my God. . . . Yes, yes. . . . You were pleased to say once that there was no philosophy in Russia, but that all people, even the paltriest, talk philosophy. But you know the philosophizing of the paltriest does not harm anyone," said Andrey Yefimitch in a tone as if he wanted to cry and complain. "Why, then, that malignant laugh, my friend, and how can these paltry creatures help philosophizing if they are not satisfied? For an intelligent, educated man, made in God's image, proud and loving freedom, to have no alternative but to be a doctor in a filthy, stupid, wretched little town, and to spend his whole life among bottles, leeches, mustard plasters! Quackery, narrowness, vulgarity! Oh, my God!"

"You are talking nonsense. If you don't like being a doctor you should have gone in for being a statesman."

"I could not, I could not do anything. We are weak, my dear friend . . . . I used to be indifferent. I reasoned boldly and soundly, but at the first coarse touch of life upon me I have lost heart. . . . Prostration. . . . . We are weak, we are poor creatures . . . and you, too, my dear friend, you are intelligent, generous, you drew in good impulses with your mother's milk, but you had hardly entered upon life when you were exhausted and fell ill. . . . Weak, weak!"

Andrey Yefimitch was all the while at the approach of evening tormented by another persistent sensation besides terror and the feeling of resentment. At last he realized that he was longing for a smoke and for beer.

"I am going out, my friend," he said. "I will tell them to bring a light; I can't put up with this. . . . I am not equal to it. . . ."

Andrey Yefimitch went to the door and opened it, but at once Nikita jumped up and barred his way.

"Where are you going? You can't, you can't!" he said. "It's bedtime."

"But I'm only going out for a minute to walk about the yard," said Andrey Yefimitch.

"You can't, you can't; it's forbidden. You know that yourself."

"But what difference will it make to anyone if I do go out?" asked Andrey Yefimitch, shrugging his shoulders. "I don't understand. Nikita, I must go out!" he said in a trembling voice. "I must."

"Don't be disorderly, it's not right," Nikita said peremptorily.

"This is beyond everything," Ivan Dmitritch cried suddenly, and he jumped up. "What right has he not to let you out? How dare they keep us here? I believe it is clearly laid down in the law that no one can be deprived of freedom without trial! It's an outrage! It's tyranny!"

"Of course it's tyranny," said Andrey Yefimitch, encouraged by Ivan Dmitritch's outburst. "I must go out, I want to. He has no right! Open, I tell you."

"Do you hear, you dull-witted brute?" cried Ivan Dmitritch, and he banged on the door with his fist. "Open the door, or I will break it open! Torturer!"

"Open the door," cried Andrey Yefimitch, trembling all over; "I insist!"

"Talk away!" Nikita answered through the door, "talk away. . . ."

"Anyhow, go and call Yevgeny Fyodoritch! Say that I beg him to come for a minute!"

"His honour will come of himself to-morrow."

"They will never let us out," Ivan Dmitritch was going on meanwhile. "They will leave us to rot here! Oh, Lord, can there really be no hell in the next world, and will these wretches be forgiven? Where is justice? Open the door, you wretch! I am choking!" he cried in a hoarse voice, and flung himself upon the door. "I'll dash out my brains, murderers!"

Nikita opened the door quickly, and roughly with both his hands and his knee shoved Andrey Yefimitch back, then swung his arm and punched him in the face with his fist. It seemed to Andrey Yefimitch as though a huge salt wave enveloped him from his head downwards and dragged him to the bed; there really was a salt taste in his mouth: most likely the blood was running from his teeth. He waved his arms as though he were trying to swim out and clutched at a bedstead, and at the same moment felt Nikita hit him twice on the back.

Ivan Dmitritch gave a loud scream. He must have been beaten too.

Then all was still, the faint moonlight came through the grating, and a shadow like a net lay on the floor. It was terrible. Andrey Yefimitch lay and held his breath: he was expecting with horror to be struck again. He felt as though someone had taken a sickle, thrust it into him, and turned it round several times in his breast and bowels. He bit the pillow from pain and clenched his teeth, and all at once through the chaos in his brain there flashed the terrible unbearable thought that these people, who seemed now like black shadows in the moonlight, had to endure such pain day by day for years. How could it have happened that for more than twenty years he had not known it and had refused to know it? He knew nothing of pain, had no conception of it, so he was not to blame, but his conscience, as inexorable and as rough as Nikita, made him turn cold from the crown of his head to his heels. He leaped up, tried to cry out with all his might, and to run in haste to kill Nikita, and then Hobotov, the superintendent and the assistant, and then himself; but no sound came from his chest, and his legs would not obey him. Gasping for breath, he tore at the dressing-gown and the shirt on his breast, rent them, and fell senseless on the bed.

XIX

Next morning his head ached, there was a droning in his ears and a feeling of utter weakness all over. He was not ashamed at recalling his weakness the day before. He had been cowardly, had even been afraid of the moon, had openly expressed thoughts and feelings such as he had not expected in himself before; for instance, the thought that the paltry people who philosophized were really dissatisfied. But now nothing mattered to him.

He ate nothing; he drank nothing. He lay motionless and silent.

"It is all the same to me," he thought when they asked him questions. "I am not going to answer. . . . It's all the same to me."

After dinner Mihail Averyanitch brought him a quarter pound of tea and a pound of fruit pastilles. Daryushka came too and stood for a whole hour by the bed with an expression of dull grief on her face. Dr. Hobotov visited him. He brought a bottle of bromide and told Nikita to fumigate the ward with something.

Towards evening Andrey Yefimitch died of an apoplectic stroke. At first he had a violent shivering fit and a feeling of sickness; something revolting as it seemed, penetrating through his whole body, even to his finger-tips, strained from his stomach to his head and flooded his eyes and ears. There was a greenness before his eyes. Andrey Yefimitch understood that his end had come, and remembered that Ivan Dmitritch, Mihail Averyanitch, and millions of people believed in immortality. And what if it really existed? But he did not want immortality—and he thought of it only for one instant. A herd of deer, extraordinarily beautiful and graceful, of which he had been reading the day before, ran by him; then a peasant woman stretched out her hand to him with a registered letter . . . . Mihail Averyanitch said something, then it all vanished, and Andrey Yefimitch sank into oblivion for ever.

The hospital porters came, took him by his arms and legs, and carried him away to the chapel.

There he lay on the table, with open eyes, and the moon shed its light upon him at night. In the morning Sergey Sergeyitch came, prayed piously before the crucifix, and closed his former chief's eyes.

Next day Andrey Yefimitch was buried. Mihail Averyanitch and Daryushka were the only people at the funeral.

The Looking-Glass

NEW year's eve. Nellie, the daughter of a landowner and general, a young and pretty girl, dreaming day and night of being married, was sitting in her room, gazing with exhausted, half-closed eyes into the looking-glass. She was pale, tense, and as motionless as the looking-glass.

The non-existent but apparent vista of a long, narrow corridor with endless rows of candles, the reflection of her face, her hands, of the frame—all this was already clouded in mist and merged into a boundless grey sea. The sea was undulating, gleaming and now and then flaring crimson. . . .

Looking at Nellie's motionless eyes and parted lips, one could hardly say whether she was asleep or awake, but nevertheless she was seeing. At first she saw only the smile and soft, charming expression of someone's eyes, then against the shifting grey background there gradually appeared the outlines of a head, a face, eyebrows, beard. It was he, the destined one, the object of long dreams and hopes. The destined one was for Nellie everything, the significance of life, personal happiness, career, fate. Outside him, as on the grey background of the looking-glass, all was dark, empty, meaningless. And so it was not strange that, seeing before her a handsome, gently smiling face, she was conscious of bliss, of an unutterably sweet dream that could not be expressed in speech or on paper. Then she heard his voice, saw herself living under the same roof with him, her life merged into his. Months and years flew by against the grey background. And Nellie saw her future distinctly in all its details.

Picture followed picture against the grey background. Now Nellie saw herself one winter night knocking at the door of Stepan Lukitch, the district doctor. The old dog hoarsely and lazily barked behind the gate. The doctor's windows were in darkness. All was silence.

"For God's sake, for God's sake!" whispered Nellie.

But at last the garden gate creaked and Nellie saw the doctor's cook.

"Is the doctor at home?"

"His honour's asleep," whispered the cook into her sleeve, as though afraid of waking her master.

"He's only just got home from his fever patients, and gave orders he was not to be waked."

But Nellie scarcely heard the cook. Thrusting her aside, she rushed headlong into the doctor's house. Running through some dark and stuffy rooms, upsetting two or three chairs, she at last reached the doctor's bedroom. Stepan Lukitch was lying on his bed, dressed, but without his coat, and with pouting lips was breathing into his open hand. A little night-light glimmered faintly beside him. Without uttering a word Nellie sat down and began to cry. She wept bitterly, shaking all over.

"My husband is ill!" she sobbed out. Stepan Lukitch was silent. He slowly sat up, propped his head on his hand, and looked at his visitor with fixed, sleepy eyes. "My husband is ill!" Nellie continued, restraining her sobs. "For mercy's sake come quickly. Make haste. . . . Make haste!"

"Eh?" growled the doctor, blowing into his hand.

"Come! Come this very minute! Or . . . it's terrible to think! For mercy's sake!"

And pale, exhausted Nellie, gasping and swallowing her tears, began describing to the doctor her husband's illness, her unutterable terror. Her sufferings would have touched the heart of a stone, but the doctor looked at her, blew into his open hand, and—not a movement.

"I'll come to-morrow!" he muttered.

"That's impossible!" cried Nellie. "I know my husband has typhus! At once . . . this very minute you are needed!"

"I . . . er . . . have only just come in," muttered the doctor. "For the last three days I've been away, seeing typhus patients, and I'm exhausted and ill myself. . . . I simply can't! Absolutely! I've caught it myself! There!"

And the doctor thrust before her eyes a clinical thermometer.

"My temperature is nearly forty. . . . I absolutely can't. I can scarcely sit up. Excuse me. I'll lie down. . . ."

The doctor lay down.

"But I implore you, doctor," Nellie moaned in despair. "I beseech you! Help me, for mercy's sake! Make a great effort and come! I will repay you, doctor!"

"Oh, dear! . . . Why, I have told you already. Ah!"

Nellie leapt up and walked nervously up and down the bedroom. She longed to explain to the doctor, to bring him to reason. . . . She thought if only he knew how dear her husband was to her and how unhappy she was, he would forget his exhaustion and his illness. But how could she be eloquent enough?

"Go to the Zemstvo doctor," she heard Stepan Lukitch's voice.

"That's impossible! He lives more than twenty miles from here, and time is precious. And the horses can't stand it. It is thirty miles from us to you, and as much from here to the Zemstvo doctor. No, it's impossible! Come along, Stepan Lukitch. I ask of you an heroic deed. Come, perform that heroic deed! Have pity on us!"

"It's beyond everything. . . . I'm in a fever . . . my head's in a whirl . . . and she won't understand! Leave me alone!"

"But you are in duty bound to come! You cannot refuse to come! It's egoism! A man is bound to sacrifice his life for his neighbour, and you . . . you refuse to come! I will summon you before the Court."

Nellie felt that she was uttering a false and undeserved insult, but for her husband's sake she was capable of forgetting logic, tact, sympathy for others. . . . In reply to her threats, the doctor greedily gulped a glass of cold water. Nellie fell to entreating and imploring like the very lowest beggar. . . . At last the doctor gave way. He slowly got up, puffing and panting, looking for his coat.

"Here it is!" cried Nellie, helping him. "Let me put it on to you. Come along! I will repay you. . . . All my life I shall be grateful to you. . . ."

But what agony! After putting on his coat the doctor lay down again. Nellie got him up and dragged him to the hall. Then there was an agonizing to-do over his goloshes, his overcoat. . . . His cap was lost. . . . But at last Nellie was in the carriage with the doctor. Now they had only to drive thirty miles and her husband would have a doctor's help. The earth was wrapped in darkness. One could not see one's hand before one's face. . . . A cold winter wind was blowing. There were frozen lumps under their wheels. The coachman was continually stopping and wondering which road to take.

Nellie and the doctor sat silent all the way. It was fearfully jolting, but they felt neither the cold nor the jolts.

"Get on, get on!" Nellie implored the driver.

At five in the morning the exhausted horses drove into the yard. Nellie saw the familiar gates, the well with the crane, the long row of stables and barns. At last she was at home.

"Wait a moment, I will be back directly," she said to Stepan Lukitch, making him sit down on the sofa in the dining-room. "Sit still and wait a little, and I'll see how he is going on."

On her return from her husband, Nellie found the doctor lying down. He was lying on the sofa and muttering.

"Doctor, please! . . . doctor!"

"Eh? Ask Domna!" muttered Stepan Lukitch.

"What?"

"They said at the meeting . . . Vlassov said . . . Who? . . . what?"

And to her horror Nellie saw that the doctor was as delirious as her husband. What was to be done?

"I must go for the Zemstvo doctor," she decided.

Then again there followed darkness, a cutting cold wind, lumps of frozen earth. She was suffering in body and in soul, and delusive nature has no arts, no deceptions to compensate these sufferings. . . .

Then she saw against the grey background how her husband every spring was in straits for money to pay the interest for the mortgage to the bank. He could not sleep, she could not sleep, and both racked their brains till their heads ached, thinking how to avoid being visited by the clerk of the Court.

She saw her children: the everlasting apprehension of colds, scarlet fever, diphtheria, bad marks at school, separation. Out of a brood of five or six one was sure to die.

The grey background was not untouched by death. That might well be. A husband and wife cannot die simultaneously. Whatever happened one must bury the other. And Nellie saw her husband dying. This terrible event presented itself to her in every detail. She saw the coffin, the candles, the deacon, and even the footmarks in the hall made by the undertaker.

"Why is it, what is it for?" she asked, looking blankly at her husband's face.

And all the previous life with her husband seemed to her a stupid prelude to this.

Something fell from Nellie's hand and knocked on the floor. She started, jumped up, and opened her eyes wide. One looking-glass she saw lying at her feet. The other was standing as before on the table.

She looked into the looking-glass and saw a pale, tear-stained face. There was no grey background now.

"I must have fallen asleep," she thought with a sigh of relief.

A Story Without A Title

N the fifth century, just as now, the sun rose every morning and every evening retired to rest. In the morning, when the first rays kissed the dew, the earth revived, the air was filled with the sounds of rapture and hope; while in the evening the same earth subsided into silence and plunged into gloomy darkness. One day was like another, one night like another. From time to time a storm-cloud raced up and there was the angry rumble of thunder, or a negligent star fell out of the sky, or a pale monk ran to tell the brotherhood that not far from the monastery he had seen a tiger—and that was all, and then each day was like the next.

The monks worked and prayed, and their Father Superior played on the organ, made Latin verses, and wrote music. The wonderful old man possessed an extraordinary gift. He played on the organ with such art that even the oldest monks, whose hearing had grown somewhat dull towards the end of their lives, could not restrain their tears when the sounds of the organ floated from his cell. When he spoke of anything, even of the most ordinary things—for instance of the trees, of the wild beasts, or of the sea—they could not listen to him without a smile or tears, and it seemed that the same chords vibrated in his soul as in the organ. If he were moved to anger or abandoned himself to intense joy, or began speaking of something terrible or grand, then a passionate inspiration took possession of him, tears came into his flashing eyes, his face flushed, and his voice thundered, and as the monks listened to him they felt that their souls were spell-bound by his inspiration; at such marvellous, splendid moments his power over them was boundless, and if he had bidden his elders fling themselves into the sea, they would all, every one of them, have hastened to carry out his wishes.

His music, his voice, his poetry in which he glorified God, the heavens and the earth, were a continual source of joy to the monks. It sometimes happened that through the monotony of their lives they grew weary of the trees, the flowers, the spring, the autumn, their ears were tired of the sound of the sea, and the song of the birds seemed tedious to them, but the talents of their Father Superior were as necessary to them as their daily bread.

Dozens of years passed by, and every day was like every other day, every night was like every other night. Except the birds and the wild beasts, not one soul appeared near the monastery. The nearest human habitation was far away, and to reach it from the monastery, or to reach the monastery from it, meant a journey of over seventy miles across the desert. Only men who despised life, who had renounced it, and who came to the monastery as to the grave, ventured to cross the desert.

What was the amazement of the monks, therefore, when one night there knocked at their gate a man who turned out to be from the town, and the most ordinary sinner who loved life. Before saying his prayers and asking for the Father Superior's blessing, this man asked for wine and food. To the question how he had come from the town into the desert, he answered by a long story of hunting; he had gone out hunting, had drunk too much, and lost his way. To the suggestion that he should enter the monastery and save his soul, he replied with a smile: "I am not a fit companion for you!"

When he had eaten and drunk he looked at the monks who were serving him, shook his head reproachfully, and said:

"You don't do anything, you monks. You are good for nothing but eating and drinking. Is that the way to save one's soul? Only think, while you sit here in peace, eat and drink and dream of beatitude, your neighbours are perishing and going to hell. You should see what is going on in the town! Some are dying of hunger, others, not knowing what to do with their gold, sink into profligacy and perish like flies stuck in honey. There is no faith, no truth in men. Whose task is it to save them? Whose work is it to preach to them? It is not for me, drunk from morning till night as I am. Can a meek spirit, a loving heart, and faith in God have been given you for you to sit here within four walls doing nothing?"

The townsman's drunken words were insolent and unseemly, but they had a strange effect upon the Father Superior. The old man exchanged glances with his monks, turned pale, and said:

"My brothers, he speaks the truth, you know. Indeed, poor people in their weakness and lack of understanding are perishing in vice and infidelity, while we do not move, as though it did not concern us. Why should I not go and remind them of the Christ whom they have forgotten?"

The townsman's words had carried the old man away. The next day he took his staff, said farewell to the brotherhood, and set off for the town. And the monks were left without music, and without his speeches and verses. They spent a month drearily, then a second, but the old man did not come back. At last after three months had passed the familiar tap of his staff was heard. The monks flew to meet him and showered questions upon him, but instead of being delighted to see them he wept bitterly and did not utter a word. The monks noticed that he looked greatly aged and had grown thinner; his face looked exhausted and wore an expression of profound sadness, and when he wept he had the air of a man who has been outraged.

The monks fell to weeping too, and began with sympathy asking him why he was weeping, why his face was so gloomy, but he locked himself in his cell without uttering a word. For seven days he sat in his cell, eating and drinking nothing, weeping and not playing on his organ. To knocking at his door and to the entreaties of the monks to come out and share his grief with them he replied with unbroken silence.

At last he came out. Gathering all the monks around him, with a tear-stained face and with an expression of grief and indignation, he began telling them of what had befallen him during those three months. His voice was calm and his eyes were smiling while he described his journey from the monastery to the town. On the road, he told them, the birds sang to him, the brooks gurgled, and sweet youthful hopes agitated his soul; he marched on and felt like a soldier going to battle and confident of victory; he walked on dreaming, and composed poems and hymns, and reached the end of his journey without noticing it.

But his voice quivered, his eyes flashed, and he was full of wrath when he came to speak of the town and of the men in it. Never in his life had he seen or even dared to imagine what he met with when he went into the town. Only then for the first time in his life, in his old age, he saw and understood how powerful was the devil, how fair was evil and how weak and faint-hearted and worthless were men. By an unhappy chance the first dwelling he entered was the abode of vice. Some fifty men in possession of much money were eating and drinking wine beyond measure. Intoxicated by the wine, they sang songs and boldly uttered terrible, revolting words such as a God-fearing man could not bring himself to pronounce; boundlessly free, self-confident, and happy, they feared neither God nor the devil, nor death, but said and did what they liked, and went whither their lust led them. And the wine, clear as amber, flecked with sparks of gold, must have been irresistibly sweet and fragrant, for each man who drank it smiled blissfully and wanted to drink more. To the smile of man it responded with a smile and sparkled joyfully when they drank it, as though it knew the devilish charm it kept hidden in its sweetness.

The old man, growing more and more incensed and weeping with wrath, went on to describe what he had seen. On a table in the midst of the revellers, he said, stood a sinful, half-naked woman. It was hard to imagine or to find in nature anything more lovely and fascinating. This reptile, young, long-haired, dark-skinned, with black eyes and full lips, shameless and insolent, showed her snow-white teeth and smiled as though to say: "Look how shameless, how beautiful I am." Silk and brocade fell in lovely folds from her shoulders, but her beauty would not hide itself under her clothes, but eagerly thrust itself through the folds, like the young grass through the ground in spring. The shameless woman drank wine, sang songs, and abandoned herself to anyone who wanted her.

Then the old man, wrathfully brandishing his arms, described the horse-races, the bull-fights, the theatres, the artists' studios where they painted naked women or moulded them of clay. He spoke with inspiration, with sonorous beauty, as though he were playing on unseen chords, while the monks, petrified, greedily drank in his words and gasped with rapture. . . .

After describing all the charms of the devil, the beauty of evil, and the fascinating grace of the dreadful female form, the old man cursed the devil, turned and shut himself up in his cell. . . .

When he came out of his cell in the morning there was not a monk left in the monastery; they had all fled to the town.

A Daughter Of Albion

A fine carriage with rubber tyres, a fat coachman, and velvet on the seats, rolled up to the house of a landowner called Gryabov. Fyodor Andreitch Otsov, the district Marshal of Nobility, jumped out of the carriage. A drowsy footman met him in the hall.

"Are the family at home?" asked the Marshal.

"No, sir. The mistress and the children are gone out paying visits, while the master and mademoiselle are catching fish. Fishing all the morning, sir."

Otsov stood a little, thought a little, and then went to the river to look for Gryabov. Going down to the river he found him a mile and a half from the house. Looking down from the steep bank and catching sight of Gryabov, Otsov gushed with laughter. . . . Gryabov, a large stout man, with a very big head, was sitting on the sand, angling, with his legs tucked under him like a Turk. His hat was on the back of his head and his cravat had slipped on one side. Beside him stood a tall thin Englishwoman, with prominent eyes like a crab's, and a big bird-like nose more like a hook than a nose. She was dressed in a white muslin gown through which her scraggy yellow shoulders were very distinctly apparent. On her gold belt hung a little gold watch. She too was angling. The stillness of the grave reigned about them both. Both were motionless, as the river upon which their floats were swimming.

"A desperate passion, but deadly dull!" laughed Otsov. "Good-day, Ivan Kuzmitch."

"Ah . . . is that you ?" asked Gryabov, not taking his eyes off the water. "Have you come?"

"As you see . . . . And you are still taken up with your crazy nonsense! Not given it up yet?"

"The devil's in it. . . . I begin in the morning and fish all day . . . . The fishing is not up to much to-day. I've caught nothing and this dummy hasn't either. We sit on and on and not a devil of a fish! I could scream!"

"Well, chuck it up then. Let's go and have some vodka!"

"Wait a little, maybe we shall catch something. Towards evening the fish bite better . . . . I've been sitting here, my boy, ever since the morning! I can't tell you how fearfully boring it is. It was the devil drove me to take to this fishing! I know that it is rotten idiocy for me to sit here. I sit here like some scoundrel, like a convict, and I stare at the water like a fool. I ought to go to the haymaking, but here I sit catching fish. Yesterday His Holiness held a service at Haponyevo, but I didn't go. I spent the day here with this . . . with this she-devil."

"But . . . have you taken leave of your senses?" asked Otsov, glancing in embarrassment at the Englishwoman. "Using such language before a lady and she . . . ."

"Oh, confound her, it doesn't matter, she doesn't understand a syllable of Russian, whether you praise her or blame her, it is all the same to her! Just look at her nose! Her nose alone is enough to make one faint. We sit here for whole days together and not a single word! She stands like a stuffed image and rolls the whites of her eyes at the water."

The Englishwoman gave a yawn, put a new worm on, and dropped the hook into the water.

"I wonder at her not a little," Gryabov went on, "the great stupid has been living in Russia for ten years and not a word of Russian! . . . Any little aristocrat among us goes to them and learns to babble away in their lingo, while they . . . there's no making them out. Just look at her nose, do look at her nose!"

"Come, drop it . . . it's uncomfortable. Why attack a woman?"

"She's not a woman, but a maiden lady. . . . I bet she's dreaming of suitors. The ugly doll. And she smells of something decaying . . . . I've got a loathing for her, my boy! I can't look at her with indifference. When she turns her ugly eyes on me it sends a twinge all through me as though I had knocked my elbow on the parapet. She likes fishing too. Watch her: she fishes as though it were a holy rite! She looks upon everything with disdain . . . . She stands there, the wretch, and is conscious that she is a human being, and that therefore she is the monarch of nature. And do you know what her name is? Wilka Charlesovna Fyce! Tfoo! There is no getting it out!"

The Englishwoman, hearing her name, deliberately turned her nose in Gryabov's direction and scanned him with a disdainful glance; she raised her eyes from Gryabov to Otsov and steeped him in disdain. And all this in silence, with dignity and deliberation.

"Did you see?" said Gryabov chuckling. "As though to say 'take that.' Ah, you monster! It's only for the children's sake that I keep that triton. If it weren't for the children, I wouldn't let her come within ten miles of my estate. . . . She has got a nose like a hawk's . . . and her figure! That doll makes me think of a long nail, so I could take her, and knock her into the ground, you know. Stay, I believe I have got a bite. . . ."

Gryabov jumped up and raised his rod. The line drew taut. . . . Gryabov tugged again, but could not pull out the hook.

"It has caught," he said, frowning, "on a stone I expect . . . damnation take it . . . ."

There was a look of distress on Gryabov's face. Sighing, moving uneasily, and muttering oaths, he began tugging at the line.

"What a pity; I shall have to go into the water."

"Oh, chuck it!"

"I can't. . . . There's always good fishing in the evening. . . . What a nuisance. Lord, forgive us, I shall have to wade into the water, I must! And if only you knew, I have no inclination to undress. I shall have to get rid of the Englishwoman. . . . It's awkward to undress before her. After all, she is a lady, you know!"

Gryabov flung off his hat, and his cravat.

"Meess . . . er, er . . ." he said, addressing the Englishwoman, "Meess Fyce, je voo pree . . . ? Well, what am I to say to her? How am I to tell you so that you can understand? I say . . . over there! Go away over there! Do you hear?"

Miss Fyce enveloped Gryabov in disdain, and uttered a nasal sound.

"What? Don't you understand? Go away from here, I tell you! I must undress, you devil's doll! Go over there! Over there!"

Gryabov pulled the lady by her sleeve, pointed her towards the bushes, and made as though he would sit down, as much as to say: Go behind the bushes and hide yourself there. . . . The Englishwoman, moving her eyebrows vigorously, uttered rapidly a long sentence in English. The gentlemen gushed with laughter.

"It's the first time in my life I've heard her voice. There's no denying, it is a voice! She does not understand! Well, what am I to do with her?"

"Chuck it, let's go and have a drink of vodka!"

"I can't. Now's the time to fish, the evening. . . . It's evening . . . . Come, what would you have me do? It is a nuisance! I shall have to undress before her. . . ."

Gryabov flung off his coat and his waistcoat and sat on the sand to take off his boots.

"I say, Ivan Kuzmitch," said the marshal, chuckling behind his hand. "It's really outrageous, an insult."

"Nobody asks her not to understand! It's a lesson for these foreigners!"

Gryabov took off his boots and his trousers, flung off his undergarments and remained in the costume of Adam. Otsov held his sides, he turned crimson both from laughter and embarrassment. The Englishwoman twitched her brows and blinked . . . . A haughty, disdainful smile passed over her yellow face.

"I must cool off," said Gryabov, slapping himself on the ribs. "Tell me if you please, Fyodor Andreitch, why I have a rash on my chest every summer."

"Oh, do get into the water quickly or cover yourself with something, you beast."

"And if only she were confused, the nasty thing," said Gryabov, crossing himself as he waded into the water. "Brrrr . . . the water's cold. . . . Look how she moves her eyebrows! She doesn't go away . . . she is far above the crowd! He, he, he . . . . and she doesn't reckon us as human beings."

Wading knee deep in the water and drawing his huge figure up to its full height, he gave a wink and said:

"This isn't England, you see!"

Miss Fyce coolly put on another worm, gave a yawn, and dropped the hook in. Otsov turned away, Gryabov released his hook, ducked into the water and, spluttering, waded out. Two minutes later he was sitting on the sand and angling as before.

Fat and Thin

WO friends—one a fat man and the other a thin man—met at the Nikolaevsky station. The fat man had just dined in the station and his greasy lips shone like ripe cherries. He smelt of sherry and *fleur d'orange*. The thin man had just slipped out of the train and was laden with portmanteaus, bundles, and bandboxes. He smelt of ham and coffee grounds. A thin woman with a long chin, his wife, and a tall schoolboy with one eye screwed up came into view behind his back.

"Porfiry," cried the fat man on seeing the thin man. "Is it you? My dear fellow! How many summers, how many winters!"

"Holy saints!" cried the thin man in amazement. "Misha! The friend of my childhood! Where have you dropped from?"

The friends kissed each other three times, and gazed at each other with eyes full of tears. Both were agreeably astounded.

"My dear boy!" began the thin man after the kissing. "This is unexpected! This is a surprise! Come have a good look at me! Just as handsome as I used to be! Just as great a darling and a dandy! Good gracious me! Well, and how are you? Made your fortune? Married? I am married as you see. . . .

This is my wife Luise, her maiden name was Vantsenbach
. . . of the Lutheran persuasion. . . . And this is my son
Nafanail, a schoolboy in the third class. This is the friend of
my childhood, Nafanya. We were boys at school together!"

Nafanail thought a little and took off his cap.

"We were boys at school together," the thin man went
on. "Do you remember how they used to tease you? You
were nicknamed Herostratus because you burned a hole in a
schoolbook with a cigarette, and I was nicknamed Ephialtes
because I was fond of telling tales. Ho—ho! . . . we were
children! . . . Don't be shy, Nafanya. Go nearer to him. And
this is my wife, her maiden name was Vantsenbach, of the
Lutheran persuasion. . . ."

Nafanail thought a little and took refuge behind his
father's back.

"Well, how are you doing my friend?" the fat man asked,
looking enthusiastically at his friend. "Are you in the service?
What grade have you reached?"

"I am, dear boy! I have been a collegiate assessor for the
last two years and I have the Stanislav. The salary is poor,
but that's no great matter! The wife gives music lessons, and
I go in for carving wooden cigarette cases in a private way.
Capital cigarette cases! I sell them for a rouble each. If any one
takes ten or more I make a reduction of course. We get along
somehow. I served as a clerk, you know, and now I have been
transferred here as a head clerk in the same department. I am
going to serve here. And what about you? I bet you are a civil
councillor by now? Eh?"

"No dear boy, go higher than that," said the fat man. "I
have risen to privy councillor already . . . I have two stars."

The thin man turned pale and rigid all at once, but soon
his face twisted in all directions in the broadest smile; it

seemed as though sparks were flashing from his face and eyes. He squirmed, he doubled together, crumpled up. . . His portmanteaus, bundles and cardboard boxes seemed to shrink and crumple up too. . . . His wife's long chin grew longer still; Nafanail drew himself up to attention and fastened all the buttons of his uniform.

"Your Excellency, I . . . delighted! The friend, one may say, of childhood and to have turned into such a great man! He—he!"

"Come, come!" the fat man frowned. "What's this tone for? You and I were friends as boys, and there is no need of this official obsequiousness!"

"Merciful heavens, your Excellency! What are you saying. . . ?" sniggered the thin man, wriggling more than ever. "Your Excellency's gracious attention is like refreshing manna. . . . This, your Excellency, is my son Nafanail, . . . my wife Luise, a Lutheran in a certain sense."

The fat man was about to make some protest, but the face of the thin man wore an expression of such reverence, sugariness, and mawkish respectfulness that the privy councillor was sickened. He turned away from the thin man, giving him his hand at parting.

The thin man pressed three fingers, bowed his whole body and sniggered like a Chinaman: "He—he—he!" His wife smiled. Nafanail scraped with his foot and dropped his cap. All three were agreeably overwhelmed.

The Murder

I

THE evening service was being celebrated at Progonnaya Station. Before the great ikon, painted in glaring colours on a background of gold, stood the crowd of railway servants with their wives and children, and also of the timbermen and sawyers who worked close to the railway line. All stood in silence, fascinated by the glare of the lights and the howling of the snow-storm which was aimlessly disporting itself outside, regardless of the fact that it was the Eve of the Annunciation. The old priest from Vedenyapino conducted the service; the sacristan and Matvey Terehov were singing.

Matvey's face was beaming with delight; he sang stretching out his neck as though he wanted to soar upwards. He sang tenor and chanted the "Praises" too in a tenor voice with honied sweetness and persuasiveness. When he sang "Archangel Voices" he waved his arms like a conductor, and trying to second the sacristan's hollow bass with his tenor, achieved something extremely complex, and from his face it could be seen that he was experiencing great pleasure.

At last the service was over, and they all quietly dispersed, and it was dark and empty again, and there followed that hush which is only known in stations that stand solitary in the open country or in the forest when the wind howls and nothing else is heard and when all the emptiness around, all the dreariness of life slowly ebbing away is felt.

Matvey lived not far from the station at his cousin's tavern. But he did not want to go home. He sat down at the refreshment bar and began talking to the waiter in a low voice.

"We had our own choir in the tile factory. And I must tell you that though we were only workmen, our singing was first-rate, splendid. We were often invited to the town, and when the Deputy Bishop, Father Ivan, took the service at Trinity Church, the bishop's singers sang in the right choir and we in the left. Only they complained in the town that we kept the singing on too long: 'the factory choir drag it out,' they used to say. It is true we began St. Andrey's prayers and the Praises between six and seven, and it was past eleven when we finished, so that it was sometimes after midnight when we got home to the factory. It was good," sighed Matvey. "Very good it was, indeed, Sergey Nikanoritch! But here in my father's house it is anything but joyful. The nearest church is four miles away; with my weak health I can't get so far; there are no singers there. And there is no peace or quiet in our family; day in day out, there is an uproar, scolding, uncleanliness; we all eat out of one bowl like peasants; and there are beetles in the cabbage soup. . . . God has not given me health, else I would have gone away long ago, Sergey Nikanoritch."

Matvey Terehov was a middle-aged man about forty-five, but he had a look of ill-health; his face was wrinkled and his lank, scanty beard was quite grey, and that made him seem many years older. He spoke in a weak voice, circumspectly, and held his chest when he coughed, while his eyes assumed the uneasy and anxious look one sees in very apprehensive people. He never said definitely what was wrong with him, but he was fond of describing at length how once at the factory he had lifted a heavy box and had ruptured himself, and how this had led to "the gripes," and had forced him to give up his work in the tile factory and come back to his native place; but he could not explain what he meant by "the gripes."

"I must own I am not fond of my cousin," he went on, pouring himself out some tea. "He is my elder; it is a sin to censure him, and I fear the Lord, but I cannot bear it in patience. He is a haughty, surly, abusive man; he is the torment of his relations and workmen, and constantly out of humour. Last Sunday I asked him in an amiable way, 'Brother, let us go to Pahomovo for the Mass!' but he said 'I am not going; the priest there is a gambler;' and he would not come here to-day because, he said, the priest from Vedenyapino smokes and drinks vodka. He doesn't like the clergy! He reads Mass himself and the Hours and the Vespers, while his sister acts as sacristan; he says, 'Let us pray unto the Lord'! and she, in a thin little voice like a turkey-hen, 'Lord, have mercy upon us! . . .' It's a sin, that's what it is. Every day I say to him, 'Think what you are doing, brother! Repent, brother!' and he takes no notice."

Sergey Nikanoritch, the waiter, poured out five glasses of tea and carried them on a tray to the waiting-room. He had scarcely gone in when there was a shout:

"Is that the way to serve it, pig's face? You don't know how to wait!"

It was the voice of the station-master. There was a timid mutter, then again a harsh and angry shout:

"Get along!"

The waiter came back greatly crestfallen.

"There was a time when I gave satisfaction to counts and princes," he said in a low voice; "but now I don't know how to serve tea. . . . He called me names before the priest and the ladies!"

The waiter, Sergey Nikanoritch, had once had money of his own, and had kept a buffet at a first-class station, which was a junction, in the principal town of a province. There he had worn a swallow-tail coat and a gold chain. But things had gone ill with him; he had squandered all his own money over expensive fittings and service; he had been robbed by his staff, and getting gradually into difficulties, had moved to another station less bustling. Here his wife had left him, taking with her all the silver, and he moved to a third station of a still lower class, where no hot dishes were served. Then to a fourth. Frequently changing his situation and sinking lower and lower, he had at last come to Progonnaya, and here he used to sell nothing but tea and cheap vodka, and for lunch hard-boiled eggs and dry sausages, which smelt of tar, and which he himself sarcastically said were only fit for the orchestra. He was bald all over the top of his head, and had prominent blue eyes and thick bushy whiskers, which he often combed out, looking into the little looking-glass. Memories of the past haunted him continually; he could never get used to sausage "only fit for the orchestra," to the rudeness of the station-master, and to the peasants who used to haggle over the prices, and in his opinion it was as unseemly to haggle over prices in a refreshment room as in a chemist's shop. He was ashamed of his poverty and degradation, and that shame was now the leading interest of his life.

"Spring is late this year," said Matvey, listening. "It's a good job; I don't like spring. In spring it is very muddy, Sergey Nikanoritch. In books they write: Spring, the birds sing, the sun is setting, but what is there pleasant in that?

A bird is a bird, and nothing more. I am fond of good company, of listening to folks, of talking of religion or singing something agreeable in chorus; but as for nightingales and flowers—bless them, I say!"

He began again about the tile factory, about the choir, but Sergey Nikanoritch could not get over his mortification, and kept shrugging his shoulders and muttering. Matvey said good-bye and went home.

There was no frost, and the snow was already melting on the roofs, though it was still falling in big flakes; they were whirling rapidly round and round in the air and chasing one another in white clouds along the railway line. And the oak forest on both sides of the line, in the dim light of the moon which was hidden somewhere high up in the clouds, resounded with a prolonged sullen murmur. When a violent storm shakes the trees, how terrible they are! Matvey walked along the causeway beside the line, covering his face and his hands, while the wind beat on his back. All at once a little nag, plastered all over with snow, came into sight; a sledge scraped along the bare stones of the causeway, and a peasant, white all over, too, with his head muffled up, cracked his whip. Matvey looked round after him, but at once, as though it had been a vision, there was neither sledge nor peasant to be seen, and he hastened his steps, suddenly scared, though he did not know why.

Here was the crossing and the dark little house where the signalman lived. The barrier was raised, and by it perfect mountains had drifted and clouds of snow were whirling round like witches on broomsticks. At that point the line was crossed by an old highroad, which was still called "the track." On the right, not far from the crossing, by the roadside stood Terehov's tavern, which had been a posting inn. Here there was always a light twinkling at night.

When Matvey reached home there was a strong smell of incense in all the rooms and even in the entry. His cousin Yakov Ivanitch was still reading the evening service. In the prayer-room where this was going on, in the corner opposite the door, there stood a shrine of old-fashioned ancestral ikons in gilt settings, and both walls to right and to left were decorated with ikons of ancient and modern fashion, in shrines and without them. On the table, which was draped to the floor, stood an ikon of the Annunciation, and close by a cyprus-wood cross and the censer; wax candles were burning. Beside the table was a reading desk. As he passed by the prayer-room, Matvey stopped and glanced in at the door. Yakov Ivanitch was reading at the desk at that moment, his sister Aglaia, a tall lean old woman in a dark-blue dress and white kerchief, was praying with him. Yakov Ivanitch's daughter Dashutka, an ugly freckled girl of eighteen, was there, too, barefoot as usual, and wearing the dress in which she had at nightfall taken water to the cattle.

"Glory to Thee Who hast shown us the light!" Yakov Ivanitch boomed out in a chant, bowing low.

Aglaia propped her chin on her hand and chanted in a thin, shrill, drawling voice. And upstairs, above the ceiling, there was the sound of vague voices which seemed menacing or ominous of evil. No one had lived on the storey above since a fire there a long time ago. The windows were boarded up, and empty bottles lay about on the floor between the beams. Now the wind was banging and droning, and it seemed as though someone were running and stumbling over the beams.

Half of the lower storey was used as a tavern, while Terehov's family lived in the other half, so that when drunken visitors were noisy in the tavern every word they said could be heard in the rooms. Matvey lived in a room next to the kitchen, with a big stove, in which, in old days, when this had been a posting inn, bread had been baked every day. Dashutka, who had no room of her own, lived in the same room behind the stove. A cricket chirped there always at night and mice ran in and out.

Matvey lighted a candle and began reading a book which he had borrowed from the station policeman. While he was sitting over it the service ended, and they all went to bed. Dashutka lay down, too. She began snoring at once, but soon woke up and said, yawning:

"You shouldn't burn a candle for nothing, Uncle Matvey."

"It's my candle," answered Matvey; "I bought it with my own money."

Dashutka turned over a little and fell asleep again. Matvey sat up a good time longer—he was not sleepy—and when he had finished the last page he took a pencil out of a box and wrote on the book:

"I, Matvey Terehov, have read this book, and think it the very best of all the books I have read, for which I express my gratitude to the non-commissioned officer of the Police Department of Railways, Kuzma Nikolaev Zhukov, as the possessor of this priceless book."

He considered it an obligation of politeness to make such inscriptions in other people's books.

II

On Annunciation Day, after the mail train had been sent off, Matvey was sitting in the refreshment bar, talking and drinking tea with lemon in it.

The waiter and Zhukov the policeman were listening to him.

"I was, I must tell you," Matvey was saying, "inclined to

religion from my earliest childhood. I was only twelve years old when I used to read the epistle in church, and my parents were greatly delighted, and every summer I used to go on a pilgrimage with my dear mother. Sometimes other lads would be singing songs and catching crayfish, while I would be all the time with my mother. My elders commended me, and, indeed, I was pleased myself that I was of such good behaviour. And when my mother sent me with her blessing to the factory, I used between working hours to sing tenor there in our choir, and nothing gave me greater pleasure. I needn't say, I drank no vodka, I smoked no tobacco, and lived in chastity; but we all know such a mode of life is displeasing to the enemy of mankind, and he, the unclean spirit, once tried to ruin me and began to darken my mind, just as now with my cousin. First of all, I took a vow to fast every Monday and not to eat meat any day, and as time went on all sorts of fancies came over me. For the first week of Lent down to Saturday the holy fathers have ordained a diet of dry food, but it is no sin for the weak or those who work hard even to drink tea, yet not a crumb passed into my mouth till the Sunday, and afterwards all through Lent I did not allow myself a drop of oil, and on Wednesdays and Fridays I did not touch a morsel at all. It was the same in the lesser fasts. Sometimes in St. Peter's fast our factory lads would have fish soup, while I would sit a little apart from them and suck a dry crust. Different people have different powers, of course, but I can say of myself I did not find fast days hard, and, indeed, the greater the zeal the easier it seems. You are only hungry on the first days of the fast, and then you get used to it; it goes on getting easier, and by the end of a week you don't mind it at all, and there is a numb feeling in your legs as though you were not on earth, but in the clouds. And, besides that, I laid all sorts of penances on myself; I used to get up in the night and pray, bowing down to the ground, used to drag heavy stones from place to place, used to go out barefoot in the snow, and I even wore chains, too. Only, as time went on, you know, I was confessing one day to the priest and suddenly this reflection occurred to me: why, this priest, I thought, is married, he eats meat and smokes tobacco—how can he confess me, and what power has he to absolve my sins if he is more sinful that I? I even scruple to eat Lenten oil, while he eats sturgeon, I dare say. I went to another priest, and he, as ill luck would have it, was a fat fleshy man, in a silk cassock; he rustled like a lady, and he smelt of tobacco too. I went to fast and confess in the monastery, and my heart was not at ease even there; I kept fancying the monks were not living according to their rules. And after that I could not find a service to my mind: in one place they read the service too fast, in another they sang the wrong prayer, in a third the sacristan stammered. Sometimes, the Lord forgive me a sinner, I would stand in church and my heart would throb with anger. How could one pray, feeling like that? And I fancied that the people in the church did not cross themselves properly, did not listen properly; wherever I looked it seemed to me that they were all drunkards, that they broke the fast, smoked, lived loose lives and played cards. I was the only one who lived according to the commandments. The wily spirit did not slumber; it got worse as it went on. I gave up singing in the choir and I did not go to church at all; since my notion was that I was a righteous man and that the church did not suit me owing to its imperfections—that is, indeed, like a fallen angel, I was puffed up in my pride beyond all belief. After this I began attempting to make a church for myself. I hired from a deaf woman a tiny little room, a long way out of town near the cemetery, and made a prayer-room like my cousin's, only I had big church candlesticks, too, and a real censer. In this prayer-room of mine I kept the rules of holy Mount Athos—that is, every day my matins began at midnight without fail, and on the eve of the chief of the twelve great holy days my midnight service lasted ten hours and sometimes even twelve. Monks are allowed by rule to sit during the singing of the Psalter and the reading of the Bible, but I wanted to be better than the monks, and so I used to stand all through. I used to read and sing slowly, with tears and sighing, lifting up my hands, and I used to go straight from prayer to work without sleeping; and, indeed, I was always praying at my work, too. Well, it got all over the town 'Matvey is a saint; Matvey heals the sick and senseless.' I never had healed anyone, of course, but we all know wherever any heresy or false doctrine springs up there's no keeping the female sex away. They are just like flies on the honey. Old maids and females of all sorts came trailing to me, bowing down to my feet, kissing my hands and crying out I was a saint and all the rest of it, and one even saw a halo round my head. It was too crowded in the prayer-room. I took a bigger room, and then we had a regular tower of Babel. The devil got hold of me completely and screened the light from my eyes with his unclean hoofs. We all behaved as though we were frantic. I read, while the old maids and other females sang, and then after standing on their legs for twenty-four hours or longer without eating or drinking, suddenly a trembling would come over them as though they were in a fever; after that, one would begin screaming and then another—it was horrible! I, too, would shiver all over like a Jew in a frying-pan, I don't know myself why, and our legs began to prance about. It's a strange thing, indeed: you don't want to, but you prance about and waggle your arms; and after that, screaming and shrieking, we all danced and ran after one another—ran till we dropped; and in that way, in wild frenzy, I fell into fornication."

The policeman laughed, but, noticing that no one else was laughing, became serious and said:

"That's Molokanism. I have heard they are all like that in the Caucasus."

"But I was not killed by a thunderbolt," Matvey went on, crossing himself before the ikon and moving his lips. "My dead mother must have been praying for me in the other world. When everyone in the town looked upon me as a saint, and even the ladies and gentlemen of good family used to come to me in secret for consolation, I happened to go into our landlord, Osip Varlamitch, to ask forgiveness—it was the Day of Forgiveness—and he fastened the door with the hook, and we were left alone face to face. And he began to reprove me, and I must tell you Osip Varlamitch was a man of brains, though without education, and everyone respected and feared him, for he was a man of stern, God-fearing life and worked hard. He had been the mayor of the town, and a warden of the church for twenty years maybe, and had done a great deal of good; he had covered all the New Moscow Road with gravel, had painted the church, and had decorated the columns to look like malachite. Well, he fastened the door, and—'I have been wanting to get at you for a long time, you rascal, . . .' he said. 'You think you are a saint,' he said. 'No you are not a saint, but a backslider from God, a heretic and an evildoer! . . .' And he went on and on. . . . I can't tell you how he said it, so eloquently and cleverly, as though it were all written down, and so touchingly. He talked for two hours. His words penetrated my soul; my eyes were opened. I listened, listened and—burst into sobs! 'Be an ordinary man,' he said, 'eat and drink, dress and pray like everyone else. All that is above the ordinary is of the devil. Your chains,' he said, 'are of the devil; your fasting is of the devil; your prayer-room is of the devil. It is all pride,' he said. Next day, on Monday in Holy Week, it pleased God I should fall ill. I ruptured myself and was taken to the hospital. I was terribly worried, and wept bitterly and trembled. I thought there was a straight road before me from the hospital to hell, and I almost died. I was in misery on a bed of sickness for six months, and when I was discharged the first thing I did I confessed, and took the sacrament in the regular way and became a man again. Osip Varlamitch saw me off home and exhorted me: 'Remember, Matvey, that anything above the ordinary is of the devil.' And now I eat and drink like everyone else and pray like everyone else . . . . If it happens now that the priest smells of tobacco or vodka I don't venture to blame him, because the priest, too, of course, is an ordinary man. But as soon as I am told that in the town or in the village a saint has set up who does not eat for weeks, and makes rules of his own, I know whose work it is. So that is how I carried on in the past, gentlemen. Now, like Osip Varlamitch, I am continually exhorting my cousins and reproaching them, but I am a voice crying in the wilderness. God has not vouchsafed me the gift."

Matvey's story evidently made no impression whatever. Sergey Nikanoritch said nothing, but began clearing the refreshments off the counter, while the policeman began talking of how rich Matvey's cousin was.

"He must have thirty thousand at least," he said.

Zhukov the policeman, a sturdy, well-fed, red-haired man with a full face (his cheeks quivered when he walked), usually sat lolling and crossing his legs when not in the presence of his superiors. As he talked he swayed to and fro and whistled carelessly, while his face had a self-satisfied replete air, as though he had just had dinner. He was making money, and he always talked of it with the air of a connoisseur. He undertook jobs as an agent, and when anyone wanted to sell an estate, a horse or a carriage, they applied to him.

"Yes, it will be thirty thousand, I dare say," Sergey Nikanoritch assented. "Your grandfather had an immense fortune," he said, addressing Matvey. "Immense it was; all left to your father and your uncle. Your father died as a young man and your uncle got hold of it all, and afterwards, of course, Yakov Ivanitch. While you were going pilgrimages with your mama and singing tenor in the factory, they didn't let the grass grow under their feet."

"Fifteen thousand comes to your share," said the policeman swaying from side to side. "The tavern belongs to you in common, so the capital is in common. Yes. If I were in your place I should have taken it into court long ago. I would have taken it into court for one thing, and while the case was going on I'd have knocked his face to a jelly."

Yakov Ivanitch was disliked because, when anyone believes differently from others, it upsets even people who are indifferent to religion. The policeman disliked him also because he, too, sold horses and carriages.

"You don't care about going to law with your cousin because you have plenty of money of your own," said the waiter to Matvey, looking at him with envy. "It is all very well for anyone who has means, but here I shall die in this position, I suppose...."

Matvey began declaring that he hadn't any money at all, but Sergey Nikanoritch was not listening. Memories of the past and of the insults which he endured every day came showering upon him. His bald head began to perspire; he flushed and blinked.

"A cursed life!" he said with vexation, and he banged the sausage on the floor.

III

The story ran that the tavern had been built in the time of Alexander I, by a widow who had settled here with her son; her name was Avdotya Terehov. The dark roofed-in courtyard and the gates always kept locked excited, especially on moonlight nights, a feeling of depression and unaccountable uneasiness in people who drove by with posting-horses, as though sorcerers or robbers were living in it; and the driver always looked back after he passed, and whipped up his horses. Travellers did not care to put up here, as the people of the house were always unfriendly and charged heavily. The yard was muddy even in summer; huge fat pigs used to lie there in the mud, and the horses in which the Terehovs dealt wandered about untethered, and often it happened that they ran out of the yard and dashed along the road like mad creatures, terrifying the pilgrim women. At that time there was a great deal of traffic on the road; long trains of loaded waggons trailed by, and all sorts of adventures happened, such as, for instance, that thirty years ago some waggoners got up a quarrel with a passing merchant and killed him, and a slanting cross is standing to this day half a mile from the tavern; posting-chaises with bells and the heavy *dormeuses* of country gentlemen drove by; and herds of horned cattle passed bellowing and stirring up clouds of dust.

When the railway came there was at first at this place only a platform, which was called simply a halt; ten years afterwards the present station, Progonnaya, was built. The traffic on the old posting-road almost ceased, and only local landowners and peasants drove along it now, but the working people walked there in crowds in spring and autumn. The posting-inn was transformed into a restaurant; the upper storey was destroyed by fire, the roof had grown yellow with rust, the roof over the yard had fallen by degrees, but huge fat pigs, pink and revolting, still wallowed in the mud in the yard. As before, the horses sometimes ran away and, lashing their tails dashed madly along the road. In the tavern they sold tea, hay oats and flour, as well as vodka and beer, to be drunk on the premises and also to be taken away; they sold spirituous liquors warily, for they had never taken out a licence.

The Terehovs had always been distinguished by their piety, so much so that they had even been given the nickname of the "Godlies." But perhaps because they lived apart like bears, avoided people and thought out all their ideas for themselves, they were given to dreams and to doubts and to changes of faith and almost each generation had a peculiar faith of its own. The grandmother Avdotya, who had built the inn, was an Old Believer; her son and both her grandsons (the fathers of Matvey and Yakov) went to the Orthodox church, entertained the clergy, and worshipped before the new ikons as devoutly as they had done before the old. The son in old age refused to eat meat and imposed upon himself the rule of silence, considering all conversation as sin; it was the peculiarity of the grandsons that they interpreted the Scripture not simply, but sought in it a hidden meaning, declaring that every sacred word must contain a mystery.

Avdotya's great-grandson Matvey had struggled from early childhood with all sorts of dreams and fancies and had been almost ruined by it; the other great-grandson, Yakov Ivanitch, was orthodox, but after his wife's death he gave up going to church and prayed at home. Following his example, his sister Aglaia had turned, too; she did not go to church herself, and did not let Dashutka go. Of Aglaia it was told that in her youth she used to attend the Flagellant meetings in Vedenyapino, and that she was still a Flagellant in secret, and that was why she wore a white kerchief.

Yakov Ivanitch was ten years older than Matvey—he was a very handsome tall old man with a big grey beard almost to his waist, and bushy eyebrows which gave his face a stern, even ill-natured expression. He wore a long jerkin of good cloth or a black sheepskin coat, and altogether tried to be clean and neat in dress; he wore goloshes even in dry weather. He did not go to church, because, to his thinking, the services were not properly celebrated and because the priests drank wine at unlawful times and smoked tobacco. Every day he read and sang the service at home with Aglaia. At Vedenyapino they left out the "Praises" at early matins, and had no evening service even on great holidays, but he used to read through at home everything that was laid down for every day, without hurrying or leaving out a single line, and even in his spare time read aloud the Lives of the Saints. And in everyday life he adhered strictly to the rules of the church; thus, if wine were allowed on some day in Lent "for the sake of the vigil," then he never failed to drink wine, even if he were not inclined.

He read, sang, burned incense and fasted, not for the sake of receiving blessings of some sort from God, but for the sake of good order. Man cannot live without religion, and religion ought to be expressed from year to year and from day to day in a certain order, so that every morning and every evening a man might turn to God with exactly those words and thoughts that were befitting that special day and hour. One must live, and, therefore, also pray as is pleasing to God, and so every day one must read and sing what is pleasing to God—that is, what is laid down in the rule of the church. Thus the first chapter of St. John must only be read on Easter Day, and "It is most meet" must not be sung from Easter to Ascension, and so on. The consciousness of this order and its importance afforded Yakov Ivanitch great gratification during his religious exercises. When he was forced to break this order by some necessity—to drive to town or to the bank, for instance his conscience was uneasy and he felt miserable.

When his cousin Matvey had returned unexpectedly from the factory and settled in the tavern as though it were his home, he had from the very first day disturbed his settled order. He refused to pray with them, had meals and drank tea at wrong times, got up late, drank milk on Wednesdays and Fridays on the pretext of weak health; almost every day he went into the prayer-room while they were at prayers and cried: "Think what you are doing, brother! Repent, brother!" These words threw Yakov into a fury, while Aglaia could not refrain from beginning to scold; or at night Matvey would steal into the prayer-room and say softly: "Cousin, your prayer is not pleasing to God. For it is written, First be reconciled with thy brother and then offer thy gift. You lend money at usury, you deal in vodka—repent!"

In Matvey's words Yakov saw nothing but the usual evasions of empty-headed and careless people who talk of loving your neighbour, of being reconciled with your brother, and so on, simply to avoid praying, fasting and reading holy books, and who talk contemptuously of profit and interest simply because they don't like working. Of course, to be poor, save nothing, and put by nothing was a great deal easier than being rich.

But yet he was troubled and could not pray as before. As soon as he went into the prayer-room and opened the book he began to be afraid his cousin would come in and hinder him; and, in fact, Matvey did soon appear and cry in a trembling voice: "Think what you are doing, brother! Repent, brother!" Aglaia stormed and Yakov, too, flew into a passion and shouted: "Go out of my house!" while Matvey answered him: "The house belongs to both of us."

Yakov would begin singing and reading again, but he could not regain his calm, and unconsciously fell to dreaming over his book. Though he regarded his cousin's words as nonsense, yet for some reason it had of late haunted his memory that it is hard for a rich man to enter the kingdom of heaven, that the year before last he had made a very good bargain over buying a stolen horse, that one day when his wife was alive a drunkard had died of vodka in his tavern. . . .

He slept badly at nights now and woke easily, and he

could hear that Matvey, too, was awake, and continually sighing and pining for his tile factory. And while Yakov turned over from one side to another at night he thought of the stolen horse and the drunken man, and what was said in the gospels about the camel.

It looked as though his dreaminess were coming over him again. And as ill-luck would have it, although it was the end of March, every day it kept snowing, and the forest roared as though it were winter, and there was no believing that spring would ever come. The weather disposed one to depression, and to quarrelling and to hatred and in the night, when the wind droned over the ceiling, it seemed as though someone were living overhead in the empty storey; little by little the broodings settled like a burden on his mind, his head burned and he could not sleep.

IV

On the morning of the Monday before Good Friday, Matvey heard from his room Dashutka say to Aglaia:

"Uncle Matvey said, the other day, that there is no need to fast."

Matvey remembered the whole conversation he had had the evening before with Dashutka, and he felt hurt all at once.

"Girl, don't do wrong!" he said in a moaning voice, like a sick man. "You can't do without fasting; our Lord Himself fasted forty days. I only explained that fasting does a bad man no good."

"You should just listen to the factory hands; they can teach you goodness," Aglaia said sarcastically as she washed the floor (she usually washed the floors on working days and was always angry with everyone when she did it). "We know how they keep the fasts in the factory. You had better ask that uncle of yours—ask him about his 'Darling,' how he used to guzzle milk on fast days with her, the viper. He teaches others; he forgets about his viper. But ask him who was it he left his money with—who was it?"

Matvey had carefully concealed from everyone, as though it were a foul sore, that during that period of his life when old women and unmarried girls had danced and run about with him at their prayers he had formed a connection with a working woman and had had a child by her. When he went home he had given this woman all he had saved at the factory, and had borrowed from his landlord for his journey, and now he had only a few roubles which he spent on tea and candles. The "Darling" had informed him later on that the child was dead, and asked him in a letter what she should do with the money. This letter was brought from the station by the labourer. Aglaia intercepted it and read it, and had reproached Matvey with his "Darling" every day since.

"Just fancy, nine hundred roubles," Aglaia went on. "You gave nine hundred roubles to a viper, no relation, a factory jade, blast you!" She had flown into a passion by now and was shouting shrilly: "Can't you speak? I could tear you to pieces, wretched creature! Nine hundred roubles as though it were a farthing. You might have left it to Dashutka—she is a relation, not a stranger—or else have it sent to Byelev for Marya's poor orphans. And your viper did not choke, may she be thrice accursed, the she-devil! May she never look upon the light of day!"

Yakov Ivanitch called to her: it was time to begin the "Hours." She washed, put on a white kerchief, and by now quiet and meek, went into the prayer-room to the brother she loved. When she spoke to Matvey or served peasants in the tavern with tea she was a gaunt, keen-eyed, ill-humoured old woman; in the prayer-room her face was serene and softened, she looked younger altogether, she curtsied affectedly, and even pursed up her lips.

Yakov Ivanitch began reading the service softly and dolefully, as he always did in Lent. After he had read a little he stopped to listen to the stillness that reigned through the house, and then went on reading again, with a feeling of gratification; he folded his hands in supplication, rolled his eyes, shook his head, sighed. But all at once there was the sound of voices. The policeman and Sergey Nikanoritch had come to see Matvey. Yakov Ivanitch was embarrassed at reading aloud and singing when there were strangers in the house, and now, hearing voices, he began reading in a whisper and slowly. He could hear in the prayer-room the waiter say:

"The Tatar at Shtchepovo is selling his business for fifteen hundred. He'll take five hundred down and an I.O.U. for the rest. And so, Matvey Vassilitch, be so kind as to lend me that five hundred roubles. I will pay you two per cent a month."

"What money have I got?" cried Matvey, amazed. "I have no money!"

"Two per cent a month will be a godsend to you," the policeman explained. "While lying by, your money is simply eaten by the moth, and that's all that you get from it."

Afterwards the visitors went out and a silence followed. But Yakov Ivanitch had hardly begun reading and singing again when a voice was heard outside the door:

"Brother, let me have a horse to drive to Vedenyapino."

It was Matvey. And Yakov was troubled again. "Which can you go with?" he asked after a moment's thought. "The man has gone with the sorrel to take the pig, and I am going with the little stallion to Shuteykino as soon as I have finished."

"Brother, why is it you can dispose of the horses and not I?" Matvey asked with irritation.

"Because I am not taking them for pleasure, but for work."

"Our property is in common, so the horses are in common, too, and you ought to understand that, brother."

A silence followed. Yakov did not go on praying, but waited for Matvey to go away from the door.

"Brother," said Matvey, "I am a sick man. I don't want possession—let them go; you have them, but give me a small share to keep me in my illness. Give it me and I'll go away."

Yakov did not speak. He longed to be rid of Matvey, but he could not give him money, since all the money was in the business; besides, there had never been a case of the family dividing in the whole history of the Terehovs. Division means ruin.

Yakov said nothing, but still waited for Matvey to go away, and kept looking at his sister, afraid that she would interfere, and that there would be a storm of abuse again, as there had been in the morning. When at last Matvey did go Yakov went on reading, but now he had no pleasure in it. There was a heaviness in his head and a darkness before his eyes from continually bowing down to the ground, and he was weary of the sound of his soft dejected voice. When such a depression of spirit came over him at night, he put it down to not being able to sleep; by day it frightened him, and he began to feel as though devils were sitting on his head and shoulders.

Finishing the service after a fashion, dissatisfied and ill-humoured, he set off for Shuteykino. In the previous autumn a gang of navvies had dug a boundary ditch near Progonnaya, and had run up a bill at the tavern for eighteen roubles, and now he had to find their foreman in Shuteykino and get the money from him. The road had been spoilt by the thaw and the snowstorm; it was of a dark colour and full of holes, and in parts it had given way altogether. The snow had sunk away at the sides below the road, so that he had to drive, as it were, upon a narrow causeway, and it was very difficult to turn off it when he met anything. The sky had been overcast ever since the morning and a damp wind was blowing. . . .

A long train of sledges met him; peasant women were carting bricks. Yakov had to turn off the road. His horse sank into the snow up to its belly; the sledge lurched over to the right, and to avoid falling out he bent over to the left, and sat so all the time the sledges moved slowly by him. Through the wind he heard the creaking of the sledge poles and the breathing of the gaunt horses, and the women saying about him, "There's Godly coming," while one, gazing with compassion at his horse, said quickly:

"It looks as though the snow will be lying till Yegory's Day! They are worn out with it!"

Yakov sat uncomfortably huddled up, screwing up his eyes on account of the wind, while horses and red bricks kept passing before him. And perhaps because he was uncomfortable and his side ached, he felt all at once annoyed, and the business he was going about seemed to him unimportant, and he reflected that he might send the labourer next day to Shuteykino. Again, as in the previous sleepless night, he thought of the saying about the camel, and then memories of all sorts crept into his mind; of the peasant who had sold him the stolen horse, of the drunken man, of the peasant women who had brought their samovars to him to pawn. Of course, every merchant tries to get as much as he can, but Yakov felt depressed that he was in trade; he longed to get somewhere far away from this routine, and he felt dreary at the thought that he would have to read the evening service that day. The wind blew straight into his face and soughed in his collar; and it seemed as though it were whispering to him all these thoughts, bringing them from the broad white plain . . . . Looking at that plain, familiar to him from childhood, Yakov remembered that he had had just this same trouble and these same thoughts in his young days when dreams and imaginings had come upon him and his faith had wavered.

He felt miserable at being alone in the open country; he turned back and drove slowly after the sledges, and the women laughed and said:

"Godly has turned back."

At home nothing had been cooked and the samovar was not heated on account of the fast, and this made the day seem very long. Yakov Ivanitch had long ago taken the horse to the stable, dispatched the flour to the station, and twice taken up the Psalms to read, and yet the evening was still far off. Aglaia has already washed all the floors, and, having nothing to do, was tidying up her chest, the lid of which was pasted over on the inside with labels off bottles. Matvey, hungry and melancholy, sat reading, or went up to the Dutch stove and slowly scrutinized the tiles which reminded him of the factory. Dashutka was asleep; then, waking up, she went to take water to the cattle. When she was getting water from the well the cord broke and the pail fell in. The labourer began looking for a boathook to get the pail out, and Dashutka, barefooted, with legs as red as a goose's, followed him about in the muddy snow, repeating: "It's too far!" She meant to say that the well was too deep for the hook to reach the bottom, but the labourer did not understand her, and evidently she bothered him, so that he suddenly turned around and abused her in unseemly language. Yakov Ivanitch, coming out that moment into the yard, heard Dashutka answer the labourer in a long rapid stream of choice abuse, which she could only have learned from drunken peasants in the tavern.

"What are you saying, shameless girl!" he cried to her, and he was positively aghast. "What language!"

And she looked at her father in perplexity, dully, not understanding why she should not use those words. He would have admonished her, but she struck him as so savage and benighted; and for the first time he realized that she had no religion. And all this life in the forest, in the snow, with drunken peasants, with coarse oaths, seemed to him as savage and benighted as this girl, and instead of giving her a lecture he only waved his hand and went back into the room.

At that moment the policeman and Sergey Nikanoritch came in again to see Matvey. Yakov Ivanitch thought that these people, too, had no religion, and that that did not trouble them in the least; and human life began to seem to him as strange, senseless and unenlightened as a dog's. Bareheaded he walked about the yard, then he went out on to the road, clenching his fists. Snow was falling in big flakes at the time. His beard was blown about in the wind. He kept shaking his head, as though there were something weighing upon his head and shoulders, as though devils were sitting on them; and it seemed to him that it was not himself walking about, but some wild beast, a huge terrible beast, and that if he were to cry out his voice would be a roar that would sound all over the forest and the plain, and would frighten everyone. . . .

V

When he went back into the house the policeman was no longer there, but the waiter was sitting with Matvey, counting something on the reckoning beads. He was in the habit of coming often, almost every day, to the tavern; in old days he had come to see Yakov Ivanitch, now he came to see Matvey. He was continually reckoning on the beads, while his face perspired and looked strained, or he would ask for money or, stroking his whiskers, would describe how he had once been in a first-class station and used to prepare champagne-punch for officers, and at grand dinners served the sturgeon-soup with his own hands. Nothing in this world interested him but refreshment bars, and he could only talk about things to eat, about wines and the paraphernalia of the dinner-table. On one occasion, handing a cup of tea to a young woman who was nursing her baby and wishing to say something agreeable to her, he expressed himself in this way:

"The mother's breast is the baby's refreshment bar."

Reckoning with the beads in Matvey's room, he asked for money; said he could not go on living at Progonnaya, and several times repeated in a tone of voice that sounded as though he were just going to cry:

"Where am I to go? Where am I to go now? Tell me that, please."

Then Matvey went into the kitchen and began peeling some boiled potatoes which he had probably put away from the day before. It was quiet, and it seemed to Yakov Ivanitch that the waiter was gone. It was past the time for evening service; he called Aglaia, and, thinking there was no one else in the house sang out aloud without embarrassment. He sang and read, but was inwardly pronouncing other words, "Lord, forgive me! Lord, save me!" and, one after another, without ceasing, he made low bows to the ground as though he wanted to exhaust himself, and he kept shaking his head, so that Aglaia looked at him with wonder. He was afraid Matvey would come in, and was certain that he would come in, and felt an anger against him which he could overcome neither by prayer nor by continually bowing down to the ground.

Matvey opened the door very softly and went into the prayer-room.

"It's a sin, such a sin!" he said reproachfully, and heaved a sigh. "Repent! Think what you are doing, brother!"

Yakov Ivanitch, clenching his fists and not looking at him for fear of striking him, went quickly out of the room. Feeling himself a huge terrible wild beast, just as he had done before on the road, he crossed the passage into the grey, dirty room, reeking with smoke and fog, in which the peasants usually drank tea, and there he spent a long time walking from one corner to the other, treading heavily, so that the crockery jingled on the shelves and the tables shook. It was clear to him now that he was himself dissatisfied with his religion, and could not pray as he used to do. He must repent, he must think things over, reconsider, live and pray in some other way. But how pray? And perhaps all this was a temptation of the devil, and nothing of this was necessary? . . . How was it to be? What was he to do? Who could guide him? What helplessness! He stopped and, clutching at his head, began to think, but Matvey's being near him prevented him from reflecting calmly. And he went rapidly into the room.

Matvey was sitting in the kitchen before a bowl of potato, eating. Close by, near the stove, Aglaia and Dashutka were sitting facing one another, spinning yarn. Between the stove and the table at which Matvey was sitting was stretched an ironing-board; on it stood a cold iron.

"Sister," Matvey asked, "let me have a little oil!"

"Who eats oil on a day like this?" asked Aglaia.

"I am not a monk, sister, but a layman. And in my weak health I may take not only oil but milk."

"Yes, at the factory you may have anything."

Aglaia took a bottle of Lenten oil from the shelf and banged it angrily down before Matvey, with a malignant smile evidently pleased that he was such a sinner.

"But I tell you, you can't eat oil!" shouted Yakov.

Aglaia and Dashutka started, but Matvey poured the oil into the bowl and went on eating as though he had not heard.

"I tell you, you can't eat oil!" Yakov shouted still more loudly; he turned red all over, snatched up the bowl, lifted it higher than his head, and dashed it with all his force to the ground, so that it flew into fragments. "Don't dare to speak!" he cried in a furious voice, though Matvey had not said a word. "Don't dare!" he repeated, and struck his fist on the table.

Matvey turned pale and got up.

"Brother!" he said, still munching—"brother, think what you are about!"

"Out of my house this minute!" shouted Yakov; he loathed Matvey's wrinkled face, and his voice, and the crumbs on his moustache, and the fact that he was munching. "Out, I tell you!"

"Brother, calm yourself! The pride of hell has confounded you!"

"Hold your tongue!" (Yakov stamped.) "Go away, you devil!"

"If you care to know," Matvey went on in a loud voice, as he, too, began to get angry, "you are a backslider from God and a heretic. The accursed spirits have hidden the true light from you; your prayer is not acceptable to God. Repent before it is too late! The deathbed of the sinner is terrible! Repent, brother!"

Yakov seized him by the shoulders and dragged him away from the table, while he turned whiter than ever, and frightened and bewildered, began muttering, "What is it? What's the matter?" and, struggling and making efforts to free himself from Yakov's hands, he accidentally caught hold of his shirt near the neck and tore the collar; and it seemed to Aglaia that he was trying to beat Yakov. She uttered a shriek, snatched up the bottle of Lenten oil and with all her force brought it down straight on the skull of the cousin she hated. Matvey reeled, and in one instant his face became calm and indifferent. Yakov, breathing heavily, excited, and feeling pleasure at the gurgle the bottle had made, like a living thing, when it had struck the head, kept him from falling and several times (he remembered this very distinctly) motioned Aglaia towards the iron with his finger; and only when the blood began trickling through his hands and he heard Dashutka's loud wail, and when the ironing-board fell with a crash, and Matvey rolled heavily on it, Yakov left off feeling anger and understood what had happened.

"Let him rot, the factory buck!" Aglaia brought out with repulsion, still keeping the iron in her hand. The white bloodstained kerchief slipped on to her shoulders and her grey hair fell in disorder. "He's got what he deserved!"

Everything was terrible. Dashutka sat on the floor near the stove with the yarn in her hands, sobbing, and continually bowing down, uttering at each bow a gasping sound. But nothing was so terrible to Yakov as the potato in the blood, on which he was afraid of stepping, and there was something else terrible which weighed upon him like a bad dream and seemed the worst danger, though he could not take it in for the first minute. This was the waiter, Sergey Nikanoritch, who was standing in the doorway with the reckoning beads in his hands, very pale, looking with horror at what was happening in the kitchen. Only when he turned and went quickly into the passage and from there outside, Yakov grasped who it was and followed him.

Wiping his hands on the snow as he went, he reflected. The idea flashed through his mind that their labourer had gone away long before and had asked leave to stay the night at home in the village; the day before they had killed a pig, and there were huge bloodstains in the snow and on the sledge, and even one side of the top of the well was splattered with blood, so that it could not have seemed suspicious even if the whole of Yakov's family had been stained with blood. To conceal the murder would be agonizing, but for the policeman, who would whistle and smile ironically, to come from the station, for the peasants to arrive and bind Yakov's and Aglaia's hands, and take them solemnly to the district courthouse and from there to the town, while everyone on the way would point at them and say mirthfully, "They are taking the Godlies!"—this seemed to Yakov more agonizing than anything, and he longed to lengthen out the time somehow, so as to endure this shame not now, but later, in the future.

"I can lend you a thousand roubles, . . ." he said, overtaking Sergey Nikanoritch. "If you tell anyone, it will do no good. . . . There's no bringing the man back, anyway;" and with difficulty keeping up with the waiter, who did not look round, but tried to walk away faster than ever, he went on: "I can give you fifteen hundred. . . ."

He stopped because he was out of breath, while Sergey Nikanoritch walked on as quickly as ever, probably afraid that he would be killed, too. Only after passing the railway crossing and going half the way from the crossing to the station, he furtively looked round and walked more slowly. Lights, red and green, were already gleaming in the station and along the line; the wind had fallen, but flakes of snow were still coming down and the road had turned white again.

But just at the station Sergey Nikanoritch stopped, thought a minute, and turned resolutely back. It was growing dark.

"Oblige me with the fifteen hundred, Yakov Ivanitch," he said, trembling all over. "I agree."

VI

Yakov Ivanitch's money was in the bank of the town and was invested in second mortgages; he only kept a little at home, Just what was wanted for necessary expenses. Going into the kitchen he felt for the matchbox, and while the sulphur was burning with a blue light he had time to make out the figure of Matvey, which was still lying on the floor near the table, but now it was covered with a white sheet, and nothing could be seen but his boots. A cricket was chirruping. Aglaia and Dashutka were not in the room, they were both sitting behind the counter in the tea-room, spinning yarn in silence. Yakov Ivanitch crossed to his own room with a little lamp in his hand, and pulled from under the bed a little box in which he kept his money. This time there were in it four hundred and twenty one-rouble notes and silver to the amount of thirty-five roubles; the notes had an unpleasant heavy smell. Putting the money together in his cap, Yakov Ivanitch went out into the yard and then out of the gate. He walked, looking from side to side, but there was no sign of the waiter.

"Hi!" cried Yakov.

A dark figure stepped out from the barrier at the railway crossing and came irresolutely towards him.

"Why do you keep walking about?" said Yakov with vexation, as he recognized the waiter. "Here you are; there is a little less than five hundred. . . . I've no more in the house."

"Very well; . . . very grateful to you," muttered Sergey

Nikanoritch, taking the money greedily and stuffing it into his pockets. He was trembling all over, and that was perceptible in spite of the darkness. "Don't worry yourself, Yakov Ivanitch. . . . What should I chatter for: I came and went away, that's all I've had to do with it. As the saying is, I know nothing and I can tell nothing . . ." And at once he added with a sigh "Cursed life!"

For a minute they stood in silence, without looking at each other.

"So it all came from a trifle, goodness knows how, . . ." said the waiter, trembling. "I was sitting counting to myself when all at once a noise. . . . I looked through the door, and just on account of Lenten oil you. . . . Where is he now?"

"Lying there in the kitchen."

"You ought to take him somewhere. . . . Why put it off?"

Yakov accompanied him to the station without a word, then went home again and harnessed the horse to take Matvey to Limarovo. He had decided to take him to the forest of Limarovo, and to leave him there on the road, and then he would tell everyone that Matvey had gone off to Vedenyapino and had not come back, and then everyone would think that he had been killed by someone on the road. He knew there was no deceiving anyone by this, but to move, to do something, to be active, was not as agonizing as to sit still and wait. He called Dashutka, and with her carried Matvey out. Aglaia stayed behind to clean up the kitchen.

When Yakov and Dashutka turned back they were detained at the railway crossing by the barrier being let down. A long goods train was passing, dragged by two engines, breathing heavily, and flinging puffs of crimson fire out of their funnels.

The foremost engine uttered a piercing whistle at the crossing in sight of the station.

"It's whistling, . . ." said Dashutka.

The train had passed at last, and the signalman lifted the barrier without haste.

"Is that you, Yakov Ivanitch? I didn't know you, so you'll be rich."

And then when they had reached home they had to go to bed.

Aglaia and Dashutka made themselves a bed in the tea-room and lay down side by side, while Yakov stretched himself on the counter. They neither said their prayers nor lighted the ikon lamp before lying down to sleep. All three lay awake till morning, but did not utter a single word, and it seemed to them that all night someone was walking about in the empty storey overhead.

Two days later a police inspector and the examining magistrate came from the town and made a search, first in Matvey's room and then in the whole tavern. They questioned Yakov first of all, and he testified that on the Monday Matvey had gone to Vedenyapino to confess, and that he must have been killed by the sawyers who were working on the line.

And when the examining magistrate had asked him how it had happened that Matvey was found on the road, while his cap had turned up at home—surely he had not gone to Vedenyapino without his cap?—and why they had not found a single drop of blood beside him in the snow on the road, though his head was smashed in and his face and chest were black with blood, Yakov was confused, lost his head and answered:

"I cannot tell."

And just what Yakov had so feared happened: the policeman came, the district police officer smoked in the prayer-room and Aglaia fell upon him with abuse and was rude to the police inspector; and afterwards when Yakov and Aglaia were led out to the yard, the peasants crowded at the gates and said, "They are taking the Godlies!" and it seemed that they were all glad.

At the inquiry the policeman stated positively that Yakov and Aglaia had killed Matvey in order not to share with him, and that Matvey had money of his own, and that if it was not found at the search evidently Yakov and Aglaia had got hold of it. And Dashutka was questioned. She said that Uncle Matvey and Aunt Aglaia quarrelled and almost fought every day over money, and that Uncle Matvey was rich, so much so that he had given someone—"his Darling"—nine hundred roubles.

Dashutka was left alone in the tavern. No one came now to drink tea or vodka, and she divided her time between cleaning up the rooms, drinking mead and eating rolls; but a few days later they questioned the signalman at the railway crossing, and he said that late on Monday evening he had seen Yakov and Dashutka driving from Limarovo. Dashutka, too, was arrested, taken to the town and put in prison. It soon became known, from what Aglaia said, that Sergey Nikanoritch had been present at the murder. A search was made in his room, and money was found in an unusual place, in his snowboots under the stove, and the money was all in small change, three hundred one-rouble notes. He swore he had made this money himself, and that he hadn't been in the tavern for a year, but witnesses testified that he was poor and had been in great want of money of late, and that he used to go every day to the tavern to borrow from Matvey; and the policeman described how on the day of the murder he had himself gone twice to the tavern with the waiter to help him to borrow. It was recalled at this juncture that on Monday evening Sergey Nikanoritch had not been there to meet the passenger train, but had gone off somewhere. And he, too, was arrested and taken to the town.

The trial took place eleven months later.

Yakov Ivanitch looked much older and much thinner, and spoke in a low voice like a sick man. He felt weak, pitiful, lower in stature that anyone else, and it seemed as though his soul, too, like his body, had grown older and wasted, from the pangs of his conscience and from the dreams and imaginings which never left him all the while he was in prison. When it came out that he did not go to church the president of the court asked him:

"Are you a dissenter?"

"I can't tell," he answered.

He had no religion at all now; he knew nothing and understood nothing; and his old belief was hateful to him now, and seemed to him darkness and folly. Aglaia was not in the least subdued, and she still went on abusing the dead man, blaming him for all their misfortunes. Sergey Nikanoritch had grown a beard instead of whiskers. At the trial he was red and perspiring, and was evidently ashamed of his grey prison coat and of sitting on the same bench with humble peasants. He defended himself awkwardly, and, trying to prove that he had not been to the tavern for a whole year, got into an altercation with every witness, and the spectators laughed at him. Dashutka had grown fat in prison. At the trial she did not understand the questions put to her, and only said that when they killed Uncle Matvey she was dreadfully frightened, but afterwards she did not mind.

All four were found guilty of murder with mercenary motives. Yakov Ivanitch was sentenced to penal servitude for twenty years; Aglaia for thirteen and a half; Sergey Nikanoritch to ten; Dashutka to six.

VII

Late one evening a foreign steamer stopped in the roads of Dué in Sahalin and asked for coal. The captain was asked to wait till morning, but he did not want to wait over an hour, saying that if the weather changed for the worse in the night there would be a risk of his having to go off without coal. In the Gulf of Tartary the weather is liable to violent changes in the course of half an hour, and then the shores of Sahalin are dangerous. And already it had turned fresh, and there was a considerable sea running.

A gang of convicts were sent to the mine from the Voevodsky prison, the grimmest and most forbidding of all the prisons in Sahalin. The coal had to be loaded upon barges, and then they had to be towed by a steam-cutter alongside the steamer which was anchored more than a quarter of a mile from the coast, and then the unloading and reloading had to begin—an exhausting task when the barge kept rocking against the steamer and the men could scarcely keep on their legs for sea-sickness. The convicts, only just roused from their sleep, still drowsy, went along the shore, stumbling in the darkness and clanking their fetters. On the left, scarcely visible, was a tall, steep, extremely gloomy-looking cliff, while on the right there was a thick impenetrable mist, in which the sea moaned with a prolonged monotonous sound, "Ah! . . . ah! . . . ah! . . . ah! . . ." And it was only when the overseer was lighting his pipe, casting as he did so a passing ray of light on the escort with a gun and on the coarse faces of two or three of the nearest convicts, or when he went with his lantern close to the water that the white crests of the foremost waves could be discerned.

One of this gang was Yakov Ivanitch, nicknamed among the convicts the "Brush," on account of his long beard. No one had addressed him by his name or his father's name for a long time now; they called him simply Yashka.

He was here in disgrace, as, three months after coming to Siberia, feeling an intense irresistible longing for home, he had succumbed to temptation and run away; he had soon been caught, had been sentenced to penal servitude for life and given forty lashes. Then he was punished by flogging twice again for losing his prison clothes, though on each occasion they were stolen from him. The longing for home had begun from the very time he had been brought to Odessa, and the convict train had stopped in the night at Progonnaya; and Yakov, pressing to the window, had tried to see his own home, and could see nothing in the darkness. He had no one with whom to talk of home. His sister Aglaia had been sent right across Siberia, and he did not know where she was now. Dashutka was in Sahalin, but she had been sent to live with some ex-convict in a far away settlement; there was no news of her except that once a settler who had come to the Voevodsky Prison told Yakov that Dashutka had three children. Sergey Nikanoritch was serving as a footman at a government official's at Dué, but he could not reckon on ever seeing him, as he was ashamed of being acquainted with convicts of the peasant class.

The gang reached the mine, and the men took their places on the quay. It was said there would not be any loading, as the weather kept getting worse and the steamer was meaning to set off. They could see three lights. One of them was moving: that was the steam-cutter going to the steamer, and it seemed to be coming back to tell them whether the work was to be done or not. Shivering with the autumn cold and the damp sea mist, wrapping himself in his short torn coat, Yakov Ivanitch looked intently without blinking in the direction in which lay his home. Ever since he had lived in prison together with men banished here from all ends of the earth—with Russians, Ukrainians, Tatars, Georgians,

Chinese, Gypsies, Jews—and ever since he had listened to their talk and watched their sufferings, he had begun to turn again to God, and it seemed to him at last that he had learned the true faith for which all his family, from his grandmother Avdotya down, had so thirsted, which they had sought so long and which they had never found. He knew it all now and understood where God was, and how He was to be served, and the only thing he could not understand was why men's destinies were so diverse, why this simple faith which other men receive from God for nothing and together with their lives, had cost him such a price that his arms and legs trembled like a drunken man's from all the horrors and agonies which as far as he could see would go on without a break to the day of his death. He looked with strained eyes into the darkness, and it seemed to him that through the thousand miles of that mist he could see home, could see his native province, his district, Progonnaya, could see the darkness, the savagery, the heartlessness, and the dull, sullen, animal indifference of the men he had left there. His eyes were dimmed with tears; but still he gazed into the distance where the pale lights of the steamer faintly gleamed, and his heart ached with yearning for home, and he longed to live, to go back home to tell them there of his new faith and to save from ruin if only one man, and to live without sufferingif only for one day.

The cutter arrived, and the overseer announced in a loud voice that there would be no loading.

"Back!" he commanded. "Steady!"

They could hear the hoisting of the anchor chain on the steamer. A strong piercing wind was blowing by now; somewhere on the steep cliff overhead the trees were creaking. Most likely a storm was coming.

A Dead Body

A still August night. A mist is rising slowly from the fields and casting an opaque veil over everything within eyesight. Lighted up by the moon, the mist gives the impression at one moment of a calm, boundless sea, at the next of an immense white wall. The air is damp and chilly. Morning is still far off. A step from the by-road which runs along the edge of the forest a little fire is gleaming. A dead body, covered from head to foot with new white linen, is lying under a young oak-tree. A wooden ikon is lying on its breast. Beside the corpse almost on the road sits the "watch"—two peasants performing one of the most disagreeable and uninviting of peasants' duties. One, a tall young fellow with a scarcely perceptible moustache and thick black eyebrows, in a tattered sheepskin and bark shoes, is sitting on the wet grass, his feet stuck out straight in front of him, and is trying to while away the time with work. He bends his long neck, and breathing loudly through his nose, makes a spoon out of a big crooked bit of wood; the other—a little scraggy, pock-marked peasant with an aged face, a scanty moustache, and a little goat's beard—sits with his hands dangling loose on his knees, and without moving gazes listlessly at the light. A small camp-fire is lazily burning down between them, throwing a red glow on their faces. There is perfect stillness. The only sounds are the scrape of the knife on the wood and the crackling of damp sticks in the fire.

"Don't you go to sleep, Syoma . . ." says the young man.

"I . . . I am not asleep . . ." stammers the goat-beard.

"That's all right. . . . It would be dreadful to sit here alone, one would be frightened. You might tell me something, Syoma."

"You are a queer fellow, Syomushka! Other people will laugh and tell a story and sing a song, but you—there is no making you out. You sit like a scarecrow in the garden and roll your eyes at the fire. You can't say anything properly . . . when you speak you seem frightened. I dare say you are fifty, but you have less sense than a child. Aren't you sorry that you are a simpleton?"

"I am sorry," the goat-beard answers gloomily.

"And we are sorry to see your foolishness, you may be sure. You are a good-natured, sober peasant, and the only trouble is that you have no sense in your head. You should have picked up some sense for yourself if the Lord has afflicted you and given you no understanding. You must make an effort, Syoma. . . . You should listen hard when anything good's being said, note it well, and keep thinking and thinking. . . . If there is any word you don't understand, you should make an effort and think over in your head in what meaning the word is used. Do you see? Make an effort! If you don't gain some sense for yourself you'll be a simpleton and of no account at all to your dying day."

All at once a long drawn-out, moaning sound is heard in the forest. Something rustles in the leaves as though torn from the very top of the tree and falls to the ground. All this is faintly repeated by the echo. The young man shudders and looks enquiringly at his companion.

"It's an owl at the little birds," says Syoma, gloomily.

"Why, Syoma, it's time for the birds to fly to the warm countries!"

"To be sure, it is time."

"It is chilly at dawn now. It is co-old. The crane is a chilly creature, it is tender. Such cold is death to it. I am not a crane, but I am frozen. . . . Put some more wood on!"

Syoma gets up and disappears in the dark undergrowth. While he is busy among the bushes, breaking dry twigs, his companion puts his hand over his eyes and starts at every sound. Syoma brings an armful of wood and lays it on the fire. The flame irresolutely licks the black twigs with its little tongues, then suddenly, as though at the word of command, catches them and throws a crimson light on the faces, the road, the white linen with its prominences where the hands and feet of the corpse raise it, the ikon. The "watch" is silent. The young man bends his neck still lower and sets to work with still more nervous haste. The goat-beard sits motionless as before and keeps his eyes fixed on the fire. . . .

"Ye that love not Zion . . . shall be put to shame by the Lord." A falsetto voice is suddenly heard singing in the stillness of the night, then slow footsteps are audible, and the dark figure of a man in a short monkish cassock and a broad-brimmed hat, with a wallet on his shoulders, comes into sight on the road in the crimson firelight.

"Thy will be done, O Lord! Holy Mother!" the figure says in a husky falsetto. "I saw the fire in the outer darkness and my soul leapt for joy. . . . At first I thought it was men grazing a drove of horses, then I thought it can't be that, since no horses were to be seen. 'Aren't they thieves,' I wondered, 'aren't they robbers lying in wait for a rich Lazarus? Aren't they the gypsy people offering sacrifices to idols? And my soul leapt for joy. 'Go, Feodosy, servant of God,' I said to myself, 'and win a martyr's crown!' And I flew to the fire like a light-winged moth. Now I stand before you, and from your outer aspect I judge of your souls: you are not thieves and you are not heathens. Peace be to you!"

"Good-evening."

"Good orthodox people, do you know how to reach the Makuhinsky Brickyards from here?"

"It's close here. You go straight along the road; when you have gone a mile and a half there will be Ananova, our village. From the village, father, you turn to the right by the river-bank, and so you will get to the brickyards. It's two miles from Ananova."

"God give you health. And why are you sitting here?

"We are sitting here watching. You see, there is a dead body. . . ."

"What? what body? Holy Mother!"

The pilgrim sees the white linen with the ikon on it, and starts so violently that his legs give a little skip. This unexpected sight has an overpowering effect upon him. He huddles together and stands as though rooted to the spot, with wide-open mouth and staring eyes. For three minutes he is silent as though he could not believe his eyes, then begins muttering:

"O Lord! Holy Mother! I was going along not meddling with anyone, and all at once such an affliction."

"What may you be?" enquires the young man. "Of the clergy?"

"No . . . no. . . . I go from one monastery to another. . . . Do you know Mi . . . Mihail Polikarpitch, the foreman of the brickyard? Well, I am his nephew. . . . Thy will be done, O Lord! Why are you here?"

"We are watching . . . we are told to."

"Yes, yes . . ." mutters the man in the cassock, passing his hand over his eyes. "And where did the deceased come from?"

"He was a stranger."

"Such is life! But I'll . . . er . . . be getting on, brothers. . . . I feel flustered. I am more afraid of the dead than of anything, my dear souls! And only fancy! while this man was alive he wasn't noticed, while now when he is dead and given over to corruption we tremble before him as before some famous general or a bishop. . . . Such is life; was he murdered, or what?"

"The Lord knows! Maybe he was murdered, or maybe he died of himself."

"Yes, yes. . . . Who knows, brothers? Maybe his soul is now tasting the joys of Paradise."

"His soul is still hovering here, near his body," says the young man. "It does not depart from the body for three days."

"H'm, yes! . . . How chilly the nights are now! It sets one's teeth chattering. . . . So then I am to go straight on and on? . . ."

"Till you get to the village, and then you turn to the right by the river-bank."

"By the river-bank. . . . To be sure. . . . Why am I standing still? I must go on. Farewell, brothers."

The man in the cassock takes five steps along the road and stops.

"I've forgotten to put a kopeck for the burying," he says. "Good orthodox friends, can I give the money?"

"You ought to know best, you go the round of the monasteries. If he died a natural death it would go for the good of his soul; if it's a suicide it's a sin."

"That's true. . . . And maybe it really was a suicide! So I had better keep my money. Oh, sins, sins! Give me a thousand roubles and I would not consent to sit here. . . . Farewell, brothers."

The cassock slowly moves away and stops again.

"I can't make up my mind what I am to do," he mutters. "To stay here by the fire and wait till daybreak. . . . I am frightened; to go on is dreadful, too. The dead man will haunt me all the way in the darkness. . . . The Lord has chastised me indeed! Over three hundred miles I have come on foot and nothing happened, and now I am near home and there's trouble. I can't go on. . . ."

"It is dreadful, that is true."

"I am not afraid of wolves, of thieves, or of darkness, but I am afraid of the dead. I am afraid of them, and that is all about it. Good orthodox brothers, I entreat you on my knees, see me to the village."

"We've been told not to go away from the body."

"No one will see, brothers. Upon my soul, no one will see! The Lord will reward you a hundredfold! Old man, come with me, I beg! Old man! Why are you silent?"

"He is a bit simple," says the young man.

"You come with me, friend; I will give you five kopecks."

"For five kopecks I might," says the young man, scratching his head, "but I was told not to. If Syoma here, our simpleton, will stay alone, I will take you. Syoma, will you stay here alone?"

"I'll stay," the simpleton consents.

"Well, that's all right, then. Come along!" The young man gets up, and goes with the cassock. A minute later the sound of their steps and their talk dies away. Syoma shuts his eyes and gently dozes. The fire begins to grow dim, and a big black shadow falls on the dead body.

A Tripping Tongue

NATALYA Mihalovna, a young married lady who had arrived in the morning from Yalta, was having her dinner, and in a never-ceasing flow of babble was telling her husband of all the charms of the Crimea. Her husband, delighted, gazed tenderly at her enthusiastic face, listened, and from time to time put in a question.

"But they say living is dreadfully expensive there?" he asked, among other things.

"Well, what shall I say? To my thinking this talk of its being so expensive is exaggerated, hubby. The devil is not as black as he is painted. Yulia Petrovna and I, for instance, had very decent and comfortable rooms for twenty roubles a day. Everything depends on knowing how to do things, my dear. Of course if you want to go up into the mountains . . . to Aie-Petri for instance . . . if you take a horse, a guide, then of course it does come to something. It's awful what it comes to! But, Vassitchka, the mountains there! Imagine high, high mountains, a thousand times higher than the church. . . . At the top—mist, mist, mist. . . . At the bottom— enormous stones, stones, stones. . . . And pines. . . . Ah, I can't bear to think of it!"

"By the way, I read about those Tatar guides there, in some magazine while you were away . . . . such abominable stories!

Tell me is there really anything out of the way about them?"

Natalya Mihalovna made a little disdainful grimace and shook her head.

"Just ordinary Tatars, nothing special . . ." she said, "though indeed I only had a glimpse of them in the distance. They were pointed out to me, but I did not take much notice of them. You know, hubby, I always had a prejudice against all such Circassians, Greeks . . . Moors!"

"They are said to be terrible Don Juans."

"Perhaps! There are shameless creatures who . . . ."

Natalya Mihalovna suddenly jumped up from her chair, as though she had thought of something dreadful; for half a minute she looked with frightened eyes at her husband and said, accentuating each word:

"Vassitchka, I say, the im-mo-ral women there are in the world! Ah, how immoral! And it's not as though they were working-class or middle-class people, but aristocratic ladies, priding themselves on their _bon-ton!_ It was simply awful, I could not believe my own eyes! I shall remember it as long as I live! To think that people can forget themselves to such a point as . . . ach, Vassitchka, I don't like to speak of it! Take my companion, Yulia Petrovna, for example. . . . Such a good husband, two children . . . she moves in a decent circle, always poses as a saint—and all at once, would you believe it. . . . Only, hubby, of course this is *entre nous*. . . . Give me your word of honour you won't tell a soul?"

"What next! Of course I won't tell."

"Honour bright? Mind now! I trust you. . . ."

The little lady put down her fork, assumed a mysterious air, and whispered:

"Imagine a thing like this. . . . That Yulia Petrovna rode up into the mountains . . . . It was glorious weather! She rode on ahead with her guide, I was a little behind. We had ridden two or three miles, all at once, only fancy, Vassitchka, Yulia cried out and clutched at her bosom. Her Tatar put his arm round her waist or she would have fallen off the saddle. . . . I rode up to her with my guide. . . . 'What is it? What is the matter?' 'Oh,' she cried, 'I am dying! I feel faint! I can't go any further' Fancy my alarm! 'Let us go back then,' I said. 'No, *Natalie*,' she said, 'I can't go back! I shall die of pain if I move another step! I have spasms.' And she prayed and besought my Suleiman and me to ride back to the town and fetch her some of her drops which always do her good."

"Stay. . . . I don't quite understand you," muttered the husband, scratching his forehead. "You said just now that you had only seen those Tatars from a distance, and now you are talking of some Suleiman."

"There, you are finding fault again," the lady pouted, not in the least disconcerted. "I can't endure suspiciousness! I can't endure it! It's stupid, stupid!"

"I am not finding fault, but . . . why say what is not true? If you rode about with Tatars, so be it, God bless you, but . . . why shuffle about it?"

"H'm! . . . you are a queer one!" cried the lady, revolted. "He is jealous of Suleiman! as though one could ride up into the mountains without a guide! I should like to see you do it! If you don't know the ways there, if you don't understand, you had better hold your tongue! Yes, hold your tongue. You can't take a step there without a guide."

"So it seems!"

"None of your silly grins, if you please! I am not a Yulia. . . . I don't justify her but I . . . ! Though I don't pose as a saint, I don't forget myself to that degree. My Suleiman never overstepped the limits. . . . No-o! Mametkul used to be sitting at Yulia's all day long, but in my room as soon as it struck eleven: 'Suleiman, march! Off you go!' And my foolish Tatar boy would depart. I made him mind his p's and q's, hubby! As soon as he began grumbling about money or anything, I would say 'How? Wha-at? Wha-a-a-t?' And his heart would be in his mouth directly. . . . Ha-ha-ha! His eyes, you know, Vassitchka, were as black, as black, like coals, such an amusing little Tatar face, so funny and silly! I kept him in order, didn't I just!"

"I can fancy . . ." mumbled her husband, rolling up pellets of bread.

"That's stupid, Vassitchka! I know what is in your mind! I know what you are thinking . . . But I assure you even when we were on our expeditions I never let him overstep the limits. For instance, if we rode to the mountains or to the U-Chan-Su waterfall, I would always say to him, 'Suleiman, ride behind! Do you hear!' And he always rode behind, poor boy. . . . Even when we . . . even at the most dramatic moments I would say to him, 'Still, you must not forget that you are only a Tatar and I am the wife of a civil councillor!' Ha-ha. . . ."

The little lady laughed, then, looking round her quickly and assuming an alarmed expression, whispered:

"But Yulia! Oh, that Yulia! I quite see, Vassitchka, there is no reason why one shouldn't have a little fun, a little rest from the emptiness of conventional life! That's all right, have your fling by all means—no one will blame you, but to take the thing seriously, to get up scenes . . . no, say what you like, I cannot understand that! Just fancy, she was jealous! Wasn't that silly? One day Mametkul, her _grande passion_, came to see her . . . she was not at home. . . . Well, I asked him into my room . . . there was conversation, one thing and another . . . they're awfully amusing, you know! The evening passed without our noticing it. . . . All at once Yulia rushed in. . . .

She flew at me and at Mametkul—made such a scene . . . fi! I can't understand that sort of thing, Vassitchka."

Vassitchka cleared his throat, frowned, and walked up and down the room.

"You had a gay time there, I must say," he growled with a disdainful smile.

"How stu-upid that is!" cried Natalya Mihalovna, offended. "I know what you are thinking about! You always have such horrid ideas! I won't tell you anything! No, I won't!"

The lady pouted and said no more.

After the Theatre

NADYA Zelenin had just come back with her mamma from the theatre where she had seen a performance of "Yevgeny Onyegin." As soon as she reached her own room she threw off her dress, let down her hair, and in her petticoat and white dressing-jacket hastily sat down to the table to write a letter like Tatyana's.

"I love you," she wrote, "but you do not love me, do not love me!"

She wrote it and laughed.

She was only sixteen and did not yet love anyone. She knew that an officer called Gorny and a student called Gruzdev loved her, but now after the opera she wanted to be doubtful of their love. To be unloved and unhappy—how interesting that was. There is something beautiful, touching, and poetical about it when one loves and the other is indifferent. Onyegin was interesting because he was not in love at all, and Tatyana was fascinating because she was so much in love; but if they had been equally in love with each other and had been happy, they would perhaps have seemed dull.

"Leave off declaring that you love me," Nadya went on writing, thinking of Gorny. "I cannot believe it. You are very clever, cultivated, serious, you have immense talent, and perhaps a brilliant future awaits you, while I am an uninteresting girl of no importance, and you know very well that I should be only a hindrance in your life. It is true that you were attracted by me and thought you had found your ideal in me, but that was a mistake, and now you are asking yourself in despair: 'Why did I meet that girl?' And only your goodness of heart prevents you from owning it to yourself...."

Nadya felt sorry for herself, she began to cry, and went on:

"It is hard for me to leave my mother and my brother, or I should take a nun's veil and go whither chance may lead me. And you would be left free and would love another. Oh, if I were dead!"

She could not make out what she had written through her tears; little rainbows were quivering on the table, on the floor, on the ceiling, as though she were looking through a prism. She could not write, she sank back in her easy-chair and fell to thinking of Gorny.

My God! how interesting, how fascinating men were! Nadya recalled the fine expression, ingratiating, guilty, and soft, which came into the officer's face when one argued about music with him, and the effort he made to prevent his voice from betraying his passion. In a society where cold haughtiness and indifference are regarded as signs of good breeding and gentlemanly bearing, one must conceal one's passions. And he did try to conceal them, but he did not succeed, and everyone knew very well that he had a passionate love of music. The endless discussions about music and the bold criticisms of people who knew nothing about it kept him always on the strain; he was frightened, timid, and silent. He played the piano magnificently, like a professional pianist, and if he had not been in the army he would certainly have been a famous musician.

The tears on her eyes dried. Nadya remembered that Gorny had declared his love at a Symphony concert, and again downstairs by the hatstand where there was a tremendous draught blowing in all directions.

"I am very glad that you have at last made the acquaintance of Gruzdev, our student friend," she went on writing. "He is a very clever man, and you will be sure to like him. He came to see us yesterday and stayed till two o'clock. We were all delighted with him, and I regretted that you had not come. He said a great deal that was remarkable."

Nadya laid her arms on the table and leaned her head on them, and her hair covered the letter. She recalled that the student, too, loved her, and that he had as much right to a letter from her as Gorny. Wouldn't it be better after all to write to Gruzdev? There was a stir of joy in her bosom for no reason whatever; at first the joy was small, and rolled in her bosom like an india-rubber ball; then it became more massive, bigger, and rushed like a wave. Nadya forgot Gorny and Gruzdev; her thoughts were in a tangle and her joy grew and grew; from her bosom it passed into her arms and legs, and it seemed as though a light, cool breeze were breathing on her head and ruffling her hair. Her shoulders quivered with subdued laughter, the table and the lamp chimney shook, too, and tears from her eyes splashed on the letter. She could not stop laughing, and to prove to herself that she was not laughing about nothing she made haste to think of something funny.

"What a funny poodle," she said, feeling as though she would choke with laughter. "What a funny poodle!"

She thought how, after tea the evening before, Gruzdev had played with Maxim the poodle, and afterwards had told them about a very intelligent poodle who had run after a crow in the yard, and the crow had looked round at him and said: "Oh, you scamp!"

The poodle, not knowing he had to do with a learned crow, was fearfully confused and retreated in perplexity, then began barking....

"No, I had better love Gruzdev," Nadya decided, and she tore up the letter to Gorny.

She fell to thinking of the student, of his love, of her love; but the thoughts in her head insisted on flowing in all directions, and she thought about everything—about her mother, about the street, about the pencil, about the piano.... She thought of them joyfully, and felt that everything was good, splendid, and her joy told her that this was not all, that in a little while it would be better still. Soon it would be spring, summer, going with her mother to Gorbiki. Gorny would come for his furlough, would walk about the garden with her and make love to her. Gruzdev would come too. He would play croquet and skittles with her, and would tell her wonderful things. She had a passionate longing for the garden, the darkness, the pure sky, the stars. Again her shoulders shook with laughter, and it seemed to her that there was a scent of wormwood in the room and that a twig was tapping at the window.

She went to her bed, sat down, and not knowing what to do with the immense joy which filled her with yearning, she looked at the holy image hanging at the back of her bed, and said:

"Oh, Lord God! Oh, Lord God!"

A Lady's Story

INE years ago Pyotr Sergeyitch, the deputy prosecutor, and I were riding towards evening in hay-making time to fetch the letters from the station.

The weather was magnificent, but on our way back we heard a peal of thunder, and saw an angry black storm-cloud which was coming straight towards us. The storm-cloud was approaching us and we were approaching it.

Against the background of it our house and church looked white and the tall poplars shone like silver. There was a scent of rain and mown hay. My companion was in high spirits. He kept laughing and talking all sorts of nonsense. He said it would be nice if we could suddenly come upon a medieval castle with turreted towers, with moss on it and owls, in which we could take shelter from the rain and in the end be killed by a thunderbolt....

Then the first wave raced through the rye and a field of oats, there was a gust of wind, and the dust flew round and round in the air. Pyotr Sergeyitch laughed and spurred on his horse.

"It's fine!" he cried, "it's splendid!"

Infected by his gaiety, I too began laughing at the thought that in a minute I should be drenched to the skin and might be struck by lightning.

Riding swiftly in a hurricane when one is breathless with the wind, and feels like a bird, thrills one and puts one's heart in a flutter. By the time we rode into our courtyard the wind had gone down, and big drops of rain were pattering on the grass and on the roofs. There was not a soul near the stable.

Pyotr Sergeyitch himself took the bridles off, and led the horses to their stalls. I stood in the doorway waiting for him to finish, and watching the slanting streaks of rain; the sweetish, exciting scent of hay was even stronger here than in the fields; the storm-clouds and the rain made it almost twilight.

"What a crash!" said Pyotr Sergeyitch, coming up to me after a very loud rolling peal of thunder when it seemed as though the sky were split in two. "What do you say to that?"

He stood beside me in the doorway and, still breathless from his rapid ride, looked at me. I could see that he was admiring me.

"Natalya Vladimirovna," he said, "I would give anything only to stay here a little longer and look at you. You are lovely to-day."

His eyes looked at me with delight and supplication, his face was pale. On his beard and mustache were glittering raindrops, and they, too, seemed to be looking at me with love.

"I love you," he said. "I love you, and I am happy at seeing you. I know you cannot be my wife, but I want nothing, I ask nothing; only know that I love you. Be silent, do not answer me, take no notice of it, but only know that you are dear to me and let me look at you."

His rapture affected me too; I looked at his enthusiastic face, listened to his voice which mingled with the patter of the rain, and stood as though spellbound, unable to stir.

I longed to go on endlessly looking at his shining eyes and listening.

"You say nothing, and that is splendid," said Pyotr Sergeyitch. "Go on being silent."

I felt happy. I laughed with delight and ran through the drenching rain to the house; he laughed too, and, leaping as he went, ran after me.

Both drenched, panting, noisily clattering up the stairs like children, we dashed into the room. My father and brother, who were not used to seeing me laughing and light-hearted, looked at me in surprise and began laughing too.

The storm-clouds had passed over and the thunder had ceased, but the raindrops still glittered on Pyotr Sergeyitch's beard. The whole evening till supper-time he was singing, whistling, playing noisily with the dog and racing about the room after it, so that he nearly upset the servant with the samovar. And at supper he ate a great deal, talked nonsense, and maintained that when one eats fresh cucumbers in winter there is the fragrance of spring in one's mouth.

When I went to bed I lighted a candle and threw my window wide open, and an undefined feeling took possession of my soul. I remembered that I was free and healthy, that I had rank and wealth, that I was beloved; above all, that I had rank and wealth, rank and wealth, my God! how nice that was!... Then, huddling up in bed at a touch of cold which reached me from the garden with the dew, I tried to discover whether I loved Pyotr Sergeyitch or not,... and fell asleep unable to reach any conclusion.

And when in the morning I saw quivering patches of sunlight and the shadows of the lime trees on my bed, what had happened yesterday rose vividly in my memory. Life seemed to me rich, varied, full of charm. Humming, I dressed quickly and went out into the garden....

And what happened afterwards? Why—nothing. In the winter when we lived in town Pyotr Sergeyitch came to see us from time to time. Country acquaintances are charming only in the country and in summer; in the town and in winter they lose their charm. When you pour out tea for them in the town it seems as though they are wearing other people's coats, and as though they stirred their tea too long. In the town, too, Pyotr Sergeyitch spoke sometimes of love, but the effect was not at all the same as in the country. In the town we were more vividly conscious of the wall that stood between us. I had rank and wealth, while he was poor, and he was not even a nobleman, but only the son of a deacon and a deputy public prosecutor; we both of us—I through my youth and he for some unknown reason—thought of that wall as very high and thick, and when he was with us in the town he would criticize aristocratic society with a forced smile, and maintain a sullen silence when there was anyone else in the drawing-room. There is no wall that cannot be broken through, but the heroes of the modern romance, so far as I know them, are too timid, spiritless, lazy, and oversensitive, and are too ready to resign themselves to the thought that they are doomed to failure, that personal life has disappointed them; instead of struggling they merely criticize, calling the world vulgar and forgetting that their criticism passes little by little into vulgarity.

I was loved, happiness was not far away, and seemed to be almost touching me; I went on living in careless ease without trying to understand myself, not knowing what I expected or what I wanted from life, and time went on and on.... People passed by me with their love, bright days and warm nights flashed by, the nightingales sang, the hay smelt fragrant, and all this, sweet and overwhelming in remembrance, passed with me as with everyone rapidly, leaving no trace, was not prized, and vanished like mist.... Where is it all?

My father is dead, I have grown older; everything that delighted me, caressed me, gave me hope—the patter of the rain, the rolling of the thunder, thoughts of happiness, talk of love—all that has become nothing but a memory, and I see before me a flat desert distance; on the plain not one living soul, and out there on the horizon it is dark and terrible....

A ring at the bell.... It is Pyotr Sergeyitch. When in the winter I see the trees and remember how green they were for me in the summer I whisper:

"Oh, my darlings!"

And when I see people with whom I spent my spring-time, I feel sorrowful and warm and whisper the same thing.

He has long ago by my father's good offices been transferred to town. He looks a little older, a little fallen away. He has long given up declaring his love, has left off talking nonsense, dislikes his official work, is ill in some way and disillusioned; he has given up trying to get anything out of life, and takes no interest in living. Now he has sat down by the hearth and looks in silence at the fire....

Not knowing what to say I ask him:

"Well, what have you to tell me?"

"Nothing," he answers.

And silence again. The red glow of the fire plays about his melancholy face.

I thought of the past, and all at once my shoulders began quivering, my head dropped, and I began weeping bitterly. I felt unbearably sorry for myself and for this man, and passionately longed for what had passed away and what life refused us now. And now I did not think about rank and wealth.

I broke into loud sobs, pressing my temples, and muttered:

"My God! my God! my life is wasted!"

And he sat and was silent, and did not say to me: "Don't weep." He understood that I must weep, and that the time for this had come.

I saw from his eyes that he was sorry for me; and I was sorry for him, too, and vexed with this timid, unsuccessful man who could not make a life for me, nor for himself.

When I saw him to the door, he was, I fancied, purposely a long while putting on his coat. Twice he kissed my hand without a word, and looked a long while into my tear-stained face. I believe at that moment he recalled the storm, the streaks of rain, our laughter, my face that day; he longed to say something to me, and he would have been glad to say it; but he said nothing, he merely shook his head and pressed my hand. God help him!

After seeing him out, I went back to my study and again sat on the carpet before the fireplace; the red embers were covered with ash and began to grow dim. The frost tapped still more angrily at the windows, and the wind droned in the chimney.

The maid came in and, thinking I was asleep, called my name.

The Student

T first the weather was fine and still. The thrushes were calling, and in the swamps close by something alive droned pitifully with a sound like blowing into an empty bottle. A snipe flew by, and the shot aimed at it rang out with a gay, resounding note in the spring air. But when it began to get dark in the forest a cold, penetrating wind blew inappropriately from the east, and everything sank into silence. Needles of ice stretched across the pools, and it felt cheerless, remote, and lonely in the forest. There was a whiff of winter.

Ivan Velikopolsky, the son of a sacristan, and a student of the clerical academy, returning home from shooting, walked all the time by the path in the water-side meadow. His fingers were numb and his face was burning with the wind. It seemed to him that the cold that had suddenly come on had destroyed the order and harmony of things, that nature itself felt ill at ease, and that was why the evening darkness was falling more rapidly than usual. All around it was deserted and peculiarly gloomy. The only light was one gleaming in the widows' gardens near the river; the village, over three miles away, and everything in the distance all round was plunged in the cold evening mist. The student remembered that, as he went out from the house, his mother was sitting barefoot on the floor in the entry, cleaning the samovar, while his father lay on the stove coughing; as it was Good Friday nothing had been cooked, and the student was terribly hungry. And now, shrinking from the cold, he thought that just such a wind had blown in the days of Rurik and in the time of Ivan the Terrible and Peter, and in their time there had been just the same desperate poverty and hunger, the same thatched roofs with holes in them, ignorance, misery, the same desolation around, the same darkness, the same feeling of oppression—all these had existed, did exist, and would exist, and the lapse of a thousand years would make life no better. And he did not want to go home.

The gardens were called the widows' because they were kept by two widows, mother and daughter. A camp fire was burning brightly with a crackling sound, throwing out light far around on the ploughed earth. The widow Vasilisa, a tall, fat old woman in a man's coat, was standing by and looking thoughtfully into the fire; her daughter Lukerya, a little pock-marked woman with a stupid-looking face, was sitting on the ground, washing a caldron and spoons. Apparently they had just had supper. There was a sound of men's voices; it was the labourers watering their horses at the river.

"Here you have winter back again," said the student, going up to the camp fire. "Good evening."

Vasilisa started, but at once recognized him and smiled cordially.

"I did not know you; God bless you," she said. "You'll be rich."

They talked. Vasilisa, a woman of experience, who had been in service with the gentry, first as a wet-nurse, afterwards as a children's nurse, expressed herself with refinement, and a soft, sedate smile never left her face; her daughter Lukerya, a village peasant woman, who had been beaten by her husband, simply screwed up her eyes at the student and said nothing, and she had a strange expression like that of a deaf mute.

"At just such a fire the Apostle Peter warmed himself," said the student, stretching out his hands to the fire, "so it must have been cold then, too. Ah, what a terrible night it must have been, granny! An utterly dismal long night!"

He looked round at the darkness, shook his head abruptly and asked:

"No doubt you have been at the reading of the Twelve Gospels?"

"Yes, I have," answered Vasilisa.

"If you remember at the Last Supper Peter said to Jesus, 'I am ready to go with Thee into darkness and unto death.' And our Lord answered him thus: 'I say unto thee, Peter, before the cock croweth thou wilt have denied Me thrice.' After the supper Jesus went through the agony of death in the garden and prayed, and poor Peter was weary in spirit and faint, his eyelids were heavy and he could not struggle against sleep. He fell asleep. Then you heard how Judas the same night kissed Jesus and betrayed Him to His tormentors. They took Him bound to the high priest and beat Him, while Peter, exhausted, worn out with misery and alarm, hardly awake, you know, feeling that something awful was just going to happen on earth, followed behind.... He loved Jesus passionately, intensely, and now he saw from far off how He was beaten..."

Lukerya left the spoons and fixed an immovable stare upon the student.

"They came to the high priest's," he went on; "they began to question Jesus, and meantime the labourers made a fire in the yard as it was cold, and warmed themselves. Peter, too, stood with them near the fire and warmed himself as I am doing. A woman, seeing him, said: 'He was with Jesus, too'—that is as much as to say that he, too, should be taken to be questioned. And all the labourers that were standing near the fire must have looked sourly and suspiciously at him, because he was confused and said: 'I don't know Him.' A little while after again someone recognized him as one of Jesus' disciples and said: 'Thou, too, art one of them,' but again he denied it. And for the third time someone turned to him: 'Why, did I not see thee with Him in the garden to-day?' For the third time he denied it. And immediately after that time the cock crowed, and Peter, looking from afar off at Jesus, remembered the words He had said to him in the evening.... He remembered, he came to himself, went out of the yard and wept bitterly—bitterly. In the Gospel it is written: 'He went out and wept bitterly.' I imagine it: the still, still, dark, dark garden, and in the stillness, faintly audible, smothered sobbing..."

The student sighed and sank into thought. Still smiling, Vasilisa suddenly gave a gulp, big tears flowed freely down her cheeks, and she screened her face from the fire with her sleeve as though ashamed of her tears, and Lukerya, staring immovably at the student, flushed crimson, and her expression became strained and heavy like that of someone enduring intense pain.

The labourers came back from the river, and one of them riding a horse was quite near, and the light from the fire quivered upon him. The student said good-night to the widows and went on. And again the darkness was about him and his fingers began to be numb. A cruel wind was blowing, winter really had come back and it did not feel as though Easter would be the day after to-morrow.

Now the student was thinking about Vasilisa: since she had shed tears all that had happened to Peter the night before the Crucifixion must have some relation to her....

He looked round. The solitary light was still gleaming in the darkness and no figures could be seen near it now. The student thought again that if Vasilisa had shed tears, and her daughter had been troubled, it was evident that what he had just been telling them about, which had happened nineteen centuries ago, had a relation to the present—to both women, to the desolate village, to himself, to all people. The old woman had wept, not because he could tell the story touchingly, but because Peter was near to her, because her whole being was interested in what was passing in Peter's soul.

And joy suddenly stirred in his soul, and he even stopped for a minute to take breath. "The past," he thought, "is linked with the present by an unbroken chain of events flowing one out of another." And it seemed to him that he had just seen both ends of that chain; that when he touched one end the other quivered.

When he crossed the river by the ferry boat and afterwards, mounting the hill, looked at his village and towards the west where the cold crimson sunset lay a narrow streak of light, he thought that truth and beauty which had guided human life there in the garden and in the yard of the high priest had continued without interruption to this day, and had evidently always been the chief thing in human life and in all earthly life, indeed; and the feeling of youth, health, vigour— he was only twenty-two—and the inexpressible sweet expectation of happiness, of unknown mysterious happiness, took possession of him little by little, and life seemed to him enchanting, marvellous, and full of lofty meaning.

A Day in the Country

ETWEEN eight and nine o'clock in the morning. A dark leaden-coloured mass is creeping over the sky towards the sun. Red zigzags of lightning gleam here and there across it. There is a sound of far-away rumbling. A warm wind frolics over the grass, bends the trees, and stirs up the dust. In a minute there will be a spurt of May rain and a real storm will begin.

Fyokla, a little beggar-girl of six, is running through the village, looking for Terenty the cobbler. The white-haired, barefoot child is pale. Her eyes are wide-open, her lips are trembling.

"Uncle, where is Terenty?" she asks every one she meets. No one answers. They are all preoccupied with the approaching storm and take refuge in their huts. At last she meets Silanty Silitch, the sacristan, Terenty's bosom friend. He is coming along, staggering from the wind.

"Uncle, where is Terenty?"

"At the kitchen-gardens," answers Silanty.

The beggar-girl runs behind the huts to the kitchen-gardens and there finds Terenty; the tall old man with a thin, pock-marked face, very long legs, and bare feet, dressed in a woman's tattered jacket, is standing near the vegetable plots, looking with drowsy, drunken eyes at the dark storm-cloud. On his long crane-like legs he sways in the wind like a starling-cote.

"Uncle Terenty!" the white-headed beggar-girl addresses him. "Uncle, darling!"

Terenty bends down to Fyokla, and his grim, drunken face is overspread with a smile, such as come into people's faces when they look at something little, foolish, and absurd, but warmly loved.

"Ah! servant of God, Fyokia," he says, lisping tenderly, "where have you come from?"

"Uncle Terenty," says Fyokia, with a sob, tugging at the lapel of the cobbler's coat. "Brother Danilka has had an accident! Come along!"

"What sort of accident? Ough, what thunder! Holy, holy, holy. . . . What sort of accident?"

"In the count's copse Danilka stuck his hand into a hole in a tree, and he can't get it out. Come along, uncle, do be kind and pull his hand out!"

"How was it he put his hand in? What for?"

"He wanted to get a cuckoo's egg out of the hole for me."

"The day has hardly begun and already you are in trouble. . . ." Terenty shook his head and spat deliberately. "Well, what am I to do with you now? I must come . . . I must, may the wolf gobble you up, you naughty children! Come, little orphan!"

Terenty comes out of the kitchen-garden and, lifting high his long legs, begins striding down the village street. He walks quickly without stopping or looking from side to side, as though he were shoved from behind or afraid of pursuit. Fyokla can hardly keep up with him.

They come out of the village and turn along the dusty road towards the count's copse that lies dark blue in the distance. It is about a mile and a half away. The clouds have by now covered the sun, and soon afterwards there is not a speck of blue left in the sky. It grows dark.

"Holy, holy, holy . . ." whispers Fyokla, hurrying after Terenty. The first rain-drops, big and heavy, lie, dark dots on the dusty road. A big drop falls on Fyokla's cheek and glides like a tear down her chin.

"The rain has begun," mutters the cobbler, kicking up the dust with his bare, bony feet. "That's fine, Fyokla, old girl. The grass and the trees are fed by the rain, as we are by bread. And as for the thunder, don't you be frightened, little orphan. Why should it kill a little thing like you?"

As soon as the rain begins, the wind drops. The only sound is the patter of rain dropping like fine shot on the young rye and the parched road.

"We shall get soaked, Fyolka," mutters Terenty. "There won't be a dry spot left on us. . . . Ho-ho, my girl! It's run down my neck! But don't be frightened, silly. . . . The grass will be dry again, the earth will be dry again, and we shall be dry again. There is the same sun for us all."

A flash of lightning, some fourteen feet long, gleams above their heads. There is a loud peal of thunder, and it seems to Fyokla that something big, heavy, and round is rolling over the sky and tearing it open, exactly over her head.

"Holy, holy, holy . . ." says Terenty, crossing himself. "Don't be afraid, little orphan! It is not from spite that it thunders."

Terenty's and Fyokla's feet are covered with lumps of heavy, wet clay. It is slippery and difficult to walk, but Terenty strides on more and more rapidly. The weak little beggar-girl is breathless and ready to drop.

But at last they go into the count's copse. The washed trees, stirred by a gust of wind, drop a perfect waterfall upon them. Terenty stumbles over stumps and begins to slacken his pace.

"Whereabouts is Danilka?" he asks. "Lead me to him."

Fyokla leads him into a thicket, and, after going a quarter of a mile, points to Danilka. Her brother, a little fellow of eight, with hair as red as ochre and a pale sickly face, stands leaning against a tree, and, with his head on one side, looking sideways at the sky. In one hand he holds his shabby old cap, the other is hidden in an old lime tree. The boy is gazing at the stormy sky, and apparently not thinking of his trouble. Hearing footsteps and seeing the cobbler he gives a sickly smile and says:

"A terrible lot of thunder, Terenty. . . . I've never heard so much thunder in all my life."

"And where is your hand?"

"In the hole. . . . Pull it out, please, Terenty!"

The wood had broken at the edge of the hole and jammed Danilka's hand: he could push it farther in, but could not pull it out. Terenty snaps off the broken piece, and the boy's hand, red and crushed, is released.

"It's terrible how it's thundering," the boy says again, rubbing his hand. "What makes it thunder, Terenty?"

"One cloud runs against the other," answers the cobbler. The party come out of the copse, and walk along the edge of it towards the darkened road. The thunder gradually abates, and its rumbling is heard far away beyond the village.

"The ducks flew by here the other day, Terenty," says Danilka, still rubbing his hand. "They must be nesting in the Gniliya Zaimishtcha marshes. . . . Fyolka, would you like me to show you a nightingale's nest?"

"Don't touch it, you might disturb them," says Terenty, wringing the water out of his cap. "The nightingale is a singing-bird, without sin. He has had a voice given him in his throat, to praise God and gladden the heart of man. It's a sin to disturb him."

"What about the sparrow?"

"The sparrow doesn't matter, he's a bad, spiteful bird. He is like a pickpocket in his ways. He doesn't like man to be happy. When Christ was crucified it was the sparrow brought nails to the Jews, and called 'alive! alive!'"

A bright patch of blue appears in the sky.

"Look!" says Terenty. "An ant-heap burst open by the rain! They've been flooded, the rogues!"

They bend over the ant-heap. The downpour has damaged it; the insects are scurrying to and fro in the mud, agitated, and busily trying to carry away their drowned companions.

"You needn't be in such a taking, you won't die of it!" says Terenty, grinning. "As soon as the sun warms you, you'll come to your senses again. . . . It's a lesson to you, you stupids. You won't settle on low ground another time."

They go on.

"And here are some bees," cries Danilka, pointing to the branch of a young oak tree.

The drenched and chilled bees are huddled together on the branch. There are so many of them that neither bark nor leaf can be seen. Many of them are settled on one another.

"That's a swarm of bees," Terenty informs them. "They were flying looking for a home, and when the rain came down upon them they settled. If a swarm is flying, you need only sprinkle water on them to make them settle. Now if, say, you wanted to take the swarm, you would bend the branch with them into a sack and shake it, and they all fall in."

Little Fyokla suddenly frowns and rubs her neck vigorously. Her brother looks at her neck, and sees a big swelling on it.

"Hey-hey!" laughs the cobbler. "Do you know where you got that from, Fyokia, old girl? There are Spanish flies on some tree in the wood. The rain has trickled off them, and a drop has fallen on your neck—that's what has made the swelling."

The sun appears from behind the clouds and floods the wood, the fields, and the three friends with its warm light. The dark menacing cloud has gone far away and taken the storm with it. The air is warm and fragrant. There is a scent of bird-cherry, meadowsweet, and lilies-of-the-valley.

"That herb is given when your nose bleeds," says Terenty, pointing to a woolly-looking flower. "It does good."

They hear a whistle and a rumble, but not such a rumble as the storm-clouds carried away. A goods train races by before the eyes of Terenty, Danilka, and Fyokla. The engine, panting and puffing out black smoke, drags more than twenty vans after it. Its power is tremendous. The children are interested to know how an engine, not alive and without the help of horses, can move and drag such weights, and Terenty undertakes to explain it to them:

"It's all the steam's doing, children.... The steam does the work.... You see, it shoves under that thing near the wheels, and it ... you see ... it works...."

They cross the railway line, and, going down from the embankment, walk towards the river. They walk not with any object, but just at random, and talk all the way.... Danilka asks questions, Terenty answers them....

Terenty answers all his questions, and there is no secret in Nature which baffles him. He knows everything. Thus, for example, he knows the names of all the wild flowers, animals, and stones. He knows what herbs cure diseases, he has no difficulty in telling the age of a horse or a cow. Looking at the sunset, at the moon, or the birds, he can tell what sort of weather it will be next day. And indeed, it is not only Terenty who is so wise. Silanty Silitch, the innkeeper, the market-gardener, the shepherd, and all the villagers, generally speaking, know as much as he does. These people have learned not from books, but in the fields, in the wood, on the river bank. Their teachers have been the birds themselves, when they sang to them, the sun when it left a glow of crimson behind it at setting, the very trees, and wild herbs.

Danilka looks at Terenty and greedily drinks in every word. In spring, before one is weary of the warmth and the monotonous green of the fields, when everything is fresh and full of fragrance, who would not want to hear about the golden may-beetles, about the cranes, about the gurgling streams, and the corn mounting into ear?

The two of them, the cobbler and the orphan, walk about the fields, talk unceasingly, and are not weary. They could wander about the world endlessly. They walk, and in their talk of the beauty of the earth do not notice the frail little beggar-girl tripping after them. She is breathless and moves with a lagging step. There are tears in her eyes; she would be glad to stop these inexhaustible wanderers, but to whom and where can she go? She has no home or people of her own; whether she likes it or not, she must walk and listen to their talk.

Towards midday, all three sit down on the river bank. Danilka takes out of his bag a piece of bread, soaked and reduced to a mash, and they begin to eat. Terenty says a prayer when he has eaten the bread, then stretches himself on the sandy bank and falls asleep. While he is asleep, the boy gazes at the water, pondering. He has many different things to think of. He has just seen the storm, the bees, the ants, the train. Now, before his eyes, fishes are whisking about. Some are two inches long and more, others are no bigger than one's nail. A viper, with its head held high, is swimming from one bank to the other.

Only towards the evening our wanderers return to the village. The children go for the night to a deserted barn, where the corn of the commune used to be kept, while Terenty, leaving them, goes to the tavern. The children lie huddled together on the straw, dozing.

The boy does not sleep. He gazes into the darkness, and it seems to him that he is seeing all that he has seen in the day: the storm-clouds, the bright sunshine, the birds, the fish, lanky Terenty. The number of his impressions, together with exhaustion and hunger, are too much for him; he is as hot as though he were on fire, and tosses from, side to side. He longs to tell someone all that is haunting him now in the darkness and agitating his soul, but there is no one to tell. Fyokla is too little and could not understand.

"I'll tell Terenty to-morrow," thinks the boy.

The children fall asleep thinking of the homeless cobbler, and, in the night, Terenty comes to them, makes the sign of the cross over them, and puts bread under their heads. And no one sees his love. It is seen only by the moon which floats in the sky and peeps caressingly through the holes in the wall of the deserted barn.

A Work of Art

SASHA Smirnov, the only son of his mother, holding under his arm, something wrapped up in No. 223 of the _Financial News_, assumed a sentimental expression, and went into Dr. Koshelkov's consulting-room.

"Ah, dear lad!" was how the doctor greeted him. "Well! how are we feeling? What good news have you for me?"

Sasha blinked, laid his hand on his heart and said in an agitated voice: "Mamma sends her greetings to you, Ivan Nikolaevitch, and told me to thank you. . . . I am the only son of my mother and you have saved my life . . . you have brought me through a dangerous illness and . . . we do not know how to thank you."

"Nonsense, lad!" said the doctor, highly delighted. "I only did what anyone else would have done in my place."

"I am the only son of my mother . . . we are poor people and cannot of course repay you, and we are quite ashamed, doctor, although, however, mamma and I . . . the only son of my mother, earnestly beg you to accept in token of our gratitude . . . this object, which . . . An object of great value, an antique bronze. . . . A rare work of art."

"You shouldn't!" said the doctor, frowning. "What's this for!"

"No, please do not refuse," Sasha went on muttering as he unpacked the parcel. "You will wound mamma and me by refusing. . . . It's a fine thing . . . an antique bronze. . . . It was left us by my deceased father and we have kept it as a precious souvenir. My father used to buy antique bronzes and sell them to connoisseurs . . . Mamma and I keep on the business now."

Sasha undid the object and put it solemnly on the table. It was a not very tall candelabra of old bronze and artistic workmanship. It consisted of a group: on the pedestal stood two female figures in the costume of Eve and in attitudes for the description of which I have neither the courage nor the fitting temperament. The figures were smiling coquettishly and altogether looked as though, had it not been for the necessity of supporting the candlestick, they would have skipped off the pedestal and have indulged in an orgy such as is improper for the reader even to imagine.

Looking at the present, the doctor slowly scratched behind his ear, cleared his throat and blew his nose irresolutely.

"Yes, it certainly is a fine thing," he muttered, "but . . . how shall I express it? . . . it's . . . h'm . . . it's not quite for family reading. It's not simply decolleté but beyond anything, dash it all. . . ."

"How do you mean?"

"The serpent-tempter himself could not have invented anything worse . . . . Why, to put such a phantasmagoria on the table would be defiling the whole flat."

"What a strange way of looking at art, doctor!" said Sasha, offended. "Why, it is an artistic thing, look at it! There is so much beauty and elegance that it fills one's soul with a feeling of reverence and brings a lump into one's throat! When one sees anything so beautiful one forgets everything earthly. . . .

Only look, how much movement, what an atmosphere, what expression!"

"I understand all that very well, my dear boy," the doctor interposed, "but you know I am a family man, my children run in here, ladies come in."

"Of course if you look at it from the point of view of the crowd," said Sasha, "then this exquisitely artistic work may appear in a certain light. . . . But, doctor, rise superior to the crowd, especially as you will wound mamma and me by refusing it. I am the only son of my mother, you have saved my life. . . . We are giving you the thing most precious to us and . . . and I only regret that I have not the pair to present to you. . . ."

"Thank you, my dear fellow, I am very grateful . . . Give my respects to your mother but really consider, my children run in here, ladies come. . . . However, let it remain! I see there's no arguing with you."

"And there is nothing to argue about," said Sasha, relieved. "Put the candlestick here, by this vase. What a pity we have not the pair to it! It is a pity! Well, good-bye, doctor."

After Sasha's departure the doctor looked for a long time at the candelabra, scratched behind his ear and meditated.

"It's a superb thing, there's no denying it," he thought, "and it would be a pity to throw it away. . . . But it's impossible for me to keep it. . . . H'm! . . . Here's a problem! To whom can I make a present of it, or to what charity can I give it?"

After long meditation he thought of his good friend, the lawyer Uhov, to whom he was indebted for the management of legal business.

"Excellent," the doctor decided, "it would be awkward for him as a friend to take money from me, and it will be very suitable for me to present him with this. I will take him the devilish thing! Luckily he is a bachelor and easy-going."

Without further procrastination the doctor put on his hat and coat, took the candelabra and went off to Uhov's.

"How are you, friend!" he said, finding the lawyer at home. "I've come to see you . . . to thank you for your efforts. . . . You won't take money so you must at least accept this thing here. . . . See, my dear fellow. . . . The thing is magnificent!"

On seeing the bronze the lawyer was moved to indescribable delight.

"What a specimen!" he chuckled. "Ah, deuce take it, to think of them imagining such a thing, the devils! Exquisite! Ravishing! Where did you get hold of such a delightful thing?"

After pouring out his ecstasies the lawyer looked timidly towards the door and said: "Only you must carry off your present, my boy . . . . I can't take it. . . ."

"Why?" cried the doctor, disconcerted.

"Why . . . because my mother is here at times, my clients . . . besides I should be ashamed for my servants to see it."

"Nonsense! Nonsense! Don't you dare to refuse!" said the doctor, gesticulating. "It's piggish of you! It's a work of art! . . . What movement . . . what expression! I won't even talk of it! You will offend me!"

"If one could plaster it over or stick on fig-leaves . . ."

But the doctor gesticulated more violently than before, and dashing out of the flat went home, glad that he had succeeded in getting the present off his hands.

When he had gone away the lawyer examined the candelabra, fingered it all over, and then, like the doctor, racked his brains over the question what to do with the present.

"It's a fine thing," he mused, "and it would be a pity to throw it away and improper to keep it. The very best thing would be to make a present of it to someone. . . . I know what! I'll take it this evening to Shashkin, the comedian. The rascal is fond of such things, and by the way it is his benefit tonight."

No sooner said than done. In the evening the candelabra, carefully wrapped up, was duly carried to Shashkin's. The whole evening the comic actor's dressing-room was besieged by men coming to admire the present; the dressing-room was filled with the hum of enthusiasm and laughter like the neighing of horses. If one of the actresses approached the door and asked: "May I come in?" the comedian's husky voice was heard at once: "No, no, my dear, I am not dressed!"

After the performance the comedian shrugged his shoulders, flung up his hands and said: "Well what am I to do with the horrid thing? Why, I live in a private flat! Actresses come and see me! It's not a photograph that you can put in a drawer!"

"You had better sell it, sir," the hairdresser who was disrobing the actor advised him. "There's an old woman living about here who buys antique bronzes. Go and enquire for Madame Smirnov . . . everyone knows her."

The actor followed his advice. . . . Two days later the doctor was sitting in his consulting-room, and with his finger to his brow was meditating on the acids of the bile. All at once the door opened and Sasha Smirnov flew into the room. He was smiling, beaming, and his whole figure was radiant with happiness. In his hands he held something wrapped up in newspaper.

"Doctor!" he began breathlessly, "imagine my delight!

Happily for you we have succeeded in picking up the pair to your candelabra! Mamma is so happy. . . . I am the only son of my mother, you saved my life. . . ."

And Sasha, all of a tremor with gratitude, set the candelabra before the doctor. The doctor opened his mouth, tried to say something, but said nothing: he could not speak.

A Joke

IT was a bright winter midday. . . . There was a sharp snapping frost and the curls on Nadenka's temples and the down on her upper lip were covered with silvery frost. She was holding my arm and we were standing on a high hill. From where we stood to the ground below there stretched a smooth sloping descent in which the sun was reflected as in a looking-glass. Beside us was a little sledge lined with bright red cloth.

"Let us go down, Nadyezhda Petrovna!" I besought her. "Only once! I assure you we shall be all right and not hurt."

But Nadenka was afraid. The slope from her little goloshes to the bottom of the ice hill seemed to her a terrible, immensely deep abyss. Her spirit failed her, and she held her breath as she looked down, when I merely suggested her getting into the sledge, but what would it be if she were to risk flying into the abyss! She would die, she would go out of her mind.

"I entreat you!" I said. "You mustn't be afraid! You know it's poor-spirited, it's cowardly!"

Nadenka gave way at last, and from her face I saw that she gave way in mortal dread. I sat her in the sledge, pale and trembling, put my arm round her and with her cast myself down the precipice.

The sledge flew like a bullet. The air cleft by our flight beat in our faces, roared, whistled in our ears, tore at us, nipped us cruelly in its anger, tried to tear our heads off our shoulders. We had hardly strength to breathe from the pressure of the wind. It seemed as though the devil himself had caught us in his claws and was dragging us with a roar to hell. Surrounding objects melted into one long furiously racing streak . . . another moment and it seemed we should perish.

"I love you, Nadya!" I said in a low voice.

The sledge began moving more and more slowly, the roar of the wind and the whirr of the runners was no longer so terrible, it was easier to breathe, and at last we were at the bottom. Nadenka was more dead than alive. She was pale and scarcely breathing. . . . I helped her to get up.

"Nothing would induce me to go again," she said, looking at me with wide eyes full of horror. "Nothing in the world! I almost died!"

A little later she recovered herself and looked enquiringly into my eyes, wondering had I really uttered those four words or had she fancied them in the roar of the hurricane. And I stood beside her smoking and looking attentively at my glove.

She took my arm and we spent a long while walking near the ice-hill. The riddle evidently would not let her rest. . . . Had those words been uttered or not? . . . Yes or no? Yes or no? It was the question of pride, or honour, of life—a very important question, the most important question in the world. Nadenka kept impatiently, sorrowfully looking into my face with a penetrating glance; she answered at random, waiting to see whether I would not speak. Oh, the play of feeling on that sweet face! I saw that she was struggling with herself, that she wanted to say something, to ask some question, but she could not find the words; she felt awkward and frightened and troubled by her joy. . . .

"Do you know what," she said without looking at me.

"Well?" I asked.

"Let us . . . slide down again."

We clambered up the ice-hill by the steps again. I sat Nadenka, pale and trembling, in the sledge; again we flew into the terrible abyss, again the wind roared and the runners whirred, and again when the flight of our sledge was at its swiftest and noisiest, I said in a low voice:

"I love you, Nadenka!"

When the sledge stopped, Nadenka flung a glance at the hill down which we had both slid, then bent a long look upon my face, listened to my voice which was unconcerned and passionless, and the whole of her little figure, every bit of it, even her muff and her hood expressed the utmost bewilderment, and on her face was written: "What does it mean? Who uttered _those_ words? Did he, or did I only fancy it?"

The uncertainty worried her and drove her out of all patience. The poor girl did not answer my questions, frowned, and was on the point of tears.

"Hadn't we better go home?" I asked.

"Well, I . . . I like this tobogganning," she said, flushing. "Shall we go down once more?"

She "liked" the tobogganning, and yet as she got into the sledge she was, as both times before, pale, trembling, hardly able to breathe for terror.

We went down for the third time, and I saw she was looking at my face and watching my lips. But I put my handkerchief to my lips, coughed, and when we reached the middle of the hill I succeeded in bringing out:

"I love you, Nadya!"

And the mystery remained a mystery! Nadenka was silent, pondering on something. . . . I saw her home, she tried to walk slowly, slackened her pace and kept waiting to see whether I would not say those words to her, and I saw how her soul was suffering, what effort she was making not to say to herself:

"It cannot be that the wind said them! And I don't want it to be the wind that said them!"

Next morning I got a little note:

"If you are tobogganning to-day, come for me.—N."

And from that time I began going every day tobogganning with Nadenka, and as we flew down in the sledge, every time I pronounced in a low voice the same words: "I love you, Nadya!"

Soon Nadenka grew used to that phrase as to alcohol or morphia. She could not live without it. It is true that flying down the ice-hill terrified her as before, but now the terror and danger gave a peculiar fascination to words of love— words which as before were a mystery and tantalized the soul. The same two—the wind and I were still suspected. . . . Which of the two was making love to her she did not know, but apparently by now she did not care; from which goblet one drinks matters little if only the beverage is intoxicating.

It happened I went to the skating-ground alone at midday; mingling with the crowd I saw Nadenka go up to the ice-hill and look about for me . . . then she timidly mounted the steps. . . . She was frightened of going alone—oh, how frightened! She was white as the snow, she was trembling, she went as though to the scaffold, but she went, she went without looking back, resolutely. She had evidently determined to put it to the test at last: would those sweet amazing words be heard when I was not there? I saw her, pale, her lips parted with horror, get into the sledge, shut her eyes and saying good-bye for ever to the earth, set off. . . . "Whrrr!" whirred the runners. Whether Nadenka heard those words I do not know. I only saw her getting up from the sledge looking faint and exhausted. And one could tell from her face that she could not tell herself whether she had heard anything or not. Her terror while she had been flying down had deprived of her all power of hearing, of discriminating sounds, of understanding.

But then the month of March arrived . . . the spring sunshine was more kindly. . . . Our ice-hill turned dark, lost its brilliance and finally melted. We gave up tobogganning. There was nowhere now where poor Nadenka could hear those words, and indeed no one to utter them, since there was no wind and I was going to Petersburg—for long, perhaps for ever.

It happened two days before my departure I was sitting in the dusk in the little garden which was separated from the yard of Nadenka's house by a high fence with nails in it. . . . It was still pretty cold, there was still snow by the manure heap, the trees looked dead but there was already the scent of spring and the rooks were cawing loudly as they settled for their night's rest. I went up to the fence and stood for a long while peeping through a chink. I saw Nadenka come out into the porch and fix a mournful yearning gaze on the sky . . . The spring wind was blowing straight into her pale dejected face. . . . It reminded her of the wind which roared at us on the ice-hill when she heard those four words, and her face became very, very sorrowful, a tear trickled down her cheek, and the poor child held out both arms as though begging the wind to bring her those words once more. And waiting for the wind I said in a low voice:

"I love you, Nadya!"

Mercy! The change that came over Nadenka! She uttered a cry, smiled all over her face and looking joyful, happy and beautiful, held out her arms to meet the wind.

And I went off to pack up. . . .

That was long ago. Now Nadenka is married; she married—whether of her own choice or not does not matter—a secretary of the Nobility Wardenship and now she has three children. That we once went tobogganning together, and that the wind brought her the words "I love you, Nadenka," is not forgotten; it is for her now the happiest, most touching, and beautiful memory in her life. . . .

But now that I am older I cannot understand why I uttered those words, what was my motive in that joke. . . .

A Country Cottage

WO young people who had not long been married were walking up and down the platform of a little country station. His arm was round her waist, her head was almost on his shoulder, and both were happy.

The moon peeped up from the drifting cloudlets and frowned, as it seemed, envying their happiness and regretting her tedious and utterly superfluous virginity. The still air was heavy with the fragrance of lilac and wild cherry. Somewhere in the distance beyond the line a corncrake was calling.

"How beautiful it is, Sasha, how beautiful!" murmured the young wife. "It all seems like a dream. See, how sweet and inviting that little copse looks! How nice those solid, silent telegraph posts are! They add a special note to the landscape, suggesting humanity, civilization in the distance. . . . Don't you think it's lovely when the wind brings the rushing sound of a train?"

"Yes. . . . But what hot little hands you've got. . . That's because you're excited, Varya. . . . What have you got for our supper to-night?"

"Chicken and salad. . . . It's a chicken just big enough for two . . . . Then there is the salmon and sardines that were sent from town."

The moon as though she had taken a pinch of snuff hid her face behind a cloud. Human happiness reminded her of her own loneliness, of her solitary couch beyond the hills and dales.

"The train is coming!" said Varya, "how jolly!"

Three eyes of fire could be seen in the distance. The stationmaster came out on the platform. Signal lights flashed here and there on the line.

"Let's see the train in and go home," said Sasha, yawning. "What a splendid time we are having together, Varya, it's so splendid, one can hardly believe it's true!"

The dark monster crept noiselessly alongside the platform and came to a standstill. They caught glimpses of sleepy faces, of hats and shoulders at the dimly lighted windows.

"Look! look!" they heard from one of the carriages. "Varya and Sasha have come to meet us! There they are! . . . Varya! . . . Varya. . . . Look!"

Two little girls skipped out of the train and hung on Varya's neck. They were followed by a stout, middle-aged lady, and a tall, lanky gentleman with grey whiskers; behind them came two schoolboys, laden with bags, and after the schoolboys, the governess, after the governess the grandmother.

"Here we are, here we are, dear boy!" began the whiskered gentleman, squeezing Sasha's hand. "Sick of waiting for us, I expect! You have been pitching into your old uncle for not coming down all this time, I daresay! Kolya, Kostya, Nina, Fifa . . . children! Kiss your cousin Sasha! We're all here, the whole troop of us, just for three or four days. . . . I hope we shan't be too many for you? You mustn't let us put you out!"

At the sight of their uncle and his family, the young couple were horror-stricken. While his uncle talked and kissed them, Sasha had a vision of their little cottage: he and Varya giving up their three little rooms, all the pillows and bedding to their guests; the salmon, the sardines, the chicken all devoured in a single instant; the cousins plucking the flowers in their little garden, spilling the ink, filled the cottage with noise and confusion; his aunt talking continually about her ailments and her papa's having been Baron von Fintich. . . .

And Sasha looked almost with hatred at his young wife, and whispered:

"It's you they've come to see! . . . Damn them!"

"No, it's you," answered Varya, pale with anger. "They're your relations! they're not mine!"

And turning to her visitors, she said with a smile of welcome: "Welcome to the cottage!"

The moon came out again. She seemed to smile, as though she were glad she had no relations. Sasha, turning his head away to hide his angry despairing face, struggled to give a note of cordial welcome to his voice as he said:

"It is jolly of you! Welcome to the cottage!"

JAICO PUBLISHING HOUSE

Elevate Your Life. Transform Your World.

ESTABLISHED IN 1946, Jaico Publishing House is home to world-transforming authors such as Sri Sri Paramahansa Yogananda, Osho, The Dalai Lama, Sri Sri Ravi Shankar, Sadhguru, Robin Sharma, Deepak Chopra, Jack Canfield, Eknath Easwaran, Devdutt Pattanaik, Khushwant Singh, John Maxwell, Brian Tracy and Stephen Hawking.

Our late founder Mr. Jaman Shah first established Jaico as a book distribution company. Sensing that independence was around the corner, he aptly named his company Jaico ('Jai' means victory in Hindi). In order to service the significant demand for affordable books in a developing nation, Mr. Shah initiated Jaico's own publications. Jaico was India's first publisher of paperback books in the English language.

While self-help, religion and philosophy, mind/body/spirit, and business titles form the cornerstone of our non-fiction list, we publish an exciting range of travel, current affairs, biography, and popular science books as well. Our renewed focus on popular fiction is evident in our new titles by a host of fresh young talent from India and abroad. Jaico's recently established Translations Division translates selected English content into nine regional languages.

In addition to being a publisher and distributor of its own titles, Jaico is a major national distributor of books of leading international and Indian publishers. With its headquarters in Mumbai, Jaico has branches and sales offices in Ahmedabad, Bangalore, Bhopal, Bhubaneswar, Chennai, Delhi, Hyderabad, Kolkata and Lucknow.

SINCE 1946

9 788184 958546